WET DREAMS ON LOCKDOWN

The Captain

TN JONES

URBAN AINT DEAD

Contact Author on FB: TN Jones / Clubhouse: @novelisttnjones / IG: @thetnjones / Pinterest: @thetnjones / TikTok: @thetnjones / Threads: @thetnjones

Contact Publisher at www.urbanaintdead.com

Email: urbanaintdead@gmail.com

CONTENTS

SOUNDTRACKS

Scan the QR Code below to listen to the Soundtracks/Singles of some of your favorite U.A.D titles:

Don't have Spotify or Apple Music?
No Sweat!
Visit your choice streaming platform and search URBAN AINT DEAD.

Currently on lock serving a bid?
JPay, iHeartRadio, WHATEVER!
We got you covered.

Simply log into your facility's kiosk or tablet, go to music and
search URBAN AINT DEAD.

URBAN AINT DEAD

Like & Follow us on social media:

FB - URBAN AINT DEAD

IG: @urbanaintdead

Tik Tok - @urbanaintdead

<hr>

SUBMISSIONS

<hr>

Submit the first three chapters of your completed manuscript to urbanaintdead@gmail.com, subject line: Your book's title. The manuscript must be in a .doc file and sent as an attachment. The document should be in Times New Roman, double-spaced, and in size 12 font. Also, provide your synopsis and full contact information. If sending multiple submissions, they must each be in a separate email. Have a story but no way to submit it electronically? You can still submit to URBAN AINT DEAD. Send in the first three chapters, written or typed, of your completed manuscript to:

URBAN AINT DEAD
P.O Box 448
Maybrook, NY 12543

DO NOT send original manuscript. Must be a duplicate.
Provide your synopsis and a cover letter containing your full
contact information.
Thanks for considering URBAN AINT DEAD.

ACKNOWLEDGMENTS

First, thanks most definitely go to my Pretty Prin; you mean the world to me. Without you, I wouldn't be anything. Mommy loves you. Yes, I do!

Second, Elijah 'don't forget the R.' Freeman. Thank you for everything. You are a true gem, a kind soul. Much love and respect to URBAN AINT DEAD PRESENTS!

Third, to the lovely readers and supporters!

Peace and blessings to all! Much love and plenty of respect!

Chapter 1

RICHARDO METS

Tuesday, March 22, 2022

I need some fucking pussy before I lose my shits again. Not any kind of pussy, either. I need hers. Pussy that'll wash my face like God wash away sins. Pussy that'll throw a tantrum when I blow on it. Pussy that'll drown me when I smile at it. Pussy that'll cause me to lock up like a car with no oil in the motor. Pussy from the woman whose mugshot had me in a chokehold since her file landed on my desk at seven fifteen yesterday morning, I thought, gripping my dick while wanting to end the unnecessary phone call.

"Richardo." Dad sighed heavily as if he shook his head.

"Sir?" I responded, unwilling to continue a conversation that didn't need to be had.

"Son, I know you enjoy the job that you have worked hard to obtain," he carefully spoke, causing me to rapidly shake my head, so I didn't lie to him about getting off the phone due to a sharp pain.

"Dad," I lowly held out, hoping he heard the desperation in my voice for him not to continue down the path he was going. "You know I'll lock up if I'm too angry or agitated. It is not wise for me to take on that responsibility."

"Son, hear me out. You were accepted to every Ivy League school. You had no interest in going to any. You needed to know if you had what it took to be accepted. You possessed it and so much more. Your innovative thoughts about the cotton fields have been remarkable. I take your brother's suggestions, but I listen to you more. What you say, I make it happen. I'm tired of being the big man in charge. I look forward to passing the torch to you in April next year. Glover isn't going to do what you have done for our family business. He can't conduct a successful meeting because he doesn't do what you do. Research. I need you to consider taking this position for our family's company, Richardo. You have enough time to do so. Just think about it, Son," he begged as I dropped my head on the clean window and stared into the gloomy day.

After exhaling sharply, I closed my eyes. "Dad, you are acting like I can't flip out at any moment when I'm not in a positive mind state or overly possessive. I am not a great candidate to take over the family lands. I'll destroy it."

"There is nothing wrong with you, Richardo! We had you checked!" he loudly voiced, causing my right eye to twitch.

"Do not yell at me. My right eye just twitched," I slowly spoke.

Hurriedly, he apologetically said, "I'm sorry, Son."

"Apology accepted." I exhaled, eager to get him off my phone. "Come back on the date, and we will redo this conversation."

"Okay. Have a good day at work, Son. I love you," he confessed as several knocks sounded at the door.

"I love you more," I responded before looking at the rectangular object. "Come in."

"Go be the best captain those people have seen," he calmly spoke as I eyed my partners since grammar school.

"As always," I voiced before we said our goodbyes.

Shoving my phone into my pocket, I stared into my curious best friends' faces, C. O. Terry Daniels, C.O. Avery Lee, and Lieutenant Palmer Harris. As they occupied the gray sitting furniture, I ran my hand down my head and said, "Dad's on my ass about taking over the cotton fields."

"That's nothing new," Avery voiced, resting his feet on the oval table.

"So, what are you going to do?" Palmer inquired as I looked at my black work shoes.

"Train Glover's ass to do what I do. I don't need to be that close to the firing pit. I'll lock the fuck up, and they won't know how to put the idiot up," I admitted, pushing from the windowsill.

"Glover is not a good businessperson. He's going to sink your family's bread and butter, Richardo," Terry confidently stated as the others agreed.

"I know, but it's the only choice I have. Too much on my plate as it is. Again, I don't need to be close to the firing pit," I leisurely spoke, eyeing them individually.

"Understood that the first time." They chuckled, causing me to crack a smile.

"They will be ready to call a priest like every year." Avery laughed, causing us to chuckle and shake our heads.

While sitting across from them, I dropped my hands in my lap and said, "It's very dust-free in here, huh?"

"With that being said, I think I got Lockley pregnant," Avery seriously voiced.

I aggressively whipped my head in his direction and balled my lips and right hand. I wanted to knock his ass out. Every six months, he spoke the exact eleven words. While I tried not to blow on his dumb, lanky, green-eyed ass, Palmer nastily stared at our friend and hissed, "You need to contain that dick, bitch. I'm sick of hearing those words every damn year. I wished you would've stayed that shy-ass White boy I met in fourth grade. You've been out of control with that thang since those nuts dropped."

"Woof!" Avery chuckled, causing Terry to laugh loudly.

"The shit is not a laughing matter. He's getting carried away because he knows we will make some shit shake. The fucker has four kids who have been adopted. Thankfully, the other females lied about being pregnant. How many more kids do we have to ensure go to a good home before we say enough is enough?" Palmer continued fussing while looking at me.

As the two went back and forth, I felt a great cursing out was in store for my partner. I, the semi-civil-headed man, had a long chat with my closest nympho friend a year ago. In that chat, I was specific about what I would do the next time he came to me with those eleven ugly words. I was confident he thought I was talking, but I wasn't.

Sick of the low bickering between them, I hissed, "Y'all shut the fuck up with that noise."

Immediately, silence overcame my office. While focusing on a confident Avery, who was sitting in the chair like a big dog, I dropped my head, looked into my lap, and voiced, "You are getting beside your fucking self with that shit, Avery. I have to do extra shit to cover your ass. Unlike the real-money career, I don't need to work hard in this easy job. You will simmer in baby shit this time. Your sister will adopt this child if Lockley is pregnant. However, you will be with your child every fucking day unless you are here. That shit is non-negotiable. Do I make myself fucking clear, Avery Leon Lee?"

"Yeah. You made yourself clear." His deep, rich tone sounded as he shook his head.

"Good. Now to the real fucking business at hand. Dope is

needed in the following prison systems: Bibb, Elmore, Jefferson, and Ventress. Make sure it gets there by Friday. As far as this one, the addicts catching hell. Make sure they continue to catch hell. I need these women restored to who they were before they got ahold of drugs. I need cells tossed on Friday, Sunday, and Wednesday. Each week, I'll rotate the days. A new set of women coming in a few weeks. Our frequent flyer, Dedricka Willis, is amongst those women. Everything clear?" I questioned, eyeing all.

"Crystal," they responded as I stood.

"Good. See y'all later," I voiced, walking from the center of my work area.

When they arrived at the door, I comfortably sat in my black swivel chair. Quickly, I looked at the manila folder that held sensitive information about a particular inmate due to come in with a known addict and drug supplier. My friends didn't exit my office right away. They analyzed me as I never tore my eyes from the manila folder.

"What?" I asked, sliding my eyes to the five-by-eight photo on my desk.

"Eventually, you will have to pick a side, Richardo. You are driving yourself crazy with your two faces. You can't save them all. Some will slip through your hands. Maybe you should think about being that badass landowner," Palmer sincerely voiced, causing me to slide my eyes in their direction.

Resting my head on the headrest, I inquired, "Who will make sure y'all asses on point if I walk away? Who will keep Avery from running through motherfuckas' family members as if they are toilet paper? Who will keep you from shooting a person in the face if you have to repeat yourself about not going down any further than what we agreed on our prices? Who will keep Terry from egging y'all stupidity on, further causing unnecessary bullshit to happen? I need you idiots alive and doing well. I don't have to pick a side. Just like I swap my verbiage when y'all or anyone pisses me off, I can continue to have two faces. Can't nobody do what the fuck I do so easily and well. Once y'all decide to leave that life alone, I will. Another thing, if I can save a fraction of these women, then I will fucking do it. Y'all will help me as I've helped you."

As they nodded, Terry said, "You need to see somebody, Richardo. It's past time to do so."

Not in the mood to hear that shit again, I observed his eyes and softly exhaled. "I'm fine. Y'all are free to leave. I have work to do."

While shaking their heads, my crew exited my office. Crossing my legs at the ankles, I stared at the photo of my then sixteen-year-old sister, Maysha, and her best friend, Trina. Softly smiling, I said, "I miss the hell out of you two idiots. I never stopped missing y'all, but I hate you so damn much. I really hate the two of you for how y'all left me. It's been twenty-six motherfucking years, and I'm trying to forget the two of you. If I forget about y'all, then my purpose here is non-existent. I can't … I can't walk away now. Not when I know exactly how y'all's lives ended. I have two faces because of y'all stupid asses."

I stared at my sister and her best friend's photo for over an hour and a half. I didn't think about their demise nor reflect on the day I had taken their picture. I was glued to my chair, staring at the liveliest, funniest social butterflies. Analyzing the dimple in their left jaw, the happiness in their brown eyes, and the purple coloring of their braces, I tried to come to terms with the fact I would always be stuck on them with no way out until I found my special someone to take my pain away. I thought my daughter, Rayne, and my grandson, Zanning, would've done that. Their presence intensified my hurt. They never received a chance to meet the most incredible girls— who would've turned into fine young adult women—God could've ever made.

Ring. Ring. Ring.

Still eyeing the image, I reached for the black phone. After clearing my throat several times, I answered. "Captain Mets."

"Daddyyyyyyy!" Rayne eagerly shouted, causing my eyes to fall from the image.

Feeling much better by hearing her angelic, animated tone, I grinned. "What will I say yes to now, Rayne Lisa Mets?"

"To an evening of grandfather and grandson fun while I'm in my old bedroom, studying for this horrible test on Friday," she cutely voiced as a crinkling noise sounded in her background.

"I'm all for spending time with the hypest kid in the world," I acknowledged, thinking of places I could take the handsome, lanky, biracial boy who had me wrapped around his finger worse than his mother.

"Perfect. Also," she held out, which caused me to shake my head while closing my eyes.

"I'm not interested in being in a relationship with anyone you've encountered, Rayne. Would you please leave my dating life up to me?" I voiced, eyeing the manila folder containing information about my final wife.

"Absolutely not," she squealed, causing me to lightly chuckle.

"I know what I'm seeking in a woman who'll carry my last name for the rest of our lives," I admitted, fingers begging to open the manila folder so I could stare at my beautiful wife once more while praying I didn't lock up and join my friends' bandwagon.

"You deserve to have a life, Daddy. I would love to see you with someone deserving of you. You really need to get back on the market. You have much to offer," she sweetly announced for the two-hundredth time since her mother, and I divorced three years ago.

"I know you do. When the time is right, you'll see the most deserving woman on my arm, rocking an elegant gold engagement and wedding rings. That's a promise," I responded, opening the manila folder.

"Okay. Um, Dad?" Rayne seriously voiced as I studied the distraught woman's captivating face and eyes. My heart rapidly thumped for the twentieth time since I ogled her mugshot. That action had never happened whenever I looked at incoming inmates. I knew it was a sign from God that the new inmate would indeed be my wife, and I would have to join my male friends' prohibited freaky escapades once I'd gotten to know her well.

"Yes?" I oddly answered, carefully reading the information attached to my final wife's name.

"Remember the bad accident I told you about that happened this past Christmas?" she calmly spoke as chills ran through me. I had landed on information that made me think Rayne's comment would be about the female I stared at.

"Yeah. What about it?" I quizzed, double-checking the woman's charge.

"There aren't any news articles about that accident. I've been looking to find the woman I helped that night. Dad, she has no one. I know that because of what she kept repeating while they removed her deceased mother from the car. I said all of that to ask if a woman comes in with charges relating to a car accident on Christmas, will you tell me?" she kindly asked as I couldn't tear my eyes off the woman with red eyes and tear streaks on her beautiful, long, oval-shaped face.

"Rayne, you are like your Auntie Maysha in more ways

than I could've ever thought. Thoughtful. A true people's person. Caring. Loving," I softly voiced, tapping the woman's original booking date at the county jail in Montgomery County. "Is the woman you helped plus sized?"

"Yes."

"Light brown and black, curly hair?" I inquired, gliding the tip of my forefinger from the sad woman's neck until I reached her bustline.

"Yes."

"Mocha, bubbly, almond-shaped eyes?" I asked, studying the female's soft lips while tracing them.

"Yes," my daughter answered with desperation in her tone.

"Her name is Nyomi Richards. She'll be here on April 4th," I replied as my heart wouldn't stop tightening and a member that hardened.

"Ugh!" my child hollered, stunning me. "How long does she have in there? Please use terms I can understand."

Never tearing my eyes from Nyomi, I chuckled. "She was sentenced to twenty-three months, split. She will do a year and a few days here, and then, she will serve the rest of her sentence on parole."

"So, they did charge her with vehicular manslaughter," my daughter sadly voiced, making me want to know more about her encounter with her soon-to-be stepmother.

Flipping the next page, I nodded. "Yep. Rayne, what happened that night? Why are you heavily pulled to this woman?"

"We were in a two-laner. I was riding to the left of Nyomi. I was doing sixty miles per hour. We were side by side, so she was doing the same speed. There was an eighteen-wheeler, a small compact car, and her vehicle. All cars were at a safe-ish distance for a while. The compact car was close to the eighteen-wheeler when Nyomi swerved hard to the left. I came off the gas. Her car went faster. She hit the compact car. It ran into the back of the eighteen-wheeler. I saw Nyomi's airbag deploy. Immediately, she was knocked out. I hurried to park in the grass so I could assist," she voiced as I was eager to hear what made her really care for the woman.

"A guy ran to the compact car. I didn't bother to go that way. I knew the driver was dead. I felt it. That was one hard impact. So, I rushed to Nyomi's crossover vehicle. When I finally got inside to assist as best as possible, I noticed the unconscious woman holding her mother's hand. Her mother was dead. When Nyomi came to, she was disoriented. She kept saying, 'Momma, are you okay? Momma, talk to me. Please.' She didn't even know I was in the backseat until I made myself known. Eventually, she was fully aware of what had happened. She didn't talk; she cried and said, 'I caused this. I was trying to hold onto Momma. She was having a seizure. She wouldn't stop shaking, so I had to get to her. I panicked'," Rayne continued as I exhaled sharply, feeling much empathy for Nyomi.

"After the medics confirmed she had a concussion and her blood pressure was through the roof, they advised her to seek medical attention. The police became too rough. Dad, they acted as if she was a drunkard. They didn't do their job right: first, let her get medical attention. They weren't listening to her. They didn't care about the blood spilling from the left side of her face, which she continuously wiped with her shaky hand. They were too rough with a woman who suffered a concussion, lost her mother before the accident, and accidentally killed a woman trying to hold onto her dead mother. She wasn't equipped to handle a seizing person. They didn't do her right. That's why I stayed. I was able to get them to shut the fuck up and listen to her instead of making her feel like a problem. They sat her on the damn ground by her passenger door. I've never seen them do that when a person was inside the car dead. They block it off. Not that time. It was like they were punishing her. I was pissed, and I let them know just how much. I covered her eyes while they pulled her mother out of the car. I kept her eyes covered until two officers approached us. They gave her an alcohol test. She had no traces of alcohol in her system. She explained what led to the accident. Then, she was released. I drove her to the hospital. I stayed with her. She was a shell of a person while answering questions. She called her dad. I don't know what he told her, but it caused her hand to drop just as fast as the tears did. When her phone slammed onto the ground, she looked at me, and I saw no life in her eyes that wouldn't stop producing tears. She thanked me before telling me to go home," my daughter hurtfully voiced as I looked at the following paper.

"I didn't leave her. I walked into the triage room. Three hours later, she walked out, still a shell of a person. I took her to her mother's house. She tried to pay me when I pulled into the driveway, but I didn't want any money. I needed to be her friend. She asked me if my dad was in my life. I answered honestly. She asked if he was a good dad. I told her he was the best dad anyone could ever have. She softly smiled while saying, 'Very good for you. Treasure and love him dearly. My dad just tossed me to the curb. He told me I was wasting his time and was just a fling baby. Nothing special, and I needed to stop trying to have a relationship with him. I'm not a weak woman, but right now, I am. I just lost my best friend and rock. I caused a family to hurt as I do. I'm in a ton of shit because I panicked. I need a parent. That's the only reason I called him. I … I thought he would give me what I needed. Parental love and support. I said all that to say this: having a father goes a long way. Go hug your dad and tell him how much you love him. You will never look and feel how I do because he doesn't love me like I love him.' Now, Dad, you understand why I returned to the family house on Christmas. Now, you know why I analyzed you the way I did. I wondered what my life would've been like without you and whether it would hurt me if you didn't want me. I had to admit; it hurt like hell, and I knew how Nyomi felt," she choked up, causing me to close the manila folder as a horrible promise surfaced.

"Dad, I returned to her mother's house every day since the accident. It's like she vanished. Now, I know she didn't. Can you please make sure she's okay? She has no one." Rayne cried, hurting my soul.

"Yes, I'll make sure."

"Thank you." She cried.

"No thanks needed," I responded, knowing who would bunk together and where. "Rayne, I need to end the call to ensure Nyomi's as comfortable as possible. Okay?"

"Okay. I love you." She sniffled.

Feeling my heart swell with joy, I lovingly responded, "I love you more."

After ending the call, I got down to business by looking at which cells were available for the fifteen incoming inmates. While reviewing the women's profiles and the chart of who rested, I smiled when I noticed a cell was available for Nyomi and Dedricka. They weren't around the rowdy crowd, but they were surrounded by two mellow husband killers, a few civilized addicts, and many petty thieves.

Satisfied with honoring my daughter's request, I started the journey learning more about Nyomi Richards while unbuttoning my shirt. Thumbing through her social media page, I found funny and encouraging posts until the day she was arrested. Viewing her photos, I was certain Nyomi was the woman I needed. They told me everything I needed to know about her.

She was an adventurous, outgoing, and happy kindergarten teacher. She was a people person like Rayne. The photos of her and her mother were heartwarming. One could see the love running between them. I loved her smile; it was magnificent. It could brighten a room, just as it had brightened every photo.

Arriving at her boudoir images, my eyelids rapidly fluttered as my shaft rose. I lingered on all the pictures, fantasizing about being behind, on top, and under her as my tongue blessed her body. I envisioned gripping her thick thighs while gliding in the coochie as we watched the wet love organs connect. The thoughts of lifting her juicy ass just to put her on my face caused me to aggressively rub my mouth and download all her photos to my phone.

"I'm going to get you, Nyomi. You will be mine by week two of being in this place. Whatever you think won't happen will. You look like you have been seeking a nigga like me in your life. You will get this hard pressure between my legs. Every position you think you can't be in, you will be. You are fucking mine," I passionately spoke, retrieving my cell phone. Contraband I wasn't supposed to have had but didn't give a fuck. I had a family who may need me in case of an emergency. I needed to be reachable at all times. I wasn't the captain who stayed in his office. I was all over the prison, involved with all the happenings.

Calling the main fucker's number, who had to have the majority of the good-looking females' pussies, I resumed eyeing Nyomi's file. I tried to get a sense of how freaky she was. She seemed like a good girl in the sheets, and I was okay with that. Yet, I knew she would no longer be a good girl in the sheets once she received my love. She would be one nasty motherfucka.

"Talk to me." Avery smacked into my ear.

"Get Palmer and Terry. Come back to my office. ASAP." I ordered, making a heart around Nyomi's mugshot.

"Ay, Boss wants us in his office," he quickly voiced as I was in motion to end the call.

Dropping my phone into my lap, I relaxed in the chair and smiled. "Time to put all types of plays in motion. Once I see you in the flesh, Nyomi Reanna Richards, I'll know how much dick I need to drop off in you and what position you can handle this fucka in. I bet you haven't had that ass clapped like a flip phone. I'll be sure to do that. My God, I'll do that."

Against my damn office door, the only asshole within my crew knocked a familiar rap song on the rectangular object. His minions decided to lowly rap the song. Instantly, I rocked my head and chuckled. "They can't act right for shit."

Focusing on the door, I loudly voiced, "Come in."

As the head rocking, lowly rapping fuckas entered the clean, lemony-scented office, Terry, Palmer, and Lee rushed to my side.

"What's the issue?" Palmer inquired as Terry and Avery hopped on my desk.

Smiling, I harshly pointed at Nyomi's picture before sliding my forefinger to her name. As I looked at them, I gleefully spoke, "Mine!"

Astonishingly, they looked at each other before planting

their eyes on me. All smiled. Their eyes were filled with happiness as Avery knocked his middle fingers knuckles against my desk and grinned. "What you want, you get. An' we will make sure you an' her asses are covered. Welcome to unlimited playland, boss times two."

Interlocking my fingers, I stared into his long, oval-shaped face and seriously said, "Fuck an unlimited playland. That's my gotdamn wife. She will love all of me. The good, the bad, and especially the fucking ugly. Checkmate!"

Chapter 2

NYOMI RICHARDS

Monday, April 4th

I can't believe this is my gotdamn life now. I trusted my mother's neighbor to ensure the little money I had was placed on my books. I'll be broke as shit within three months, if not less. How the fuck did I go from a respected and loved kindergarten teacher to a fucking inmate? I don't deserve to be in this place. I'm not that type of person, I thought, walking beside a straight back, strutting C.O. Joseph.

With my items in my hand, I looked around the ugly-ass hallways that reeked of depression. I prayed I wouldn't have to show my face in the raggedy areas for the duration of my time. I didn't like how it made me feel less of a human. Stepping inside a women's prison had done enough of tearing me down without anyone knowing.

As we turned down another depressing ass hallway, C.O. Joseph looked at me and said, "I'm sorry you are in here, Richards. The justice system is something else."

Tell me about it, I thought while saying, "Thanks."

"I don't know you personally. I read what needed to be read. I got a sense of who you are. So, free game. Be careful who you socialize with. I would tell you to be extremely careful around some male C.O.s and lieutenants. Still, that statement doesn't apply to you. It will never apply to you. The captain is a good man. He takes unpleasant cases seriously. Very seriously. Some say his demon shows after he calls one of those guys to his office. They don't leave the same way they came in. Meaning, they beat the fuck up," she quickly spoke while stopping at the door.

As she knocked on it, I dryly responded, "Thanks for the tip. What did you mean by you would tell me to be extremely careful around some of the male C.O.s and lieutenants?"

"Come in," a robust and deep-voiced male commanded as I impatiently waited for her to answer.

When she opened the door, and my eyes caught a glimpse of the prison's gotdamn captain, my eyelids rapidly waved. The pink monster that had been dead for years was woke and at motherfucking attention. I couldn't stop gripping my bedding items as if he was fucking me from the back, hitting every spot that needed a great workout. My breathing was horrible as I analyzed the nutmeg-hued, six-footer, ripped, dripping in sex appeal authority figure. His sexy eyes held no interest. They made him seem like a cold and a pain in the ass captain.

"My God," I lowly moaned as my toes curled into the simple white shoes.

"Nyomi Richards, sir," C.O. Joseph spoke as he sat at his desk.

"You can stand outside the door, C.O. Joseph," he voiced, distant eyes still focused on me.

"Yes, sir," she answered before dashing out of his office.

The captain didn't speak once the door closed. Simply, he stared at me. I became impatient. I needed to know what was on his mind. Unhurriedly rising from the chair, his thick, rich tone ran wildly through my ears. "My name is Captain Richardo Mets. The best way to learn is how Richards?"

"Observation, sir," I responded as he crept closer.

That's a motherfucking peen right there, or is it just the drawls that have it pushed up like that? I thought, trying to keep my eyes off the bulge in his pants.

"Right. With those almond-shaped, mocha eyes, you need to do that well. Learn who to be around. Pay attention to your surroundings. Be mindful of how you speak to authority over you. Meaning, don't give me a reason to knock a motherfucka around this gotdamn office for committing acts I can't tolerate. You know what? Disregard the fifth statement, it won't apply to you. Make use of the programs available. If they don't apply to you, find ways to make yourself useful in those programs. That's it. Usually, I tell my inmates welcome, but I refuse to tell you that. So, I will say this. Make the best of your time here," he voiced, standing straight like a spruce.

That's the second time I've heard that phrase. Hmm, I wonder why it doesn't apply to me. Could such and such be keeping an eye out for me? But why would he do that? I thought, oddly responding, "Yes, sir."

Gazing into eyes that comforted me, I drank in the intoxicating scent of mint, lavender, and vanilla. A fragrance that would've made me look at him numerous times if we were in a public place.

As I could hear the soft tick from the clock across from his desk, the captain stepped closer, causing me to gasp while gently bumping into the door. His square jaw tensed, making him look more powerful and sexier. His succulent lips begged me to plant a juicy smooch on it. The thought of touching his chiseled chest was very satisfying.

"Hmm," he sexily sounded, taking a small step backward and pulling me forward. "Try to have a good day, Richards."

Before I could comprehend the softness of his palm, the brief but yearning expression in his eyes, or respond to his comment, Captain Mets put much distance between us, saying, "C.O. Joseph, she's ready to be escorted to her area."

When the door opened, it took much will to remove my eyes from the captain's watchful eye. I wasn't sure if C.O.

Joseph observed my lingering look when she arrived next to me, and a part of me didn't care. Her captain had stirred something that should've been left alone. Turning on my heels seemed a difficult task. My legs didn't want to move; they wanted to be spread.

While I walked out of his office, he mumbled. Badly, I wanted to know what the fine individual with a severe bite had to say that he didn't need two sets of ears to hear. As we strolled toward my temporary living quarters, I reflected on the man with a mean look but an even meaner talk and ogle game. I loved his strong posture, presence before my body, the intense stares, and how he made himself clear by speaking bluntly.

I didn't like the assholes who talked just to hear their voices. That was why I had kept my legs closed for the past few years. I didn't have time for the games. I was too far in life to deal with a man who didn't know what he wanted other than not to be alone. That wasn't enough for me. I needed a man to know he needed me. That would cause us to be a faithful power couple.

"You really don't have anyone to come visit you?" C.O. Joseph inquired, jarring me from my thoughts.

"No," I responded as we arrived in the loud part of the prison. I was sure it was time for me to use the eyes God blessed me with.

"I'm sorry," she sweetly stated, looking at me.

"It's okay. Everyone can't have a picture-perfect family.

I've come to terms with it. No longer bothered by those who didn't want to have an amazing life with Momma and me," I confidently spoke, softly smiling at the thought of Momma grinning at me for arriving at the point she had come to terms with before I could comprehend how to read and write.

"I feel I must put you at ease more. You aren't around the rowdy crew. Those around you are welcoming, friendly, and not with the fuck shit. So, you will be comfortable," she admitted, causing me to ponder if she was that friendly with all inmates or if the warden had something to do with her behavior toward me.

After clearing my throat, I asked, "Are you this way with all inmates?"

"Yes. I'm a kind person until you piss me off. Then, I'm a firecracker," she gently spoke as we entered my new living area.

Ah, so the asshole doesn't have anything to do with her attitude, I thought, seeing all eyes were on me.

Carefully, I scanned the many faces I would have names attached to within a few days. For some of them, I would be elated to call to chat; it would be a privilege for them to have their names rolling from my lips. I was a closed-off person who had three friends. That was until I was slapped with a vehicular manslaughter charge. Those high and mighty bitches disappeared on me as if they hadn't known me since grade school. I didn't bitch or show my ass whenever I saw them. Simply, I smiled and sashayed by those bitches like the gorgeous, genuine-hearted, but no fool woman I was.

"Well, look who is still my cellmate." Dedricka Willis grinned, showing her meth teeth. Her fucked-up smile had always been a sincere grin.

Smiling and thankful for the familiar face of a young adult whom I could tell was once beautiful, I nodded. "Yes, it is me. Seems we are destined to spend many days together. Nice seeing you after only being separated for a few moments."

"Indeed," she gleefully announced, hopping from the top bunk.

"Willis, the captain needs to see you," C.O. Joseph spoke from the iron poles.

"Yes, ma'am, C.O. Joseph," she eagerly voiced, walking in the direction of the nice woman.

Stunned, I swirled and asked, "Why does it sound like you are familiar with C.O. Joseph?"

The average-height woman looked at me and giggled. "I am. It's my fourth time here."

"Huh? You know what? That's none of my business. I hope the chat goes well. See you when you return," I shockingly spoke as I couldn't tear my eyes off the female who had me with many questions I needed answered without asking.

I strolled toward the sleeping area while observing my surroundings when they exited the cell. The only thing I liked about the personal space for two people was the barred, high-rise window. I loved the sun. If I was in a cell, unable to see the sun shining, I was sure my mental health would decline. I wasn't a gloomy person and had never done well with darkness or storms.

"I'm only here for a few months, which will go in a breeze, and I'll be free-ish," I stated, taking my personal items to the makeshift shelf.

While arranging my items, Captain Mets' face slithered across my mind. My breathing became labored as naughty thoughts consumed me. I shook my head rapidly and whispered, "I will act accordingly. I do not have any toys to entertain me. I will not work my damn fingers to death while thinking about that fine ass man. I am here for a year and a few months. That's a lot of masturbating. I will read until the horniness is no longer present. So, devil, get the fuck off my back, bitch. You've destroyed me enough."

"Knock. Knock," two proper women happily greeted, causing me to face them.

The two short but stocky women looked alike, so I assumed they were sisters. While analyzing them, I voiced, "I love dick, and if you try me, I'll smile when they do what the fuck they want to me as far as time. I am far from a weak bitch. Tread fucking lightly."

"Whoa. Whoa," they quickly voiced while bucking their eyes and waving their hands.

"I'm Patricia Hines, and this is my best friend, Lisa Betterman. We love dick as well. However, our dick got beside himself, so we killed him. We aren't those women you've probably read about or portrayed on television shows. We are civil-headed women doing a life sentence with no chance of parole. We are something like a mother figure around here. We don't get over on people. The rowdy crew do not fuck with us. We check on those who are like us. Level-headed, calm, and possess a welcoming and loving vibe. We are heavily navigated to that hardheaded ass Dedricka. She's a sweetheart until she gets back on the drugs," the softly talking woman spoke as her friend by the bars nodded.

My eyelids had never blinked as fast as they had when she mentioned 'our dick'. I told myself before landing in the women's facility that I would mind my damn business. I couldn't after analyzing their body language. They didn't pose a threat to me, so I eased a bit.

"Well, then. I'm Nyomi Richards. Since you've told me why y'all are in here, I guess I should tell you why I am." I exhaled, motioning for them to come in.

"We already know," Betterman sorrowfully voiced, shaking her head.

"How?" I asked, furrowing my eyebrows while walking toward the bed.

"Everything my children and grandchildren are involved in, I know about. I know all of their teachers. Have pictures of them with their teachers each grade year. You were my sixth grandson, Trenton Betterman's teacher, in the fall semester of 2021. I have a copy of the class Halloween picture of the two of you. According to my daughter, he's still distraught you couldn't end the year with them. He still asks about you. You have impacted him tremendously. For that, I thank you. How did you do it?" she curiously asked, causing much light and warmth to overcome me as I rehashed the handsome, pale, oval-shaped boy's face.

Arriving at the bed, feeling proud, I smiled. "I know how to make kids comfortable in their skin by using the words my mother used on me. I told him what all kids need to hear. How much they matter. How smart they are, and it's okay not to grasp something as quickly as their peers. Trenton's a sweetheart. Tell Amanda he was my best and most favorite student."

"I will. I'm sorry for the loss of your mother and having to be in this place," she voiced as they helped place the fitted sheet on the bed.

"Were you drunk?" Hines asked softly.

"No. My mom had epilepsy and stage three colon cancer. She had a seizure while I was driving," I confessed while drifting to why we were out in the chilly weather. "I needed to bring some joy into her life. The month had been hard for her. The chemotherapy was really doing a number on her body. So, I decided to do what I do every year on Christmas. We rode around the town, looking at Christmas decorations and listening to holiday songs. Something we had been doing since I was a young one. Shit went to the left the moment she squeezed my hand. Like always, I'm not great under pressure. I fucking panicked and didn't pull over. It never crossed my mind. I unintentionally mashed the pedal while placing my hand on her chest to hold her steady. I woke up, and there was a stranger in my backseat. Momma wouldn't wake up for me, no matter how many times I called her name or shook her. Even when I removed her seatbelt and pulled her to me, she wouldn't wake the fuck up. Then, I looked ahead and saw what the fuck I did. I died that evening right along with them."

As I felt tears welling, the ladies gently rubbed my back as Momma had done many times, saying, "Forgive yourself, Nyomi. Please forgive yourself. If you don't, you will miss out on a wonderful life."

"I'm trying," I honestly announced, wiping my face and reaching for the thin garment referenced as a blanket.

"Are the family going to sue?" Hines asked as I unfolded the gray item.

"Thankfully, no. I owe them bunches for digging further into the accident."

"That's a big blessing."

"Mhm." I nodded as Dedricka glided into the cell, popping her lips.

Focusing on her was a great thing. It took me away from the first of the four worst days of my life. I could meddle in her business as I swore I would not do. While ensuring the bed was made according to the prison's rules, I asked, "Dedricka, why have you been in here four times? How old are you?"

"Have you seen my mouth?" She giggled, causing Betterman and Hines to laugh. I bucked my eyes at her and rapidly blinked while balling my hand to place it under my chin.

Closing my eyes, I nodded. "Yes, I've seen your mouth, Dedricka."

"Okay. Do you know what type of mouth I possess?" she stated as if she smiled and shimmied.

I laughed at her silliness and answered. "It looks like a meth mouth."

"Correct. I'm an addict. There's no such thing as recovering long-term for me. My dealer learns I'm on the streets and back, swirling through the streets higher than a kite. I'm twenty-eight," she confidently spoke as I sat on the bed.

I patted the spot beside me and said, "Come sit by me."
"Sure."

When she did so, Betterman and Hines analyzed us. I studied Dedricka for a while before speaking. I knew she had deep troubles or could've linked with the wrong girl or guy, and they messed her world up. I lost a few classmates to the wrong person in their lives.

Friendly grabbing her hand, I calmly breathed. "Do you want to die?"

"We all have to go one day, right?" she asked as her eyes gave me her answer—no.

"Yes, we do, but that's not what I asked you," I calmly replied, gently shaking her hand.

Dedricka didn't respond, just looked at me. I saw pain and

hopelessness in her chocolate-brown eyes. Knowing I needed to pull off her case, I softly voiced, "Whenever you want to talk about anything, I will always be available to hear you. I will tell you this: get help instead of running from your past. Make use of the resources here. Let that pain go before it's too late, Dedricka. Go for everything you set out to do before drugs become a favorite thing in your life. It's okay not to be okay. It's okay to want to run but not to continue running, putting yourself in a headspace that will eventually catch up. You will bottom out and have no idea who will be affected by your passing. Regardless of how they've turned their backs on you, it was to protect themselves from an addict, not you, but the addict in you. Get back to the you they loved, and your world will change."

As a tear skated from her round peepers, I gently rubbed her hand and said, "I'm going to tell you who I am. I'm going to keep it funky with you. I am a people's person. I can adapt to any age group. I am also a bitch not to cross. Do not think you can play underneath me. I'll fold your ass the fuck up in this bitch. You would prefer the sweetheart versus the cold me. Are we clear?"

"Crystal," she sincerely voiced, rapidly nodding.

Standing, I grinned. "Good. Since you, Hines, and Betterman are well-equipped with information, I would love for y'all to give me a rundown on how this place runs and who will be in my vicinity until next year."

"Sounds great to me," they responded as Dedricka hopped

from the bed, and Hines and Betterman led the way out of the cell.

God, be with me heavily until I leave this place. Please don't let anyone test me. I'm not trying to be in this joint longer than I should. Give me much strength each morning I wake up. Give me an understanding of what I read days after burying my mother while I'm here. Please don't let the religious group be full of non-believers. I know them when I spot them. I don't need anyone fake preaching Your word.

RICHARDO

Photos of Nyomi didn't serve her. She was a phenomenal sight in person, even though she rocked state property clothing. Her sexiness seeped from her pores, begging me to act out in ways I had never. Even her respectful tone caused my arousal to rise higher. Her adorable eyes begged me to stare into them while gently caressing her body as I backed her to the door. The voluptuous thighs on a body that needed many hickeys put a hurting on the starched, white pants. Nyomi Reanna Richards was the shit inside and outside, and I needed her at my side.

Since planting my eyes on her four hours ago, all I could

think about was her. I could barely focus on doing my daily tasks. I caught hell trying not to call another of our best friends into my office so she could bring Nyomi to me. Ashley Joseph would know I had a soft spot for Nyomi, and I wasn't ready for her to know. When the time came that I could no longer hold in my sexual urge for her, Ashley would be in a place like the others.

"Another day but more dollars," Palmer voiced as we exited the prison for the day. "Are we hitting up the gym?"

"Not tonight. On granddaddy duty while Rayne studies," I answered, aiming the key fob at my truck.

"She's doing amazing, man. Do you think I tell her that enough?" he questioned, causing me to chuckle and nod.

"I think you overdo it, which says a lot coming from me." I grinned at the buff man who had become my best friend after I saved him from a girl bully who had become his wife when we turned twenty.

As we arrived at our vehicles, I exhaled sharply and looked at him. I knew what needed to be said but didn't know how to start the conversation. Thankfully, he knew me well enough to post on his car and analyze me.

"You want me to tell you it's okay to sleep with her, don't you?" he lowly questioned, studying my eyes.

"I will do that whether you say it's okay or not. My issue is how do I step into her life in a place like this. She won't take me seriously. Nyomi's far from stupid, Palmer. She won't go for bullshit. Man, she hasn't had a man in five years. I've gone so far into one of her social media pages that I stumbled across a post she was tagged in. She laughed at it. I hopped my nosey ass in the comments and saw her reply. 'Just my toys and fingers. Five years strong. I'm waiting on my king, not a little boy.' I damned lost my shits in the office. Pussy hasn't been touched by a man in five fucking years. That is a dedicated ass woman. She is certain what she needs, not wants. She's a wife, not a girlfriend or fuck buddy. A wife! I've written fifteen gotdamn baby names and haven't seen or breathed on the cat yet," I passionately expressed, observing him.

Moving his hand in a circular motion was a clue for me to continue. Staring into his sparkling eyes, I sincerely said, "I have to move strategically with her, or we will constantly play the back-and-forth game. I don't like that game. Before my conversation with Rayne, I had looked at Nyomi's file. Off her damn mugshot, I knew she was the one for me. My body did all that girly shit before I started growling and becoming possessive. The aggressiveness intensified after talking to Rayne while thoroughly reviewing Nyomi's file. She has my child in a fucking chokehold, Palmer. That speaks volumes to me. Rayne is a people person, but she's not fond of females. So, me being me, I dug into who Nyomi is. From what I've seen from social media pages, she's the one. I am one thousand percent sure. I'm feeling something I've never felt, and I need to know how to handle it, so I don't fuck up making her my wife the moment she's free."

Smiling, he strolled toward me. Plopping his large palm on my shoulder, he grinned. "Ah, now I see Glover in you."

Throwing my head back, I laughed. "Nigga, fuck you. That was a low blow."

"No, that was the truth. You have always been a hopeless romantic, Richardo. Always. Being in love and wanting unconditional love has always been your thing. You always put love first, but you never ran across it because that condom broke. Stop overthinking. Just be the hopeless romantic you are. Keep that damn sex drive at bay. Go slow with her. You can anonymously romance her while she's here. There are many ways you can put a smile on her face. Build that solid friendship by writing her a letter. Either mail it or give it to Ashley. You don't have to reveal yourself until you absolutely can't control the urge to make love to her. You are the fucking captain, bro. Make some shit shake, and we will cover your ass, just as you have been covering ours since we found all that dope in that well and became two-faced fuckers," he confidently spoke while stepping backward. "Call me when you've worn out Zanning. I'll hip your old ass into how to be a sneaky, romancy fucker."

Opening my vehicle's door, I laughed. "I'm not helpless, dude. I think I can handle it from here."

"Until The Don shows up, and your ass gets stuck like a batch of peanut butter in your mouth." He chuckled as I slid into my truck, laughing.

At the same time, I closed the door and started the engine.

While reversing, my cell phone rang. Retrieving it, I stared at my oldest brother's name. Shaking my head, I hissed, "I guarantee he's going to fuck me up from masturbating, and I'm going to kick his ass."

Zooming from the parking slot, I answered, "Talk to me, Glover."

"I think Dad doesn't want me running the land once he retires," he hurtfully spoke as I neared the front guards.

"Do you know why?" I questioned, tooting the horn at the guards employed at the prison for six years.

"He says I lack dedication to bringing innovative ideas. He states I'm not owner material because I don't do things the way you do," he confessed as I skirted from the prison ground.

"Glover, why do you want to be over the fields?" I asked to see how I could best help him get the position I didn't want.

"To show him I can be as good as you," he answered, causing me to sigh.

"Glover, that's not a good reason to want that position. You should want it to continue our family's business. You should want it because you know you can bring in more revenue. You should want it because you want our family to continue owning those fields that those before us left for generational wealth. You need to sit down and think about the responsibilities of being over that land. It's a lot of work," I offered, nearing a red traffic light.

"Do you think I can do it?" he asked hopefully.

"Yes, as I mentioned, if your head is in the right place. If it's not, you will fail."

"Can you help me do what you do, or do you want to be over it?" he kindly inquired as I stopped behind Palmer.

"Hell nawl, I don't want that responsibility. I like being in the background since I was a teenager. I will help you get better at researching and learning more about an industry your ass supposed to know. We will start this weekend. Okay?" I exhaled, needing triple shots of whiskey.

"Okay. Thank you, little brother," he gleefully voiced.

"You're welcome." I exhaled, knowing I sat myself in an ant bed.

After properly ending the call, I dropped my phone into my lap and sighed heavily. "Mannn, I don't have time to end up being over those damn cotton fields that I launder our dirty money through. I'm not trying to fucking move like that. I can't move like that. Too many asses to cover. Now, I can't lick my gotdamn phone because one of Nyomi's boudoir images showing. I can't beat an inch of this fucka tonight because I have to figure out how to keep that idiotic bitch on his rightful inheritance."

I STRETCHED out on the sofa since Rayne and Zanning left two hours ago. I couldn't focus on how to keep my brother in his place as the field runner. I was too busy wondering how Nyomi settled into her temporary living place. I envisioned her horribly resting on the thin items as a tear skated from her pretty eyes. I imagined her softly weeping while praying she was in a dream.

Feeling as if she was sad, I sat upright and retrieved my device. I knew two of my people were still on duty since they took advantage of the overtime offered. Also, I knew they had their personal cell phones. Dialing Terry's personal number, I sauntered toward the kitchen, eager to hear his voice. He answered on the fifth ring, and I was at my fully stocked bar, smiling and proud.

"I need Ashley in the know about Nyomi. She needs a burner phone. Avery has a brand-new burner phone hidden well in his trunk. The row he parked on; the cameras don't work. The security company won't come out for two weeks. In an hour, I will call you back. I need Ashley next to you. Understood?" I said, filling the glass to the rim.

"Always. Hear from you in an hour."

"Bet," I responded before ending the call.

Shoving my phone into my pocket, I strolled from the bar, putting together plays. I encountered a few hurdles when I noticed Rayne's notebook and pen resting on the kitchen table.

Write her a letter. I rehashed Palmer's phrase.

"Look at this." I grinned, nodding and setting the drink on the table.

Sick of hearing the sportscaster, I hurried to the front room to place the TV on YouTube. I hadn't written a letter to a female in ages. I needed to set the mood before putting the pen on the college-ruled paper. I felt it would enable the right words to flow freely.

Freddie Jackson's "Main Course" sounded, causing me to groove to the kitchen. Indeed, I could flip the script in seconds, but I was an overly loving man. I dug the rap songs but was a love jam type of guy. Especially during sex, it made the slow, deep strokes better. It made the drenching kitty purr when I slowly rocked in it from the side. It made me a filthy ass nigga.

"Time to write this letter," I nervously spoke, pulling out the barstool and opening the notebook.

I analyzed my daughter's beautiful handwriting before reading 'Rayne's Wishes'. I tried to respect her privacy. Yet, I couldn't when I saw 'daddy' in the third sentence. Grabbing my glass, I read my daughter's thoughts. She pulled at my heartstrings, making me prouder of the woman she had become. My eyes became teary when she expressed how much she needed me to be happy and find true love because she felt deep in her soul that I never had it.

In her next set of thoughts, she confessed to wanting to move to Birmingham to continue furthering her nursing education. Yet, she wouldn't leave because I didn't have a good woman beside me. I stopped reading and called my daughter.

On the seventh ring, she sleepily answered. "Hello."

"You have your own life, Rayne. You don't have to stay here for me. I'm fine. I will always be fine," I confessed, causing her to softly sigh. "I'm going to be all right. It will take time for me to get where you need me, but I promise I will get there by next year. Go for all you seek. I'm supporting one thousand percent. I have no problem upping whatever you need. You know this."

"I hate you are by yourself. You are too handsome, kind, and loving. You deserve the world, Dad. I don't understand why you won't put yourself on the market. There are good women out there. You have to be open to meeting people. Momma is happy with Flex. You should be happy with someone, too. I know she hurt you by cheating on you. I'm sure your trust issue is high, but Daddy, all women are not the same," she confidently said, causing me to sigh and shoulder to sag. Rayne had the wrong impression of my feelings. I didn't give a damn about Zella and Flex fucking around. The less I had to fuck her and hear her bitching about me not loving her. I was thankful he aided me in signing the divorce papers I had been wanting to sling in her face two weeks after we got married.

"Daddy, did you hear me?" Rayne softly voiced.

"I did. All I have to say is that by next year, you will get everything you wish for. You will obtain your goals and not be worried about me. I've taken up enough of your time. Get some rest, and I'll have dinner ready for y'all," I said, swirling the brown liquid.

"Sounds good. I love you, Daddy. Goodnight," she lovingly announced.

"I love you more than you'll ever know. Goodnight, sweetheart," I responded before our call ended.

Placing my phone on the table, I rocked my head to King South's "What U Need". Instantly, Nyomi's boudoir image crossed my mind. Biting my bottom lip, I eyed my device and grabbed the pen. My twitching hand rushed to the power button. Brightly, my phone displayed the gorgeous woman perfectly propped up, sporting a black bra and panty set. The red lipstick resting on her full, juicy lips caused me to grip my dick. She had the perfect set of irresistible lips that would look great wrapped around my guy.

"My God. I don't think I'll act right when I get my hands on you. Those plump, pretty titties will receive many hickeys. As I write my name in cursive on your stomach, my tongue will sluggishly glide across it. While I show you how well I can dance in the twat, your trembling arms will house my birthday, social security number, and how much money is in my bank accounts. I'm going to fuck the shit out of you, Nyomi. That you can believe," I erotically confessed, unable to tear my eyes from the image saved as my home screen.

Flipping to the middle of Rayne's notebook, I stared at the blank paper while reaching for my glass. Once I placed the rim to my lips, I realized a lot of pressure was applied. I couldn't move too fast with her, so I was stuck on what to say.

"Ah, let's get to it," I voiced as the liquor cruised through my body, warming up the freak in me.

After placing the tip of the pen on the paper, I took a deep breath and wrote:

Nyomi Richards,

You don't know me, but I'm learning who you are. Social media is a semi-good way to get to know anyone.

"No, I don't like that. Redo," I huffed, ripping the paper from the notebook before balling it.

Again, I placed the tip of the pen on the paper and wrote:

Nyomi,

I need to stare into your eyes as I did earlier. I need to gently skate my knuckles across your cheeks. I need to witness the hunger in your eyes as I saw them earlier. I need to feel your body against mine. I felt complete. I was close to shoving my tongue in your mouth while slinging your arms upward. It was very welcoming. I felt the need to show you what it's like to have your pussy eaten by a mouth that has never been placed on one. I needed to slow grind in the chunky monster while our fingers were interlocked, and our eyes roamed elsewhere. The constant eye contact and the dedication and passion of my body movements will cause our souls to connect. No one will intervene in our happily ever after. They would be dumb to try to do so. I need to be in your life forever, starting now. Based on the first two lines, you know who I am.

The person who gave you this letter, tell them if you need a life of unlimited happiness, sexual bliss, and security with me.

"Hmm," I voiced, overlooking my letter. "That isn't hitting hard enough. I need to go deeper."

Flipping to the next page, I planted the tip of the pen on the paper, exhaled sharply, and coached, "Nigga, last chance before you get agitated and take your ass to that prison. That will be a fucking disaster."

Nodding, I wrote:

Nyomi,

Right now, I can't tell you who I am, but I can tell you I am interested in you. It's crazy to say this, but it's the truth. Your mugshot captured me. My eyes didn't see an inmate as my heart rapidly thumped. I saw a beautiful, intelligent, and accomplished woman in a fucked-up situation. I saw a woman who would be perfect for my daughter, grandson, and me. I saw my queen. You.

I've gone through your social media pages to get a better insight into you. I've purchased a background check but have yet to look at it. I don't want to read anything about you. I would prefer you to tell me about yourself. I need to hear your voice. Gaze into eyes that make me want to shower you with love. I know you will be skeptical of dealing with me since you are in prison, but I can assure you that I'm coming in good faith. I know what's being said about what goes on in prisons. I do not abuse my power unless it needs to be done.

May I be your anonymous friend who makes you smile? I

would love to see the bright, confident, and loving smile in all your photos. May I be your anonymous everything until I can reveal who I am?

The answers need to be given to the person who handed you this letter. Trust that if anyone gives you something, it can be trusted. You will always be protected, I promise.

Your Anonymous Admirer

"Ah." I smiled, feeling confident about my letter.

Folding it, I grooved to R. Kelly's "Freaky in the Club". Feeling myself and needing to master oral sex, I danced to the refrigerator. Eager to train a mouth to make my last wife visit the clouds, I felt a high surge of energy and positive emotions blanketing my bones.

When I opened the food keeper, I grinned at the applesauce and pudding cups. Snatching the times that would have me prepared to gobble up Nyomi, I excitedly voiced, "The ultimate pussy eating tactic. Come here!"

Grooving back to the table, ready to dive into a freaky moment, my phone rang a particular tune. I shuffled my feet and growled. Then, I realized what time it was and simmered. Immediately, I prayed nothing would disturb my plans to do my work duties and seal Nyomi into my life.

Plopping on the barstool, I answered my father's call. "Hello."

"Are you busy?" he questioned, sounding frustrated.

"Sort of," I responded, opening the applesauce and pudding cups.

"Can you put it on hold for a brief second? I need to talk about the lands," he voiced as I balled my hands and shook them.

"Of course, but may I say something first?" I calmly spoke through slightly gritted teeth.

"Sure."

"Dad, it's eleven o'clock at night. When you call this late, I get a little worried. Just a little. To talk about the fields is best during the day, say my lunch break. Not during breakfast because I'm liable to spaz. My mind is traveling faster than a jet during that time. Nothing has changed about the way my mind works. I wake up with a ton of stuff on it. The latest situation has me in a chokehold that will possibly cause me to spaz soon if I don't get a handle on it. There's a spectacular woman who has landed in my reach. I will use some of the late-night hours to prepare myself for her. I hope you understand where I'm going, Dad," I respectfully spoke.

"Um, no, I don't understand. Can you elaborate?" his nerdy ass inquired, causing me to clasp my hands and shake them. "Spill, Richardo. Bluntly but respectfully so I can understand."

Dropping my head, I confessed. "Dad, I haven't had sex in three years. I have never gone down on a female before. This mouth is forty-seven years old. I wouldn't dare put it on a woman I wasn't in love with. I've watched tons of porno, so I know what to do, but I haven't done it. I can stroke a woman until she sees Jesus, Mary, the lambs, and the Disciples. I need to do the same while orally pleasing her."

"Ah, shit, Son," he gleefully voiced, making me lift my head and look oddly around my black, tan, and cocoa brown kitchen. "Accept my video chat request. Grab an applesauce and pudding cup. I'll show you how it's done. These jaws are still strong at my age, especially when I remove my dentures."

With a turning stomach and no motivation to get my shit together for my wife, I politely ended the call without so much as giving him a head's up. I powered off my device while not giving a damn about calling Terry back to chat with Ashley. I would talk to her tomorrow when I handed her Nyomi's letter. Dad had officially weakened my stomach. He had destroyed my masturbation session to Nyomi's boudoir pictures.

From now on, if it's not anyone in your circle, do not answer any calls after ten, I thought aggressively, walking from the kitchen and shaking my head with the most disgusting facial expression.

NYOMI

Two Weeks Later

Fourteen days in the messy women's prison didn't faze me. I was deterred from the horrible feelings of being incarcerated until my release date. The mysterious person giving letters to C.O. Joseph had me closely watching all the male correctional officers. None gave me an indication they were the mystery person. I didn't need to get caught up in anyone's bullshit. So, I never answered the person's questions as they wanted. Consistently, I answered 'Uninterested. I'm here to serve my time and go home.'.

If I wasn't reading a book or a note from the beautiful

handwriting man, I had meaningful chats with Hines, Betterman, and Dedricka. They were the only females I talked to. I started to grow fond of the trio. They were a force to reckon with when I mentioned the religious program. I was yet to get them on board with me. I didn't let my faith wither because of where I was. It grew more because my rock was gone. I needed confirmation that I was on the right path even though I was where I was. I needed to see the light at the end of my fucked-up but temporary tunnel.

"Read and trash as always," C.O. Joseph whispered, startling me as she shoved her hand into my pocket as I washed the pans used for lunch.

"Will I ever get used to you scaring the shit out of me?" I whispered quickly.

"Probably not. That's why you are in the corner, hidden from snooping eyes. Thanks to the person who needs you out of sight," she rapidly voiced before dashing off.

"I would love to know who the hell that person is," I whispered, carrying on with my duties as if I didn't have a letter that wasn't quite a priority.

Scrubbing the food-stained pan, I zoned out and rehashed the simple statements in the letter from yesterday.

Trust me, please. I'm begging at this point. Just trust me.

Your Anonymous Admirer

After hurrying my hands from the soapy water to dry them, I quickly retrieved the folded paper. My heart raced every time I unfolded one; nothing changed with this letter. As

I scanned to see how long it was, I was astonished that it was five paragraphs.

Oh, my. This is going to be something. I wonder if he will reveal who he is, I thought, jumping into the note.

Nyomi Reanna Richards. Nyomi. Nyomi. Nyomi.

My Nyomi,

You are hurting my heart. I don't like that. Let me see if I can capture you this way. You've met me once and have seen me plenty of times. I've had my eyes on you before you landed in this prison. I know your entire background, what you've done, and how you are not so lonely looking anymore. Before your arrival, I ensured you had money waiting to be placed in your account, and no one disrupted your temporary life path.

I feel like I already know you. I've learned a lot about the woman who was a kindergarten teacher. I've fallen in love with you through your social media videos, photos, and dedication to speaking with the chaplain. I love how you drive Betterman, Hines, and Willis crazy about joining the religious program. I love how Betterman and Hines look at you as if you are their daughter. I love how you are turning Willis around. She's doing fantastic in trying to move from her past. That's something she's never done. You are a peaceful and knowledgeable woman. You make a man tell you he loves you and never had a proper chat with you.

I've enjoyed witnessing your beautiful smile. I ensure I receive an eyeful when you think I'm not looking. I need to see a smile filled with life and love when I open my eyes. It makes me eager to get here. You are a rare, sexy gem I must have in my life. I will wine and dine you while you finish your bid and after. I will give you my last name when you are free. I will give you children. I will aid you in putting your life back on track. Hell, it will be on track before you walk out of here.

Most importantly, I'm going to give you this dick, mouth, and fingers. There won't be a day I won't supply you with carnal bliss. Nyomi, I hope you know Brian McKnight's "The Only One for Me". I won't sing it. I'll be humming it. You will see whose heart you captured with a smile. You will see whose last name you will carry. You will see whose babies you will pop out regularly.

Once you know and accept, you will feel me. I plan our life; you are welcome to adjust anything if it's not removing me. That will hurt significantly, especially after recently adding ten more names to our baby list. I've written enough.

Your Anonymous Admirer

"Whew, shit!" I loudly voiced as my eyes bucked. I was thankful there was a lot of noise throughout the kitchen. I didn't like disrespecting my elders. There were quite a few on kitchen detail.

Instead of tearing the letter, I dipped that powerful sucker into the water before tearing it up. While discarding the note, I pondered, *who is this person? How will I react when I see his face? Can I take him seriously?*

That last question was why I pinched myself. I had officially lost my gotdamn mind, entertaining someone when I was in no position to bring shit to a table that I didn't have. I was in no position to think about sneaking around with anyone.

Hell no, I can't move fucked up against myself. I will stick with being uninterested even though I need to know who has their eyes on me. I don't give a damn if the letter is from the captain. I am not going to entertain a fucking soul in this place. I'm not dateable, fuckable, or sociable. I can't be, I thought while resuming my duties.

Forty minutes later, we were escorted from the kitchen. I was the last one in line; I had to ensure my area was spotless. I was a neat freak, had always been. As I walked behind an older woman with a permanent limp, I noticed C.O. Daniels, C.O. Lee, Lieutenant Harris, and Captain Mets chatting at the end of the hallway that led to our resting places. Like always, when they were huddled in the hallways or sleeping areas discussing prison improvement, I didn't pay them any mind. Yet, this time, I became nervous. I wasn't sure why since I had never been.

When I arrived thirty steps from turning left, Captain Mets erotically licked the lips I would gloriously capture and hold onto for dear life. My stomach caved as my hands balled. I was a thirsty female to see how long and wide a man's tongue was whenever they wet their mouth. As he slowly rolled his palms counterclockwise, he continued chatting with C.O. Lee.

Show your gotdamn tongue now, Captain Mets. I'm about to bypass you, I thought as the humming started.

The closer I approached them, the more I made out the tune. It was Brian McKnight's "The Only One for Me". My heart raced as my knees grew weak. Butterflies floated in the pit of my stomach as I couldn't control my eyelids from blinking rapidly. I sneakily eyed the four males. C.O. Lee and C.O. Daniels were smiling, so the noise wasn't coming from them. Lieutenant Harris was happily married, so I knew it couldn't have been him. When I slithered by the captain, he snapped his fingers to the beat of the song. The humming grew louder, and I was sure who had written me the letters.

"Oh shit!" I voiced oddly and loudly with bucked eyes as I hurried to cover my mouth.

"What's the issue, Richards?" C.O. Joseph asked with a blank facial expression.

Awkwardly, I pointed at my knee and stuttered, "My knee. It … um … it almost left to see Jesus nem."

"Do you need to see someone about it?" she questioned, head held high and shoulders straight,

"No, it'll be all right," I nervously voiced as Captain Met stopped humming.

"So, like I said, fellas, she's the only one for me. Get your tuxedos ready. She's mine," Captain Mets proudly stated.

Ohhhh, shit! Hmm, I might have told a massive lie in the kitchen. I might be a little dateable. A little fuckable. A little sociable. Just a little bit, though. I might do a little suckling on the captain's penis. Just a little, though. Nothing major. Ha! I lied. Much major! Pressure is applied in this place.

Wow. It's the captain. It's the gotdamn captain! I might do a little fucking. I might do a little sucking; I haven't done that in years. I might do a little riding while gripping my ankles. I won't do too much major shit. Just a little bit, I thought, grinning.

"C.O. Joseph, get your wedding attire together. The wedding and reception will be top tier. That's if that's what she wants it to be. I'm just proud to say she's my wife."

"I will be in attendance, sir," she cheerily voiced, walking behind me.

Holy fuck, I thought, sneakily pinching myself.

"Ouch," I lowly and painfully spoke.

Nope, I am not dreaming. Not at all.

LIGHTS WERE due to be out in forty minutes. I was eager for the noisy place to become settled. I had run myself ragged with rehashing Captain Mets' letters and the first time I met him. I needed my brain to be at peace. I was tired of going back and forth with myself about the situation. I hated how my mind decided to linger on thoughts of how he stared into my eyes as I was up against the door, wanting to touch him. I hated how I thought about us having sex. I hated how my clit tingled at the rehashing of him licking his lips while actively paying attention to his friend.

"Richards," C.O. Joseph stated, walking into the cell.

Opening my eyes, I rolled over to get out of bed and answered. "Yes?"

Quickly, she handed me a phone and whispered, "At eleven o'clock, he will call. You don't have to whisper or properly greet him. You will simply listen. Once the call is complete, power off the phone and stick it in your mattress. Do not let anyone know you have a phone; that includes Dedricka, Betterman, or Hines. There are only five people who know you have a device. Understood?"

With a pounding heart and slightly trembling hands, I reached for the phone and nodded. "Understood."

"Excellent. Have a good night, Nyomi," she sweetly voiced while backing away.

"You have a good night as well," I responded while getting cozy and stashing the phone underneath the pillow.

Yawning, I closed my eyes. After exhaling deeply, the phone started vibrating. My heart seemed as if it was in a stampede. My eyes popped open as I stared at the pillow as my hand traveled toward the device. The phone wasn't supposed to have rung until eleven o'clock. So, I enjoyed the simple vibration I hadn't felt in weeks.

When the phone stopped ringing, it rang again. My fingers itched to open the black flip phone. Against better judgment, I flipped that sucker open, pressed the answer option, and placed it to my left ear. As the beat of Trey Songz's "When We Make Love" sounded in his background, the deep-voiced man graciously said, "Thank you for answering, Nyomi. You are not to talk. Just listen. Sigh deeply if you understand your position on this phone."

With a racing heart and butterflies clouding my stomach, I smiled and sighed deeply. His tone was perfect. It paired well with the song playing. It relaxed me, taking me away from my reality.

"Perfect. I couldn't wait to hear your voice. I'll try not to take up too much of your time this go round. Is it okay if I tell you who I am? Fake cough if I can. Sneeze if I can't," he stated as I heard clinking in his background.

Nervously, I fake coughed.

"Again, thank you."

Out of habit, I wanted to respond that he was welcome, but I was thankful I didn't. People were heading to their cells. So, I ensured they couldn't tell I was on the phone.

"I'm the middle child; I'll be forty-eight on November 24th. My oldest brother's name is Glover. He'll be fifty. We have a baby sister. Well, depending on who you talk to, they may say have or had. I say have. She died when I was twenty-two; she was sixteen. Her name is Maysha. She's a nigga's heartbeat. She and her friend overdosed at a teen party. They died on the scene. I have a daughter; she'll be twenty-five this year. I have a five-year-old grandson. I'm family oriented. My parents and those before us were married. I'm no longer married. I was involved in that since I learned my daughter's mother was pregnant. I've been divorced for three years. I've been employed at the prison since I was nineteen. I climbed the ladder well. I'm sure you know C.O. Daniels, C.O. Lee, C.O. Joseph, Lieutenant Harris, and I go way back. From grammar school to now, we've always been a team. With the title of captain should let you know I'm the head honcho outside of here as well. I will stop talking briefly so you can take all that in." He calmly breathed as I was astonished to know he was ten years older than me. He didn't look a day over thirty.

Reflecting on his speech, I zipped back to when he chatted about his sister. I heard the hurt in his tone. I was thankful I couldn't talk. I didn't know what to say to him about it other than the usual words. I couldn't relate to losing a sibling, but I could relate to losing a loved one. I loved how he was family oriented. I'd always wanted to be part of a family. His marriage, I needed to know more. It was the word choice that made me question it.

As Delegation's "Oh Honey" played, Dedricka strutted into the cell, telling me goodnight. I pretended to be asleep and fought not to rock my head to Momma's and my favorite song to which we had often happily danced.

"I read on your social media page this is your favorite song. So, I thought it would be good for you to hear it," he said sexily as if he were relaxed on a comfortable piece of furniture.

Thank you, I thought, smiling.

"I'm sure you want to know why I'm divorced. It's because I didn't love her. She was in love with me. We had been fucking around for years, nothing major in my eyes. I let it be known. The condom broke. My beautiful kid was conceived. I needed to do the right thing for both. So, I married her mom. I gave my girl what I had: a two-parent household. I only held her mother's hand when my daughter was present. We took family photos and all that shit, but I was miserable. I never cheated on her mom. I gave her the same dick I had been giving her—toxic and condom-covered. When I learned she was fucking around with a close associate, I didn't give a damn, but that gave me ammunition to file for divorce. I was happy as fuck filing that shit and slapping my signature where needed. To date, she doesn't talk to me. I don't care. Our kid is grown with a kid. I've never found my one, so I can't say I was ever in love or deeply loved someone. I've never romanced a female and had plenty before I tied the knot. It was always suck this dick, open those legs, bend the fuck over, come sit on this thang, or leave me the fuck alone."

Basically, you were a cold-hearted whore, I thought, thankful for him telling me his truths. Yet, I needed him to finish.

"I'm an undercover hopeless romantic. I would love to take walks in the park while holding hands, sit on the beach watching the sunset, get dressed up and go on a dinner and movie date, and cook for you before feeding you. I'm with the bubble bath, champagne, and fruit tray while you sit on me talking about whatever. There is a dark side to me, like some Dr. Jekyll and Mr. Hyde shit. He's called The Don. My parents had to get me checked to make sure I didn't have multiple personality disorder when I was ten. The doctor said I was fine, so we rode with it. They let me slide with a lot of shit because I'm intelligent, and they don't know how to control me when my dark side shows up. I'm going to stop talking so you can take that in," he confessed, causing me to open my eyes and stare at the wall.

Oh, this nigga looney! Gotdamn it! It's always the fine ones! I thought, wanting to hang up the phone and call C.O. Joseph to come get it.

"Cough if I threw you off with Dr. Jekyll and Mr. Hyde. Sigh if I didn't," he erotically commanded, making my clit tingle.

I coughed, and he laughed. "Is it a turn-off? Sigh if it is. Say, 'Whew, it's a little warm in here. Let me take off a sock,' if you are stuck and can't tell."

Telling the truth, I spoke in a fake sleepy tone, "Whew, it's a little warm in this bitch. Let me take off a sock."

As he laughed, Dedricka voiced, "I was thinking the same thing."

"Go back to sleep, Dedricka. I'm not up to chat. I's tired, boss," I responded as the hearty laughter from Richardo made me smile.

"I like how you don't follow the rules. I see now you will

get eaten and fucked a lot. You are hardheaded," he thuggishly groaned as Gourdan Banks' "Keep You in Mind" played.

Immediately, my body was set ablaze as a gasp ran into the palm of my hand. The thought of his luscious lips on my hairless coochie caused my toes to curl. His mouth looked very experienced in pleasing a coochie.

"You'll be the first female I've gone down on," he sincerely said.

Astonished, I blurted, "I know you are lying."

As he chuckled my name, Dedricka said, "Huh?"

"Girl, nothing. I … um … shit, Dedricka. Don't pay me no mind," I responded, shaking my head.

While I rushed my hand to my mouth, Richardo breathed. "I'm serious. My mouth is extra exclusive, but I got a condom-covered community dick."

I couldn't help it; I laughed. It was muffled, but I was certain Dedricka heard me.

"You are so fucking hardheaded, man. I see now I can't talk to you at night." He chuckled handsomely. "Yet, I like that I can talk to you at night. When we were younger, I witnessed Terry, Avery, Ashley, and Palmer lying on the sofa, chatting on the phone with their love interest, looking love stricken. I was jealous as fuck. I didn't have anyone who made me want to lay up with my legs crossed, cheesing and shit. I do now. That's if you can handle it. Can you? Or should I be asking if you are interested in me since I have a Tasmanian devil side? To answer, softly say one or two."

"One," I whispered, trying not to smile.

"Cool," he voiced as if he grinned. "Now, answer. Softly."

Throwing the cover over my head, I smiled. "I can, but I still need to get to know you."

"You will. Can you handle The Don when he surfaces? Softly answer."

"Depends. Who is he?" I truthfully voiced, gradually sprinting my forefinger across my lips.

"He's the one who beats the shit out of those who take advantage of women. He's the possessive one. When he says 'mine', it's fucking his. All will know who and what is off-limits. He's why I can't accept owning my family's cotton fields. He's the no-nonsense fucker. He's a very intellectual, cutthroat person who owns a pharmaceutical with no LLC," he confessed before exhaling sharply.

Hmm. He references his dark side as The Don. Dons are those niggas. He's a gotdamn drug dealer and possibly a killer. The mention of owning a pharmaceutical with no LLC tells me that. He's a mighty fucker with illegal and legal money, I thought, closing my eyes and shaking my head.

I had never been with a street man. They were never of interest to me. They may have been good guys, but bad things happened to them or those they loved. I would face danger by dealing with him. It's not like people didn't know what he did or could do. I didn't want a man with ties to the streets, and I wouldn't be tied to the captain.

"Nyomi, your breathing is heavy. Is it because you caught on to what I said? Cough once, for yes. Sneeze for no."

I coughed.

"Are you no longer interested in getting to know me further? Sneeze for yes. Cough for no."

I exhaled heavily and analyzed the barren walls.

"Sneeze for yes or cough for no, Nyomi," he worriedly commanded as Tony! Toni! Tone!'s "Me and You" played.

I coughed as I wiggled my toes to the song and softly swayed to the beat.

"Fuck!" he angrily growled, causing my wiggling toes to curl and my stomach to cave. His tone was a turn-on.

After exhaling sharply, he sadly spoke, "Okay. Before I leave you alone, I must tell you this. My daughter was with you on Christmas. She's the one who covered your eyes. She was the one you told to leave the hospital, but she never left. She took you to your mother's home. You gave her a mission. She completed it with tears running from her eyes. Then, she analyzed me the entire time. Now, I know why she did. I was already looking into your file before she gave me all the accident details and y'all's encounter. I was smitten with you before my child called me the day you were in the process of coming this way. My daughter, Rayne Lisa Mets, has been worried about you. She came to your mother's house the next day and many days after. My child is like me. She doesn't give her time to anyone, regardless of the situation. My child has me in a chokehold, and I am proud to say that she does. I pay attention to my kid as she pays attention to me. I move Heaven and Hell for Rayne. You aren't interested in me, and I understand. I am not the pushy type. I know when to back off, but I have to make sure you are straight in here and once you hit the streets. Rayne made me promise to look after you because you have no one. Her words, not mine. You will never want anything because you have my child's heart more than her mother got it. Once this call ends, power it off and place it under the pillow. C.O. Lee will retrieve it. You will never be bothered by me again. It was a pleasure talking to you. Goodnight, Nyomi."

I was so caught up in knowing who had raised a fantastic woman who had helped me during the most chaotic time in my life that I couldn't tell him not to hang up. My trembling lips and stuck tongue wouldn't move fast enough to push out those words. So, he ended the call, and my shaky hand removed the phone from my ear.

Staring at the device, I pondered whether to call or text him. I needed him to pass a message to his sweet, loving child. Also, I needed to hear more about him because there was no way he was that bad of a man with a child-like Rayne. She was respectful to me, but she showed her ass to the police officer.

Tilting my head, I reflected on a scene when the police tried to handle me, and she stepped in.

"I'm The Don's motherfucking daughter. Y'all better show her some fucking respect before I call him. Officer Roy, I know

you don't want to see that nigga. I suggest you bring two more people personable officers over here before the Tasmanian devil will be on your porch because his child is fucking angry," Rayne nastily barked. She seemed to have grown taller as she held her head high.

My fingers had never moved so fast to open the call log and press the send button. When he answered, butterflies floated in my stomach as I softly whispered, "Tell Rayne I said hello and thank you. I was out of it that night, sitting on the grass, trying to comprehend things. Two officers, one was Officer Roy. She called his name when she mentioned whose daughter she was. She made it clear The Don doesn't like it when his child is upset. The Tasmanian devil will be on his porch. You can't be that much of a bad guy if you have such an amazing daughter. You can bother me if you are still interested. Cough once for no, you aren't. Laugh if you are still interested."

He laughed loudly, and my smile was brighter than ever.

"So, where was we in our conversation, sir?" I seductively whispered, twirling my forefinger into my hair.

"Softly say my name, Nyomi," he provocatively demanded, causing my nipples to harden.

To match his tone, I lowly purred, "Richardo Mets."

"I'm on the way to spend the night with you, so you can say my name all night," he sexily voiced.

"Slide through, handsome," I egged before slowly sliding my tongue across my lips.

Chapter 5

RICHARDO

The Next Day

My alarm clock blasted, causing me to slap the snooze button. Nyomi softly snored, making me smile at my latest accomplishment. I had never gone to sleep with a female on the phone. I was elated to experience it. I was delighted to hear her soft whimpers and coos. They were cute. I couldn't wait to hear them when I climbed between her legs, slowly stroking the slit while staring into her eyes. I desired to swallow her moans while digging into guts I would ensure drowned me.

Ring. Ring. Ring.

Looking at my primary phone, I stretched while grabbing

it. Seeing the birthday man's name, I hurried to answer his call, trying not to miss a single beat of Nyomi snoring.

"I'm up. I'm up." I groggily answered. "Happy Birthday, dude."

"Good, because my goddaughter brought her chipper ass over here and let the loud squad in. It's four o'clock in the morning, and Zanning is on a fucking million, just like the quads, their ringleader, my goddaughter. Terry and Palmer are ten minutes from taking three shots. So, they will be cranky today. Get Ashley up. I called thirty times, and she hasn't answered. Get dressed. We have a busy day," he gleefully voiced, as always, on his birthday.

Throwing the covers off my naked body, I yawned. "I'm exiting the bed. I'll meet y'all at the restaurant."

"Excellent!" the cheery fucker hollered before I ended the call.

"You haven't had much sleep, have you?" the sweetest voice sounded as I walked from the lonely bed.

"You crashed on me at one o'clock. I listened to your sleeping noise. It's cute. You don't sound like a bear. Thank God," I teased, stepping into a bathroom Rayne had to redecorate every three months.

"Whose birthday is it?" she whispered before yawning.

Walking toward the tub, I answered. "Lee's."

"So, is it a tradition for y'all to have breakfast before work on birthdays?" she asked while I strolled toward the toilet.

"Yes."

"Who set that in stone? You or the bossy one, The Don?" She cutely and lowly giggled.

Standing before the toilet, I whipped out the monster and chuckled. "Neither. On Avery's eighteenth birthday, he set it in stone. He's the baby of us by two months. How many babies do you want me to give you?"

"I almost clapped this bitch shut." She giggled, muffled, causing me to howl in laughter while shaking my guy.

"If you had, you would've regretted it," I seriously barked, flushing the toilet.

"Oh, really?" she whispered in a cute, hostile manner.

"Yep. Clap it if you think shit's a game, Nyomi. When you do clap it, to further let me know you think shit is a game, power it off," I egged, praying she would hang up on me and power off the phone. She would get the monster and my inexperienced mouth today.

When she hung up on me, I laughed while strolling toward the tub and dialing the burner number back. Once I received the automated voice about the phone not having a voicemail set up, I hooted, hollered, pumped my fist, and called Ashley. It was officially time for Nyomi to see me with no motherfucking clothes.

"I'm up, Richardo. My God. How am I supposed to survive the day? We are up too gotdamn early. Why am I not used to this shit?" she aggressively voiced as I stepped into the tub.

"I have no idea but put a little liquor in your coffee. That's what I'm going to do. I need you bright-eyed and bushy-tailed. I've been on the phone with Nyomi. We fell asleep. It's time for me to be alone with her. I will be thinking of how and where I need all players to be," I gleefully voiced as the warm water slammed onto my tattooed chest.

"No need to overthink how to get her isolated. Her roommate on some fuck shit. I received a tip that she had a visitor over the weekend and slipped in drugs. You need to conduct a search," she announced, making me sad and proud simultaneously.

"Then a fucking search it will be," I growled before our call ended.

Tossing the phone onto the black rug, I stood under the showerhead and thought about the praise I gave Nyomi for Dedricka's turned leaf. I thought it was hope for the girl who had a rough life due to the same motherfucka who supplied the teenagers the drugs that took my sister and her best friend's lives—her scumbag uncle, the nigga I had to make sure got caught up in the prison system just so I could flood it with drugs, made sure he became a gotdamn addict and overdosed. I was proud to hear motherfuckas watched him meet either his maker or his maker's nemesis.

Showering, dressing, and arriving at the best twenty-four-hour restaurant on the city's outskirts went in a blur. Zanning ensured I was no longer in the zone when I hopped out of my truck. The bucktooth kid, dressed to impress the little girls at school, scurried toward me.

As I kneeled to retrieve him, he shouted, "Good morning, Granddaddy!"

"Good morning, guy. Why are you so chipper at this time?" I chuckled as we hugged and walked toward the others, joking on the active child.

"I get unlimited pancakes because I'm Momma's broke best friend." He grinned, causing me to stop walking while howling in laughter.

"Come on, Daddy." Rayne giggled, waving us over. "I don't want to rush our traditional birthday gathering."

Walking off, I greeted my family as they greeted me. Stepping into the bright establishment attached to a gas station, Zanning looked at me with glowing eyes and a mischievous smile. I knew he would ask for something, and I would give Rayne the money before sitting at a booth or table.

"What you want, Zanning?" I grinned, loving that I could give him any and everything just as I had, and still did, his mother.

"I want a real giraffe, Granddaddy," he seriously voiced as everyone laughed. I couldn't because he reached too high.

"Get realistic now. What do you want?" I questioned, becoming annoyed as the hostess escorted us to our table.

"A real giraffe," he seriously voiced, searching my eyes.

"I'm not entertaining that. Pick something else."

"Why not?" he sadly voiced.

"Zanning, I said pick something else," I spoke through clenched teeth, staring into his mesmerizing eyes.

"Okay," he sadly responded as my four identical quadruplet nephews cackled and joked as if the sun was high in the sky.

"You could've said you wanted to go to Disney Land for a week, and I would've made that happen. You could've asked for a go-kart, and I could've easily made that happen. A bunny, cat, dog, or a fleet of roaches you could ask for, and I would make it happen before I finished eating," I seriously spoke, ready for my grandson to get out of my arms, raising my blood pressure.

"I wish he would ask for a fleet of roaches. They and he would be living with you." Rayne giggled as Avery pulled out a chair for her.

"If I could, I wouldn't buy no damn roaches," I responded as we sat Avery's gifts on the table behind us.

"Daddy, whatever Zanning is concocting, do not fall for it. He has enough stuff. Y'all are overdoing it by buying him stuff. He still has shoes and clothes with tags on them. I had to tell his father to stop buying him stuff. At your house, his closet is filled with things," she offered, clasping her hands while I sat him beside her.

"Okay," I replied, not hearing what she was saying. I could do whatever the hell I pleased with my money. If I saw something I knew he would like, I would purchase it.

"Speaking of his father, how's that going?" Avery inquired, cracking his knuckles. My grandson was Avery's younger brother's, Lucas, son. A motherfucka who had us close to choking him out until he was a few seconds from dying.

"Whew, it's going," she replied as I sat across from the birthday man.

Silence overcame the table once the full-figured server arrived. I prayed we didn't take long to order our food. I couldn't hold on to what I needed to say to my people who worked directly under me.

"I see that look. What's happened?" Avery questioned lowly as the quads and my daughter laughed.

"Dedricka had someone smuggle in drugs. Search today. Don't inform anyone. They will know when we stomp through that bitch. There's another matter at hand. It's time for me to cash in all favors. Starting today. It ends when she's released," I responded lowly, looking at my faithful and loving crew.

As the grinning, hardworking, yet idiotic playboy birthday man leaned back in the chair, his husky tone lowly floated amongst us. "I'm delighted to do my part."

"You better be." I cheesed, rolling my palms.

"The isolation area has six occupied cells. In the far back," Palmer whispered, staring into my eyes.

"Knowing Dedricka, she probably stashed some shit in her stuff," Ashley voiced, causing my attitude to change drastically. My growls were loud and nasty.

You are the fucking captain. She can't get fucked up with you on board. If Dedricka did put drugs in her shit, she's in isolation, and I'm right there with her. No need to spaz, I thought, closing my eyes and performing breathing exercises.

"It's too gotdamn early for this shit!" Avery laughed loudly as always. "My birthday finna be lit! Work is about to be off the chain! I can't wait! Overtime me, please!"

"Bitch, be quiet," Ashley snarled as the table grew quiet. My heart raced rapidly as I continued performing breathing exercises.

The goofiest of my nephews, Roq, laughed. "That nigga shiftin' at the gotdamn table. My God, what y'all was down there talkin' 'bout? He hotta than my motor right nih."

"Daddy let's go outside. Fresh air will do you good," Rayne softly voiced as I simmered greatly.

"Calm down, Richardo. Please. If you go into that prison like that, it will not be good. She will be fine. Trust me," Ashley softly stated, rubbing the back of my hand gently. Meanwhile, my nephews were on my ass about what they witnessed a lot in their young lives.

"Daddy let's go outside. Now," Rayne softly stated from behind me.

After opening my eyes, I eyed my worried child and exhaled. "I'm calming. Please sit down."

"Are you sure?" Rayne softly inquired, studying my eyes.

"Yes." I nodded as Roq removed his hands from around my grandson. He was in motion to whirl him from the table like always.

Ashley hurriedly voiced, "You say you are calming, but you need to be calm."

"I know that, Ashley." I exhaled, visualizing Nyomi sitting before me with the prettiest smile and bubbliest eyes. "I need to get my hands on Richards. Sooner than later."

"Richards? As in Nyomi?" Rayne softly voiced, crossing her middle and forefingers. "You were close to shifting into an angry beast. Is she in danger, Daddy? Is she the reason you almost spazzed like that? Or is she the reason you just calmed down?"

"She's not really in danger. She may have been or about to be crossed. Yes, she's the reason I almost spazzed and calming more. The breathing exercises helped kick off the calming," I voiced, rubbing my mouth.

"You like her," Rayne excitedly voiced,

Ashley softly asked, "Do you want me to get her on the phone?"

"No," I responded, eyeing her while lightly tapping on the light brown table. "You are right, Avery. Your birthday will be lit as fuck. See y'all when y'all clock in. I'm headed to see her."

As the server arrived with our drinks, they rapidly shook their heads, saying, "Not wise. All persons not in place."

Standing, I analyzed my best friends and said, "Last time I checked, I'm the captain. Last time I checked, I'm the one who put y'all onto where to be and when. I'm always the thinker before the doer. Remember that."

"And sometimes you are the doer and don't do thirty seconds of thinking, so sit your ass down before you have the worst headache of the day," Ashley calmly spoke, standing.

"It's too early for this shit." Terry exhaled sharply, shaking his head.

"Good luck putting me on my ass, Ashley, especially when I'm being civil-minded," I responded, observing her narrowed eyes. "Zanning, Granddaddy will see you later. Love you."

"Love you more," the eager kid replied as the waiter returned with our food.

"You will move recklessly, Richardo. Don't go to that place until we all step off in it," Avery seriously and loudly stated as I walked away with my daughter on my heels, asking a million questions. She was close to getting cursed the fuck out. I was a horny nigga who only needed to beat in one female's guts. I was an agitated bastard over the one female who had a hard time trusting a nigga like me.

"Daddy, what happened?" Rayne asked, grabbing my hand.

"Just like everything about you drives me insane, in a fatherly way, I'm the same way with her, but romantically. She told me to say hello and thank you. I am who I am, Rayne. I like her. I liked her from the moment I saw her mugshot. I need what the fuck I need from her. I see a future with her. I see you having a sibling or two. I see a new house with us in it. I saw what I had always seen, but it was with the wrong person. I dislike something that may involve her. I … I don't like when good people are fucked over," I spoke while pushing the door.

Standing beside me, Rayne softly patted my chest and said, "You might want to let your emotions settle before going to work. You are very irrational when a certain side of you shows up. My uncles and auntie said it's too early for you to clock in. When your heart is racing because of negative emotions, and you nor they are at fault, I suggest you listen to my auntie and uncles as they always listen to you when their hearts are racing, and they are at fault. You found your queen, Daddy. Don't fuck it up by being hotheaded over the smallest stuff. Within these three years, your beast's nastiness has increased. It's getting outrageous. You need to tame it and fast."

It's outrageous because I need some fucking pussy from my last wife, I thought, exhaling sharply and nodding. "Let's go eat."

♥♥♥♥♥♥

TWIDDLING MY THUMBS, I looked at my work boots and reflected on my behavior from this morning. Rayne was right; I needed to control my attitude. It had always been on another level since I was a child. It indeed became more uncontrollable when my voice deepened. I was a full-blown fool when I lost my sister. It doubled when I said, 'I do'.

Three years without sex because I didn't want to do the same shit that I did in my younger days had me off the fucking Richter scale. Closing my eyes, I wondered how things would play out between us. I didn't get a chance to think about it. Terry delivered my perfect package to the last isolation cell on time. As the chilly air swirled into the lifeless area, so did a nervous and softly smiling Nyomi. My heart galloped as I noticed Terry nodding three times before walking out.

When he locked the door, I walked from the bed I had personally made up. Lovingly, I observed a beautiful face I couldn't wait to wake up to every morning. I softly smiled at the strong woman posted against the wall with her arms resting at her sides.

Stepping before her, leaving no space, I gently skated my knuckles down her cheek. Sweetly, I whispered, "I like how you defied me this morning. So, I will take the privilege of saying this, Nyomi. I don't care how many lies have to be told about your whereabouts as long as you are willing to go along with them. Today and many other days and nights, we won't leave a cell until I have you folded like a gaming floor rocker chair. I need you to believe that I'm interested in getting to know you better before making you my wife. For you to believe it, I have to show it. I'm not the kind of man who does a lot of talking. I show, so will you eat with me?"

"Depends on who cooked," she cutely voiced, searching my eyes as I separated her arms.

"A certified cook from LongHorn Steakhouse," I answered, pulling her from the wall.

"You've earned a brownie point," she nervously replied, allowing me to lead her to the bed.

"Good." I smiled, loving the feel of her soft hand and her softening toward me.

As we sat on the bed, I couldn't tear my eyes from her, and I couldn't keep my nasty thoughts at bay. I needed every part of her badly. I was ready to execute my plan of hearing her moans and feeling her nails dig into my back. I was eager to shove her legs as far as they could go to face plant in the chunky monster. Yet, I didn't want to turn her off and make her feel as if that was all I wanted from her.

"Why are you lowly growling?" she inquired, snapping me from my thoughts.

"I didn't know I was growling. Sorry," I voiced embarrassingly while rubbing my palms together.

"Can I be honest right now?" she asked, tilting her head and placing the bagged food onto the floor.

"Always be honest with me," I answered, interlocking our hands.

"I need to know what your lips and tongue feel like more so than eating," she uttered, stunning me and growing my dick. "Then, I need to know what you feel like inside me."

Erotically licking my lips, I kicked off my shoes and nodded. "I have no problem giving you what you need."

"Okay," she voiced, bending forward to remove her shoes.

Hurriedly, I put her on her back and hissed, "That's my job. I take off your clothes. I clean you up after I've gotten you sweaty. I put your clothes on since I took them off. No, I am not controlling. I don't see the need for you to do anything before and after I've pleased you. Do I make myself clear?"

"Crystal," she moaned as her right eyelid flapped harder than the left.

Grabbing the bottom of her slip-in, white shoes, I teased, "I hope your feet don't stink."

"Trust me, they don't. They are topnotch smelling like the rest of my body," she admitted as I planted her shoes on the ground.

"I love the sound of that," I praised while snaking my hands toward the sides of the white pants waistline. At the same time, I dropped my mouth in the center of the waistline.

Nyomi lifted from the bed while observing me with the most peaceful eyes I could ever see. Those begging eyes relaxed me, steadied my breathing, and intensified my need for her to be in my life forever.

Pulling down her pants, I ensured my soft knuckles gently graced her soft skin as I overlooked her seductively. I needed her to remember my touches and gazes throughout the days and possibly nights I couldn't get to her.

"Hmm," she cutely cooed, balling her cute, average-sized toes.

Looking at her as if taking a photograph, barely blinking and breathing, I removed her pants and tossed them onto her shoes. With her feet in my hands, receiving light pressure from my fingertips, I drove them to my hungry mouth. She curled them and cooed.

I didn't believe in going fast when it came down to sex. It was an art that had to be done with precision and dedication. So, I catered to a toe at a time. Sweet kisses followed by rapid tongue flickers and the suckling followed by French kissing caused her fingers to twitch.

My wet tongue traveled upward as she crept her hands into the mass of her brown and black hair strands. While writing my name in cursive on her thighs, I licked her legs, nice and slow, causing a delicate whimper to slither into my ears.

The steam rolling from this chunky monster has me not wanting to go slow. This motherfucka is fat as fuck. It's going to drown me. It will please me, and it will make me lock up at the thought of another nigga trying to obtain it, I thought, arriving before the pink monster I couldn't imagine what it looked or felt like due to the many disturbances after I clocked out.

With a watery, eager mouth, my jaws clenched as Nyomi lifted so I could remove her underwear. Just as I had done her pants, I did the same with the white panties, slowly removing them while longingly staring into her thrilled eyes.

Dropping the underwear onto her pants, I asked, "Do you trust me?"

She hesitated to answer; unlike last time, I patiently waited for her to answer. While she pondered and observed me curiously, I unbuttoned my shirt, ensuring my pinky fingers glided down the crisp, white cotton material.

A soft smile formed when I tossed the shirt on the ground and asked, "You must have to see my boy to answer?"

Erratically, she breathed, "I thought I already answered."

"When was that?" I chuckled, taking my time to remove my white undershirt.

"When you asked," she panted as my nipples hardened.

"You didn't say a word, Nyomi Reanna Richards." I grinned, unbuckling the thin, black belt.

"Oh, I could've sworn I did," she cooed, eyelids fluttering and stomach lightly quivering.

"Are you nutting?" I laughed, unbuttoning my pants.

"Just about," she sensually voiced before provocatively licking her lips.

"How is that when I haven't done anything to you?" I probed, stepping from the bed to become naked, just as she would be.

"I trust you," she spoke in a tiny coo as her toes curled.

"That's good to know. It's also good to know that I can make that monkey arouse without barely doing anything to you. I won't have to worry about sliding a bullet through a nigga's cerebellum. You will keep a motherfucka out of your face once you hit the streets," I cockily announced, taking my time dropping my pants on my shoes.

"Will you always take this long to get naked?" she asked, aggressively running her fingers across her forehead. "Or are you a carrier of a little one and trying to build your confidence or whatever?"

Gripping the waistline of my tight-fitted boxers, I laughed. "A carrier of what?"

"A little one," she responded, staring and pointing at my private area. "If you have one, it's okay if you can work it."

I continued laughing while dramatically dropping my underwear. As I outstretched my arms, Nyomi rose off the bed. When she started rocking back and forth like an older person, clasped her hands, and covered her puckered lips, I made him jump fast. "Is he up to par for you?"

"Richardo, let me out of this damn cell. I'm not about to do this with you. Got me down here wasting your fucking time. I'm not grown up enough to be in this damn prison, much less have you in me," she goofily whispered, waving me over to her.

"I asked your ass if he's up to par for you?" I chuckled, grabbing a condom and staring into eyes that begged me to come to her.

"Two more inches, and he wouldn't have made the cut," she sassed as I kneeled before her, grabbing the hem of her shirt.

"Is that so?" I replied, raising an eyebrow while removing her shirt.

"Very much so," she tenderly voiced as I dropped her shirt onto her panties. "Um, what are you doing?"

"Showing instead of telling," I confessed, hurrying to unclasp her bra. "My breakfast has run its course. Time for my appetizer before eating my meal. Nyomi, if it doesn't call for me to give you a quickie, I won't rush intimacy. I can't lock you in if I rush. Understood?"

"Yes." She nodded as I erotically removed her bra, ensuring it dangled. At the same time, my hands traveled in all directions across her soft back.

"Mmm," she moaned, biting her bottom lip.

"I was a cold bastard, Nyomi. So, I can tell you exactly what type of niggas you had in your presence. Cold ones, like the old me. Ones who didn't give a damn about pleasing a woman, only getting them hooked. To me, that's a difference. I didn't do all of this with anyone. I went straight into the coochie. Your days of having a nigga rub on you for a few minutes to get you wet is over. I … will … make … your … twat … flood … before … I … breathe, finger, suck, kiss, or fuck it. That's a promise," I sluggishly voiced against her chest while looking into her hungry eyes.

Dropping her bra onto her shirt, I ogled what God had taken His time crafting. After wetting my lips, I grunted, "My gotdamn. Simply beautiful. Every motherfucking part of you. I must have you. If I don't, The Don will come out and make some shit shake, Nyomi. Once I connect us, I hope I don't have to be The Don permanently to make you see how badly you fucked up by tossing me to the side. No need to respond."

As she nervously nodded, I swiftly slithered my arms underneath her thighs and suckled her nipple into my mouth. Pushing my face into her titty and lifting it, her sweet, erotic pleasure noises lowly ran around me. Immediately, I knew we would be naked every day, minus the weekend.

Lifting her from the bed, I rapidly flicked my tongue against her erect nipple. Nyomi's legs started to tremble as I lifted her upward. The higher she rose, the more I hated I had to let her nipple go. It felt incredible as my tongue skated and rolled across it. Yet, it was time for me to have a meaningful chat with the pretty, shaved monster.

"Richardo," she whimpered, sounding like an angel, bricking me more.

With her hovering over my face, I said, "You know what you need to do with your feet, and you also need to remember where you are. Understood?"

"Yes," she panted as I stared at the glistening pussy.

"Good," I responded, bringing my appetizer to my face. "Hey, beautiful. I hope you are ready for me, and I'll try my best not to disappoint you."

Chapter 6

NYOMI

I thought Richardo was ready to devour me when he brought me toward his face. I was utterly wrong. He slung his arms upward, and I swore I was on the way to meet Jesus. My heart raced as a small screech floated around us.

Looking down at the man with the finest face in all the land, I snarled, "Do not drop me."

"Not on the floor, I won't." He grinned before dropping his arms.

"Eek," I shrieked, hurrying to cover my mouth as fear consumed me tremendously.

I felt as if I was on a motherfucking freefall carnival ride. I wanted to scream for him to help me put on my gotdamn clothes so I could return to my cell. My heart galloped as my eyes bucked; I was ready to curse his ass out for making me fearful. Yet, the moment his rapidly flickering, long, and wide tongue ran up in my kitty cat, all was, but wasn't, well. I lost the will to control everything but my feelings.

Every time he rolled his tongue through my pink tunnel, my heart turned over, and my toes gripped his shoulders. The slow tongue fucks and the sealing of his lips on my prized kitty made me desire him more. His strong hands pushed my butt, granting him less air. It was as if he was suffocating himself with the goodness my parents made. That was a major turn-on.

"Richardo," I moaned, gently bouncing on his tongue.

"Nope," he hissed into my lady pocket before slinging me off his pink flesh.

I couldn't react to the vibrations he rendered as much wind consumed my mouth and nose. At the same time, I oddly and lowly screeched, "Eet."

"Stop rushing me. I'll let you fuck my tongue when I'm ready for you to do so. I told your ass … you are the first female I have done this to," he sternly spoke before dropping his arms.

Onto his tongue, my ladylove went before he shoved me back in the air. I clasped my hands across my mouth as Richardo Mets lifted me as if I were weights. Not once did his arms shake. My heart skipped many beats like he didn't skip any by shoving his tongue into my pretty kitty before tossing me in the air as if I were a piece of tissue.

For God knows how long, Richardo continued using me as weights while passionately French kissing, suckling on my pretty folds, and quickly flickering his tongue on and around my pink tunnel of pleasure. It seemed I floated on the highest cloud every time I came on his tongue. Several times, when he suckled on my clit, I needed to passionately yodel his name. It frustrated me that I couldn't.

When he ceased tossing and dropping me, Richardo kept my pretty kitty on his face as he slowly walked toward the bed. I didn't want to fall, so I slowly turned to guide him. My vision was poor due to his quickening tongue flicks and rolls. Gripping the back of his head, my nails graced it as I moaned, "You need to get me off your face. I do not want to fall."

Without notice, the amazing oral giver tossed me in the air. "Eet!"

"You said you trusted me. You need to act like it," he lowly barked, rapidly descending his arms. I didn't land on his tongue; I was face to face with the wet, stern-faced man.

As he walked closer to the bed, I rolled my eyes and hissed, "You are already making me sick. Fine-ugly ass."

Before he could blink or reply, I hungrily slapped my mouth over his soft lips. Immediately, I fell in love with his smooth mouth as I pushed my tongue farther inside. I marveled at the sweetness embedded in his supposed inexperienced tongue. I admired our bodies meshing as his soft palms caressed my butt.

"Mhm," I cooed sweetly, resulting in him swallowing my pleasure noise.

As he laid me on my back and placed my left leg on the wall, I broke the kiss just to take in his attractive physique nestled between my thick thighs. Yet, I couldn't do to his hypnotizing gaze. When his eyes slowly and seductively moved from my eyes downward, my eyes followed where he looked. Cockily, he smiled, dropped his head, and extended his tongue. I received a clear visual of how long his tongue was.

"Ah," I moaned as he started showering my body with kisses and dragging his short-trimmed nails down the side of my body.

His slow arrival to my wetland had me eager to tell him to hurry up. I was boiling with passion. It was time for him to scratch an itch he created. As I opened my mouth to tell him to speed things up, it was stuck once he hurried to spread my wetland lips with two fingers, and French kissed my clit.

"Yes, God. That's it," I cooed as my body melted into the thin bedding.

Left to right, slow and pleasant, Richardo turned his head while tonguing my clit down. The feeling was so great that I forgot where I was. A few of my moans slithered around the room slightly too loud. The more his tongue glided and rolled, the more I found myself thrusting while cradling the back of his head. One too many thrusts rendered his beasty growl to surface. Several intense rapid flicks from the tip of his tongue against my pink bud brought a forceful tingling sensation running wildly through my pink monster. As volcanic heat rose from my toes, my body started jumping and jerking, and my eyelids blinked faster.

Unintentionally, I blurted, "Shit! Okay, *honey*, it's time to come off my clit. My body is on another level. I'm going to be honest. I don't know how to handle it."

Snatching his mouth off my sensitive spot, he glared into my face and hissed, "There's a gotdamn pillow your head is on, *honey*. Use it. Do not stop me again. I got time today, and quite frankly, so do you."

He didn't give me time to curse him out or house an ugly facial expression. The fine-ass slop mouth man resumed rapidly flickering his tongue. My body was back in hot mode; my toes were back curled, and I had aggressively removed the pillow from my head. As I damned near smothered myself, I had the urge to urinate. I heard about that feeling and knew what would happen, so I braced for impact.

With a death grip on the pillow, my stomach massively caved as I howled, "Richardooooooo."

I felt my waterworks gushing out of me as he started sloppily eating my pretty kitty. I needed to see him, but I was afraid I would be too loud since I hadn't stopped moaning, growing, and yodeling into the pillow.

His hungry slurping noises and French kisses started as a

finger entered my drenching pink tunnel. Many soft whimpers ran into the pillow I no longer had tightly pressed to my face. Three taps to my G-Spot, my back held a deep arch. Instantly, I was back to singing into the pillow I mashed into my face while shaking like a stripper.

When the quick orgasm arrived, it was different than the last one. It was a million times more powerful, and Richardo was officially at a waterpark. My mobility and voice were useless as a prickling sensation ran from the bottom of my feet to my neck. Tears tumbled down my face as I realized Richardo's loving made me weak, and I loved it. I yearned for more of it while he still gave it to me and snatched the pillow from my face.

Starvingly, he looked at me and growled, "Look at me while you drown me, Nyomi. Remember where you are, beautiful one."

Not needing any static for us, I watched Richardo devour my coochie with his mouth and finger. Meanwhile, his longing gaze took my mind to places it had never been. Deep in euphoria land, sounding like a puppy on a hot, sunny day with no water to lap, I believed my soul busted a dramatic split on his finger before dancing into his mouth.

Richardo had me feeling like I was on a white-water rafting adventure with a few rowdy friends. My sweetness splashed and squirted on his face, and he eagerly growled while pumping his fists. My hot, horribly trembling body rocked from left, right, and up continuously as he yodeled while pumping his fists.

I was a lost cause when he slowly removed his finger and mouth. Seeing his satisfied facial expression towered in my sweetness aroused me. Witnessing his charming smile melted my heart. It was filled with love, determination, and passion. I wanted to kiss him, but his longing stares kept me in a trance once I saw the twinkle in his eyes. It was magnificent to witness, but knowing I was the reason he looked that way was outstanding. I felt fucking proud. My previous boyfriends didn't look at me like I was their galaxy. Their eyes didn't sparkle, nor did they have the ability to stop me from moving or talking during sex.

Dragging his hands underneath my butt, Richardo's deep voice glided from his succulent lips. "I don't know what I'm doing, so I'm free-flowing it. I promise I'll get better the more I'm between your legs. Okay?"

"You are doing a wonderful job," I praised in a tight voice while studying him as he dropped his head to my ladylove. My breathing became erratic as I anticipated him passionately attacking me.

Slowly, he placed my legs on his shoulders and gripped my waist. In a flash, he slowly French kissed my starving girl while staring into my eyes. Antsy, I threw my snatch on his tongue while lowly groaning, "My God."

Like before, he stopped, glared at me, and hissed, "Stop rushing me."

"It feels good, Richardo," I whined.

"You need to learn patience, Nyomi. I'm romancing the chunky monkey, your heart, mind, and soul. I need all three in sync with me. I'm doing it my way. A method that will let you know that no matter the time or place, I will always take my time with you. I'm the motherfucking captain of this prison. I will say how long you will be gone. You are my captain. I must make sure you are straight before you leave my presence. Understood?" he voiced seriously.

"Yes," I cooed as he dropped his face an inch or two from my treasure box.

He didn't look at me as he passionately spoke, "I'm on my knees to ask you, pussy, to marry me an' The Don. In that order. Why I'm asking you? Because if I can't sexually satisfy you, I'm useless to her. You don't have to answer now, but in a minute, I need my answer."

This man here, I thought, in awe of his speech to my pretty lady. She had never been spoken to.

Aggressively, Richardo removed me from the bed. I was back in the air, like a kite on a sunny and windy day. With my toes planted on his broad shoulders, my coochie rested on his lips. Slowly, he danced as if we were face to face. Against my pretty kitty, Richardo sang the hook of R. Kelly featuring Plies' "Marry the Pwussy (P-Mix)".

The heat from his mouth and the movements from his lips had me aroused, but the fact he carried out an action I had dreamed about experiencing pushed me over the top. I was done! He had me! There was no more cat-and-mouse game between us as I slung my arms upward, rotated my hips, and lowly sang along with my man.

"Going to run this prison, thinking, my man, my man, my man when I see you," I lowly whimpered as Plies' verse caused Richardo to become a little too crunk while rocking from side to side. Yet, that didn't stop me from throwing my wet-wet on his lips and cradling the back of his head.

"I will put a ring on this pussy," he eagerly voiced into my pretty kitty while descending me.

As he descended me, the handsome gentleman calmly asked, "What did she say to marrying me?"

"She said yes," I breathed against his sweet lips.

"Perfect." He grinned as I felt the pole of all poles gliding between my folds. "Can I go in you raw?"

"Did you forget where I'm housed until next year?" I moaned as he slowly slid the head in.

"Fuck," he hissed, nodding. "I did. I'll have to put the condom on. It's been a while since I—"

The incredible feeling of his head in my starving hole caused me to slowly rock on it while he talked. I didn't give a damn about shit. I needed his loving. I had gotten a whiff of his inexperienced mouth, and I needed to see what his condom-covered community thang could do.

"Nyomi," he stuttered, gripping my waist and slowly sliding himself into a suckling hole.

"What?" I growled, rotating my hips and eyeing him through lowered eyelids.

"You will get nutted in if you don't stop moving," he moaned, walking toward the bed.

"That shouldn't happen if you have self-control and pull out," I cooed, rising from the shaft. I needed to have his head beating up my G-Spot.

"I can't fuck you raw, Nyomi. I'm going to nut in you," he announced, lying me on the bed—fucking up my groove, which pissed me off.

"Richardo Mets, if you don't stop pussyfooting with a coochie that said it would marry you, I'm going to put your ass in the no zone. In five motherfucking years, I have not found a man to pique my interest. I come up in this raggedy-ass bitch, and my stuff wakes up for a fine-ass captain. You, Keith Sweat, my ass to death to get me where I'm at. Fuck me. Damn it. Fuckkkkk. Meeeee," I lowly and nastily snarled, glaring at him.

His jaws locked as his stomach caved massively. The grip around my waist became tighter as his eyes narrowed. Richardo's head rocked awkwardly as his right eyelid flapped. The mighty stick grew harder as he growled and closed his eyes. I had no idea what the fuck was going on with him or why my body thought the shit was sexy.

"You got it," he thuggishly spoke, dropping his nose on mine.

Observing my eyes, a wickedly grinning Richardo artistically and passionately glided himself inside me. Immediately, I melted into the thin mattress as the hissing man rapidly rotated his hips. My eyelids flickered when I noticed the dick touching areas that hadn't had any visitors since I started having sex. Sprinting his mouth to my neck, Richardo outstretched my legs, leaned to the left, and started boxing out my guts. My watery sweetness shot out of me like a ton of small pieces of confetti in a popper.

"Ah! Shit amighty. My God. This fantastic dick is all over the motherfucking place," I poorly whimpered as he devilishly chuckled, turning me on more.

"Mine!" he growled in my neck while digging in my guts.

"Amen," I praised as he bit my neck hard as fuck, causing my arousal to increase. It took everything in me not to yodel his name. I had a thing for pain during sex, but I wouldn't dare tell him.

"I don't give a fuck 'bout nuttin' in you, sassy mother-fucka you. You'll have a swoll ass womb fuckin' wit' me, an' I'mma take care of mine."

"Oooou, shit amighty," I moaned, unsure who had my body locked as my ladylove had a nasty tantrum.

Standing up in my goodness, Richardo grinned wickedly and said, "Brace."

I didn't have time to acknowledge him before receiving the best whacking. I had to cover my mouth when he played Whack-a-Mole with my A-Spot and G-Spot. My body started playing Hopscotch as my throat was part of the choir team.

So many thrusts and gut-wrenching muffled moans later, Richardo snatched me off the bed and fucked me until I cried happy tears. Up against the wall, still fucking me gloriously, Richardo rested his lips against mine. Cockily, he smiled. "This dick must not be good to you. You ain't said shit since I been in you."

Looking at him as if he had lost his mind, I weakly voiced, "I'm a prisoner, Richardo. Doing something prohibited. I can't sound off."

"Shiddd," he snarled, snatching me from the wall.

God, get his mind right and fast, I thought as he placed me on the ground.

"Bend over," he ordered, rubbing his palms together.

As I did so, his phone vibrated, and his firm, sweaty palm graced my right cheek. The bite of pain and the loud smack were pure pleasure. Yet, I didn't moan, thanks to focusing on the tight curling of my toes.

"Put this in yo' mouth, baby. You like pain, an' I ain't got no fuckin' problem deliverin' that," he voiced, extending his shirt.

Shit, he knows, I thought, stuffing my mouth with the cotton item.

I barely had my mouth sealed around the shirt when I felt him slowly sliding inside me. Gripping my ponytail, he undid it. As my hair flowed onto my face and neck, Richardo said, "Don't ever snarl at me. I don't like that. I'm gon' make sure you never snarl at yo' king because I will never snarl at my queen."

Before I could acknowledge him, Richardo bent his knees, spread my ass cheeks, snatched my head back, and jackhammered me while rotating his hips. Again, that thang was everywhere as I yodeled into the shirt and dug my nails into my ankles. The more he banged in those spots, the more I craved him. The more I craved him, the more I needed him next to me, in me, making me feel everything I had never.

Zit. Zit. Zit.

Aggressively grabbing my waist before lifting me from the ground—still fucking me—he sexily growled, "Today, you will learn who to play wit'. It ain't me. It's this fat ass motherfucka suckin' my dick you will play wit'."

"Richardo," I screeched into the wet pieces of cloth as my body was a mess from being swiftly removed from the ground.

Zit. Zit. Zit.

"Don't say shit 'bout me droppin' you. The fuck I look like lettin' my queen fall on the fuckin' ground. You said you trust me. You need to fuckin' act like it. Make that my last motherfuckin' time sayin' that shit. Can you still bust a split?" he hissed.

Turned on that he did know much about me, I nodded.

"Bust it," he savagely spoke, making his mighty pipe rapidly jump in my clenching hole.

Quickly, I spread my legs and dropped my head.

"I can't wait 'til next year. We will have much fun wit' an' without clothes on, baby. I promise," he sincerely spoke while standing tall.

Richardo held tightly to my waist as he pushed me off his stick and pulled me back onto it. By the fourth time he slowly entered and exited me, his beautiful singing voice graced the cell. My eyes were filled with tears as he lovingly sang Brian McKnight's "The Only One for Me".

Zit. Zit. Zit.

Increasing his thrusts, Richardo savagely announced, "You got two months to fall in love wit' me, Nyomi. Two months."

Shit, I'm in love now, I thought as my pretty kitty vomited on the coochie clogger clawing into my drenching tunnel.

His phone vibrated seventeen times before he stopped rocking my violently shaking, sweaty, and satisfied body. Breathing heavily, the sex god held tightly to me while walking toward our clothes and shoes.

"Grab my phone fo' me, baby," he panted, stopping before our clothes.

"Okay, but um, did you cum?" I questioned curiously. I was pretty good at detecting it.

"Yeah," he proudly voiced as my eyes bucked, and I hopped off the firing gun.

Before I could stand tall, cum ran from between my legs. Fear consumed me as I stumbled toward the bed and tried to move my mouth to ask what was next. As I thought about every worst scenario of what would happen to me and a child I wasn't supposed to have, the fucker walked toward me, grinning. At that moment, he made me feel like the biggest idiot in the world.

Standing before me, the smiling bitch cuffed my chin while wiping my tears. Slowly sliding his eyes from my teary peepers to my stomach, he happily spoke, "Make me proud, lil' ones. Rayne a siblin'; Zannin' need someone to help him spend my money, an' I need my queen to carry her first child proudly."

Before I could catch my hand, I slapped him, causing him to lean to the right. With quivering lips and tears tumbling down my face, I hissed, "You had no right to do that shit."

Gently grabbing the back of my neck, his dreamy eyes stared into mine as he slowly enunciated, "I told yo' ass while you was bouncin' on me I needed to put on a condom, or I would nut in you. Then, I told you I didn't give a fuck 'bout nuttin' in you. 'Cause I'm gon' take care of mine. You ain't say shit. So, who is really at fault fo' my nut sprintin' through that good ass snatch, Nyomi?"

Zit. Zit. Zit.

"Get me back to my cell, Richardo," I choked up, not looking at him.

Placing his face in my vision, he shook his head and said, "Not while you like this. You gon' get those tears offa you while you in here. You too emotional. You will tell on yo'self. You don't need to let anyone know you too emotional. They'll know you got som' dick. So, cry on me an' when it's all out, C.O. Joseph will come get you, so you can shower."

As he lifted me from the bed, I dropped my head on his shoulder and softly wept while thinking, *I have fucked up. I can't do this with him. Not here. Sex is so fucking good I can't talk or move. I can't tell when he's going to nut. I can't do what I did with the others. Control our sex life. He's a sex demon, so I am, but I'm a fucking inmate. I can't get wild like that. I need to cut this shit off with him until I'm released. This shit is a major risk to my freedom. The loving is all that, but not enough for me to risk going home in April of next year.*

♥♥♥♥♥♥

How could he do that to me? Why didn't I ask to leave? I knew better when C.O. Daniels removed me from the library. I had no business being in that cell with him. He's a gotdamn hot oven, not meant to be touched. God, why was I tempted like that? Why did I submit to the devil's demand? I was weak, God. He makes me weak. I don't know how or why because I don't know him, but he knows so much about me. Is that why I'm weak towards him? I highly doubt I'm that way because of my connection to Rayne. I was already attracted to him when I met him. I was already thinking of nasty things we could do, I thought as Dedricka sauntered into the room, whistling.

"You've been in this cell since you returned. You look

scared and depressed. What is wrong?" she curiously announced, sitting beside me.

Exhaling sharply, I never tore my eyes from the barred window. I felt the tears welling. I tried to stop them from dropping, but once my stomach caved, the floodgates opened. Covering my face, I wept lowly.

"What's wrong? What happened? You were gone for a long time. This isn't my first rodeo here. I know certain people move particular people for sexual reasons. Willingly or not, Nyomi. Were you sexually assaulted?" she lowly asked, rubbing my back.

Rapidly, I shook my head and semi-lied, "No. Just miss my mom, and I hate I'm in here."

"Whew, thank God." She exhaled, resting her head on my back.

"Who are the people that move others for sexual reasons?" I whispered, looking at her. "Have any of them moved you for someone?"

"I'm not saying who they are, and no," she answered as I felt good about her not snitching. That would've been a problem for Richardo and his close pals.

"I was told in therapy that it helps to talk about what hurts you. I would love for you to tell me about your mother, Nyomi," she softly voiced, gently rubbing my back, which relaxed me much.

Wiping my face, I softly grinned. "She was kind, sweet, and homely. She loved to cook, bake, and garden. She was a thorn when she tried to drive her point to me. She was a warrior while battling colon cancer and heart issues. She never skipped a beat while handling her health problems. She was a down-to-earth woman."

"Sound like a remarkable woman," she kindly voiced, extending a paper to me.

"She was," I oddly voiced, staring at the college-ruled paper.

"Are you going to accept it?" she lightly questioned, eyeing me as I couldn't move my hand to retrieve the letter.

"Who gave you that?" I asked through quivering lips. I had to play my part and act like I didn't know who the sender was.

"I was told not to tell you. Just like I didn't receive the answer to who is the sender," she voiced as I shook my head and grabbed the letter from Richardo.

"How do I shut this shit down? I don't want to be involved with anyone here," I whispered, hand terribly shaking.

"Speak to the captain. He's gotten rid of the bad ones. They left with a few broken ribs or an arm. He despises them," she whispered as I forced myself to smile and nod.

"Then, I'll do that," I lied, opening the letter.

"I'll give you some type of privacy," Dedricka voiced, standing and gripping her bunk.

"Thanks." I breathed, analyzing Richardo's sleek, beautiful handwriting.

Baby, I'm sorry. I went too far. Please don't toss us away. It hurt holding you while you cried. It pained me to feel your sad tears drip on my shoulder. I never want to see you cry again unless it's from happiness. I'll use a condom from now on until you are released. I won't fuck up again. I promise.

You will get a morning-after pill. So, dry your face, please. Get back to the bubbly woman you are. People notice you are different since you've returned. A few inmates came to me, stating that they think you've been touched without consent. That hurt me because I hurt you by placing you in a worried state. I don't need you to worry about shit. I see and hear everything, Nyomi. I will always protect you. I'm too powerful not to do that. I'll make sure you survive in this place with no mishaps. I meant that. Can you please smile for me? I love it when you do. It's filled with life and love. Can I redo what I botched in a few hours? If so, find her and simply say yes.

RTD in that order

As Dedricka rolled over on her bunk, I tilted my head and stared at the last two statements. While re-reading them, my body reacted, leaving me to rehash our time together before our cum blended. Honestly, I loved how he gazed into my eyes while on top. Constant eye contact during sex had always been my thing. I didn't care what position I was in; I needed to view my partner's eyes.

The way he touched me was different from the others. His soft lips touching skin that hadn't been caressed in years set my soul ablaze. He needed to take his time, and I rushed him. I rushed him because that's what I was used to. The others never glided their hands delicately and passionately across my body as Richardo had. Their touches didn't make me shiver, let alone yearn for it while they touched me. They looked at me but didn't look at me as he did. His longing stares were dire; theirs were ... shit, I don't know what it was, but it wasn't anything like the captain's. He was tender even when he turned into a sexy-ass street beast. Even his thuggish dark side had significant love in his eyes while he damned near ate and stroked me off the bed. Phew, the fucking me from the back before lifting me as if I was a sack of potatoes fucked with my respiratory system. I had never had that happen. My ass clapped on his stomach while my pussy massively vomited on his naked, juicy, veiny, three inches above average length and four inches above the average girth-size dick. A mighty tool I thought was little but was the perfect size and girth for me. I can't lie every part of our sexing was the shit and a total turn-on. I've never let a bad boy get the kitty. It takes me to go to prison to get the type of sex I craved, I thought as my under-yonder begged me to find C.O. Joseph. It was time to redo getting my back blown out, but I needed to know some things first, and only Dedricka could lead me in the right direction.

Tearing up the letter, I cleared my mind while walking toward the toilet. As I approached it, the cheery ladies, Hines and Betterman, strolled into the cell. While I dropped the torn paper into the toilet, Hines grinned. "Hey, sweetheart. I was told that you were very upset— well, sadder—when you returned. What happened, and where did you go?"

"Hey, ladies. I had to talk to a psychiatrist. Sadness overcame me rapidly. I guess it finally hit that I'm not a free woman, and I can't talk to my mom," I lied smoothly while looking at them, just as Richardo told me to say and do. "I'm surprised y'all came this way since the Tic-Tac-Toe game sounds fun."

"It was but making sure no one touched you when you didn't want it was more important," Betterman sincerely announced, standing beside our sleeping quarters as I flushed the toilet.

Hmm, was she the one who went to the captain about my behavior? I thought, proud to know I was really amongst the good people.

"Oh, no, nothing like that happened. I heard the captain is pretty stern about stuff like that." I exhaled, walking toward my bunk.

"Come hang out with us. You need to be around silliness, happy spirits, and genuine people. Being in this cell by yourself isn't a good thing. It causes you to think about what you should be doing instead of what you are actually doing," Betterman softly voiced, studying my eyes.

"Maybe later. I'm going to read a book." I told them, hoping they received the hint I needed them to leave. It was time to have a deeper, personal conversation with Dedricka. She blended well with the rowdy and the quiet individuals.

"I will hold you to that." Hines nodded, faintly smiling.

Filled with relief they didn't detest me, I softly nodded and said, "As you should."

When they left, I focused on the reformed drug addict with silky, long, jet-black hair turning the page of a thick novel. After clearing my throat, I asked, "I know the warden's name, but does he have any ties to the captain or anyone here? Prisoners included."

"He's the captain's maternal great-uncle. So, he's real cool with C.O. Joseph, C.O. Daniels, C.O. Lee, and Lieutenant Harris," she answered, narrowing her eyes. "Why?"

Say it isn't so, I thought, trying my best not to laugh at Richardo telling me he was very powerful nor show anger toward the warden. At that moment, my mind was slung into a whirlwind.

After exhaling and nodding, I quickly stated, "One, I'm nosey, and two, an inmate should always know who is over them. How do you know he's the captain's maternal great-uncle?"

"His maternal family lives in Lowndes County. That's where my family is from. Everybody knows everybody down there," she offered as I exhaled and stretched out on my bed, unsure how to feel.

"Gotcha."

"Soooo, what was up with that letter, roomie?" She grinned, hanging over her bed.

"A bunch of gibberish from an unknown person," I lied while closing my eyes.

Clapping, she gleefully but lowly asked, "If you could fuck one of the staff, who would it be?"

The fuck I would tell you for, I thought, draping my arm over my face as I replied, "No one until I'm released."

"Are you serious?" she shrieked, causing me to giggle.

"Yes, Dedricka, I'm serious," I lied through my pretty, white teeth.

"Girl, I wish my mouth was pretty like yours. I would let the captain, C.O. Daniels, and C.O. Lee's fine White ass run a train on meeee," she happily sang as I frowned.

All right now, bitch. You are pushing it, I thought as the always-moving chick hopped from the top bunk.

"I see you aren't in the mood to talk. I'll check on you later," she said, walking toward the shiny steely bars.

So, Richardo, Donovan Rawlinson, your great uncle, is the warden. The same motherfucker I have a bone to pick with if he ever calls me into his office for a fucking chit chat, I thought, aggressively rising from my bed.

"I think I will slide out of this shoebox for a bit," I softly voiced, not wanting to seem extremely eager.

"That's the damn spirit!" Dedricka grinned, waiting for me.

Sassily walking toward the bars, my face was as it always was—free of worry. I had a huge smile and confident eyes. Yet, my attitude was on another level, all thanks to the captain's eye on me and his maternal uncle's deep feelings for my mother and me. I was ready to confidently yet secretly step into the prohibited land many females did with the correctional facility staff.

While I exited the cell with my shoulders squared and head held high, Dedricka excitedly rattled some shit that went into one ear and out of the other as I saw the captain step to C.O. Joseph.

Slowly licking my lips, I eyed him facing the wall while tossing many words into her ear. Raising an eyebrow, I *wonder how he would make things up.*

While nearing the chatty friends, my heart raced as my palms became sweaty. I wasn't sure how to get the two apart so I could deliver his answer. They were in a deep discussion. From my angle, I could tell C.O. Joseph was going off on him. Her plump lips were tighter than my asshole.

I wonder what she's saying to him, I thought as we closed into them.

Their communication ceased as Hines happily yelled, "There's my girl! I'm glad you took my advice, Richards!"

Baby, I'm down here so he can whisk me away like the queen I am, I thought, smiling as Richardo and C.O. Joseph briefly looked at me.

Three paces from them, I showed all that my mother and our church members knew well when I hit the first line of Brian McKnight's "The Only One for Me".

"La la la la la la la la! Yes! Yes! Yes! I can sing! Don't y'all get used to it." I grinned, slowly turning around to view all who had stopped what they were doing to look at me. When I saw the stunned best friends staring at me, I put on a great act while blushing. "Shoot, was I not supposed to do that? I'm new here, so please just give me a warning. I'll re-read the inmate handbook tonight. Promise."

"You are fine, Richards," the fine fucker responded with a blank facial expression. I saw the twitching of his hands. He needed to touch, suck, and dig in my pretty kitty while hearing me yodel.

"Cool beans. Um, C.O. Joseph, the answer is yes. I'll be delighted to come up with a proposal for another women's outreach program," I replied, quickly moving my eyes to Richardo, who smiled but quickly removed it.

"Good. I'm eager to review it before passing it where it needs to go," she calmly spoke.

After nodding, I quickly arrived before Hines, Betterman, and four older ladies. Meanwhile, I caught a glimpse of Richardo walking toward the door. His hands moved faster than his legs. I had to remove my eyes from him as the older Black woman tsk'd.

Eyeing her, she showed the few teeth in her mouth while saying, "Eyes off that one. He's possessed by another person in that head. I don't know how he got this job."

"Don't start that mess, Jones," Betterman scolded, narrowing her eyes. "He's saved your old ass from being face down ass up when you didn't want to be. Who gives a fuck if he does have another person in his head? He's loyal and dedicated to women's rights. Much change has happened since he's been the captain. Focus on that before talking shit."

Ooh, yeah, I'm digging you a lot, Captain Mets. Loyal and dedicated to women's rights.

"I'm with you when you are right, Betterman, but still, she needs to keep her little twat to herself while she's here. So, many inmates fall for the bullshit a staff member says. She looks naïve. If we are going to lace her boots up, we better do it the right way. How many times have we been tricked and lied to?" Jones stated as I sat beside Dedricka, soaking in the juicy news.

While Jones continued with her assumptions of me being a weak woman, I wanted to laugh. Yet, I acted like the naïve woman she thought I was. My father made sure I was never naïve to a man. Momma taught me to pay attention to everyone around me and listen to them, and the one I couldn't shake.

At that moment, Richardo Mets was the one I couldn't shake. So, my gotdamn eyes were on him heavily.

Chapter 7

RICHARDO

*Y*ou *better not cut up, nigga,* I thought, quietly stepping toward the bars of a cell Nyomi and I would always meet.

Peeking at the beautifully nervous woman staring through the barred window, a smile crept across my pleased face as I calmly voiced, "Hi, gorgeous one. Thank you for singing to me and saying yes."

While I sauntered inside, Nyomi whipped her head in my direction and smiled brightly. "You are welcome. Communication goes a long way, you know."

Confused, I furrowed my eyebrows and said, "Elaborate."

"You wouldn't have gotten slapped if you told me exactly how powerful you are, Captain Mets," she sexily voiced, tilting her head to the right. "To know you are the warden's great-nephew would've rendered our blissful sexual encounter very much differently."

Sitting beside her, I asked, "How do you know that? My crew and I kept that part well hidden."

"Dedricka," she stated matter-of-factly while crossing her legs at the ankle.

Immediately, my lips upturned as I growled and balled my hands. That bitch was starting to agitate me more than I needed to be.

"Calm down. Talk instead of growling," Nyomi chastised, planting her warm hands on me.

Searching her carefree eyes, I nodded and asked, "How did that conversation go?"

"I knew the warden's name, but I needed to know if he had ties to prisoners and staff. She gave me the relation. She asked why I wanted to know, and I was truthful. I am nosey, and I need to know who was temporarily over me. Like I told her, knowing stuff like that is helpful, just as knowing who the wrong inmates are to mix and mingle with," she calmly expressed as her eyes searched mine.

"Be careful around her. She's a sneaky bitch," I snarled, pulling her into my lap.

"Why has your radio changed about her?" she questioned, observing me and dragging her nails down my neck.

Shivering from her touches, I reclined on the bed and said, "I really don't want to tell you because it will fuck up my plans. Then, I do want to tell you because I don't want to keep anything from you. I mean nothing. But I don't think you will react as I need so people can believe what they see."

Dragging her hand from the back of my neck to the front, Nyomi raised an eyebrow and said, "You are beating around the bush."

After exhaling sharply, I breathed. "One, she's giddy as fuck. She wasn't like that when she came, and she wasn't like that a week after being here. Her being giddy means that dope in her system, and she's a gotdamn supplier. Yes, it's been confirmed the dope's here. We are searching once we part ways. We are letting her move around a bit, thinking she is out-slicking a nigga like me. I'm confident drugs are in that room, possibly hidden in your things."

"I told that bitch not to cross me," Nyomi snarled, causing me to chuckle at her mean facial expression. It was cute.

"In a way, I need her to cross you. I am banking on her stashing her shit into yours. That will grant you the right to be here for fifteen days. Everyone will think you are in isolation for beating her ass. We will let them think that, and when you return, you will give them a description of being isolated as I tell you." I grinned, placing my arms behind my head. "Or we can continue having you pulled for whatever odd reason someone sees fit."

"Here's fine," she quickly stated, covering her face.

Pulling her hands from the prettiest face I needed to be in mine for life, I smiled. "So, my plan is a go?"

"Yeah, but what if she confesses to the drugs being hers?" she asked, unbuttoning my shirt.

"Then, the playing field will be the same. You being pulled for whatever odd reason," I spoke, sitting upright.

"Okay." She nodded, dropping her lips on mine. "I need a kiss, Captain Richardo Mets."

My guy bricked at the sound of her calling my name. Gripping her neck, I traced her juicy lips.

"Mhm," she moaned, finally unbuttoning the last button.

After planting a kiss on her lips, I gazed into her sex-crazed face and said, "If you are going to say my name, you need to say it correctly. You will see it on our marriage license anyway. Richardo Vincent Mets. Now, say that sentence with my title and name so I can give you what you demanded."

Hunching me, her delicate hands cradled as she beautifully cooed. "I need a kiss, Captain Richardo Vincent Mets."

Gripping her butt, I whispered, "Then a kiss Mrs. Captain Richardo Vincent Mets gets."

As we stared into each other's eyes, our heads closed in. She didn't rush as I thought she would. She was in the moment the right way; her head was clear, and she was comfortable. When my lips touched hers, it was a delicious sensation. My spine tingled, causing me to grip her butt tighter.

When I slowly slithered my tongue into her mouth, our

eyes closed. Sparks flew as our pink flesh passionately clashed. The slow, drugging kiss and her pushing that hot monkey on my man had me wanting to turn her lips loose and dive back into her goodness, but I couldn't.

"Richardo," she whimpered, gliding her hands to my belt.

Slowly pulling my tongue from her mouth, I opened my eyes and grabbed her hands. Shaking my head, I voiced, "Not now. Before I have you, I would love to dance with you … clothed. May we dance?"

"You are really something else," she cutely announced, nodding. "I would be honored to dance with your multiple personalities having ass."

As I had to control the volume of my laughter, I lifted us from the bed while digging into my pocket. While wrapping her legs around my waist, Nyomi's steady breaths smothered my face, sending a prickling buzz skating around my dome, causing me to grunt.

"What's your problem now?" she teased as I improperly removed my shoes.

"Your breaths gave me a good feeling," I answered, placing a black earbud into her ear.

"Oou, we have music. I'm excited." She giggled, making me kiss the tip of her nose.

"Good," I responded, retrieving my phone and pressing play on the music app.

With my hands resting on her juicy ass, Brian McKnight's "The Only One for Me" played. The twinkle in her eyes was everything as I slowly danced and happily said, "This is our song. Agree or disagree?"

"I agree," she cooed, staring into my eyes while draping her arms over my shoulders.

"Every word he's singing is dedicated to you. You don't know much about me as I know a lot about you. You will be well acquainted with me before the end of the week. If things go according to how we think, after your supposed isolation time, you will be here every day, minus the weekend, getting to know me, feeling me, and falling in love with me. During the weekends, you will receive letters from me. You will be my wife, Nyomi. I can't have it any other way. I swear I can't," I confessed, slowly dragging my hand to her thick thigh.

As I lifted her, a sexy coo escaped her mouth, causing the tiny hairs on my neck to rise. Slowly dragging her fat monster across my hard-on, I grinned. "Since you will have a morning-after pill tomorrow, may I let him throw up in you while your legs are pointing in the east and west direction and your nipple is in my mouth?"

"Abso-fucking-lutely," she sexily whimpered, bringing much delight to me.

Moone Walker's "Lizzo" sounded, further setting me in a dancing mood. I grind on her as if we were in bed. My guy had a job to do; that was to make her extra gushy. I needed the seat of her panties drenching when I spread her legs to pull them off with my teeth.

"Don't think you are the only one who can dance, Richardo," she cutely spoke, seductively rocking and rolling from the side.

Honestly, I laughed. "You walk like an uptight White woman who's an elementary principal. So, I assumed you couldn't move."

"Ut," she comically broadcasted, rocking her head and erotically grooving on me.

While gazing into eyes I was grateful matched mine, I gently skated my nose across hers. Sincerely, I whispered, "I need you to trust me, Nyomi. Me. Not because I'm the warden's great-nephew. I'm not with the games. I'm too old for that. There's so much I can do to and for you. I will show you while you are here that I am the man you need in your life, just as you are the woman I must have in mine."

"Okay." She easily breathed, body tensing as I held tightly to her while rapidly rocking from left to right thanks to Big Boogie's "Pop Out".

"I know damn well you are not going to have me acting like we are in the club." She lightly giggled, pumping her fist.

"Frrrt." I grinned, causing her to laugh.

Together, we jammed and rapped the song while enjoying the happiness in each other's eyes. That's all I ever needed to see from her. Anything less would hurt me, hurt us.

"Do you visit clubs on the weekends?" she asked, stopping me from entertaining the song.

"Only when we go out of town."

"How often y'all do that?" she inquired, gently gliding the tip of her nose across mine.

"Second and fourth weekend of each month," I admitted as Ball Greezy's "Dats My Bae" slipped into our ears, resulting in Nyomi sliding her hot snatch up and down the hardheaded nigga.

"Yep, it's time to get naked so you can wet the mattress and me." I hurried to speak to the horny woman.

"Indeed, Captain Richardo Vincent Mets," she purred, erotically staring at me and unbuckling my belt.

Walking to the bed, I felt Nyomi grabbing my soul through her delicious gaze and gentle knuckle touches. I loved the feeling of belonging to her.

"Wherever your mind is, let it go," she smoothly voiced against my lips.

"It was nowhere for you to slap me. That's for sure," I responded, causing her to grin while unzipping my pants. "I thought about how you got my soul wallowing around your fingers. I remember many people telling me that love at first sight doesn't exist. I can't wait to show them how wrong they were. Pictures show things, Nyomi. No matter how much people fake the funk, they will always tell on a person. Yours spoke loud and clear to me that I had to have you. What was your first impression of me?"

"It wasn't love at first sight, but you had my full attention. I went into fantasy land about what sex was like with you," she replied sincerely.

Partially pleased with her answer, I dragged my fingers from her hand to her neck and confessed, "When freed, you will move in with me. Your life will really begin. Intimacy will change drastically. It will be longer."

"Okay," she erratically spoke, trying to remove her shirt.

Furrowing my eyebrows and slowly shaking my head, I hurried to remove her hands. Searching eyes that posed a question, I calmly chastised. "No, baby. I spoke once about you not removing anything because that's my job. Another thing that'll drive me mad is I don't like repeating myself more than three times because I know I'm heard the first time, just like you will always be heard the first time."

"My God. Tomorrow's my release day, isn't it? Because you are talking grown man shit I've been begging to hear for years," she stated before hungrily parting my lips with her slender, sweet tongue.

Suckling on her pink flesh, I slowly peeled off her clothes, ensuring my smooth touches brought delight to her frame. When she moaned in my mouth and shivered, I was proud that I had done my job. I deepened the ardent kiss that had the pit of my stomach in a wild swirl. With the slow turning of our heads, I caressed her soft skin and marveled at the thought of seeing my sexy woman standing proud in her birthday suit. I needed to view the dimples in her thighs before kissing and licking them.

"Mhm," Nyomi moaned as Tyrese's "On Top of Me" blasted.

Seductively dancing backward, I slid the masterful mouth to the hollow of her neck and pulled her head back. She needed a love bite on the most visible part of her body, but it wasn't time to put one there. So, I gently suckled but didn't stay in one spot for long.

"It's time for you to mount me, Captain Mets," she moaned.

"In a minute, I will, Nyomi Mets. Right now, I need to see you," I replied against her neck, placing her on the pretty feet that I would show tremendous love to.

"Well," she cutely and lowly sang, swaying from side to side, stepping into the piece of light that graced the cell.

Rolling my palms, I admired my perfect view of a highly confident, adaptable woman. Nyomi didn't cuff her enormous titties. She let them be; I loved that. She didn't suck in her stomach; I truly loved that. Her confidence level was off the charts, making me want her more. There was nothing sexier than a woman owning everything about her—the good, bad, and ugly.

Once she slowly turned around, I groaned and smiled at the dimples in her ass. I would have much fun putting hickeys on her round, dimpled-out butt cheeks.

"Mhm. All mine," I lowly groaned, needing her next to me. "Come to me."

"Like you told me, stop rushing me," she provocatively responded, sluggishly touching her toes and clapping her ass nice and slow.

"Hannit the fuck here," I hissed through clenched teeth as I observed her ass rolling like a slowing fidget spinner. "You are mine, Nyomi."

I eyed the gorgeous woman giving me a great show while spinning on her tiptoes. The sound of Moone Walker's "She Wanna F@%K!" turned Nyomi up in ways I could've never imagined. Her calm yet erotic behind slowly dragged her right hand toward the pink monster.

"Ooou, shit. Show out for me then," I groaned, sitting on the edge of the bed, barely blinking. I didn't want to miss a thing.

My baby rocked her fingers and cooed, "Richardo, I rocked on my fingers like this my fifth day here. I saw you lick your lips. It was slow, just like the way you licked my pussy earlier. You were extraordinarily sexy while wetting your juicy lips with that skillful tongue your parents created. I came hard while biting my bottom lip. A little blood trickled into my mouth, but that didn't stop me from doing this when I came again."

"When you did what, baby? When you did what?" I grunted, gripping my man and slowly jacking it.

Silk's "Meeting in My Bedroom" sounded as she sexily slid her fingers from her slit. Gazing at me, she moaned, "I did this."

I held my breath to ensure I didn't blink. The shaft hardened more as she twirled her tongue around her slender fingers. Like a sweet slut, she sucked her juices from fingers that would be in my mouth the moment she brought her fine ass to me.

Slowly rising, she sexily cooed, "Mhm. Super tasty."

"No lies told. Bring me my super wet wet wet." I ordered as she pranced toward me. "You know how to put on a show. Don't spoil me and then snatch it away. Asshole will come out."

Eyeing me, she grinned. "Thank you, and one day soon, you need to give me the rundown on how asshole came to."

"I have no problem doing that," I responded as she whimpered while sitting on the bed and erotically spreading her legs.

"My God. Oh, how do I love what's before me," I confessed as she had me in a trance.

Seductively running her fingers from her thick thighs to her titties, Nyomi cuffed them and softly asked, "Well, why are you still over there, Richardo?"

Lloyd's "Feels So Right" boomed through our ears as I face-planted into the saturated goodness, slowly rolling my face around, ensuring I received a great facial. Instantly, she gasped and slithered her warm palms to the back of my head. With the heat from her palms and paying attention to the song in my ear, I slowly nibbled on her folds.

"Ooou, I didn't know nibbling could feel like that on that," she cooed, body relaxing. At the moment, I needed her body tense.

Quickly, I rushed my mouth to her clit and suckled.

"Ah," she moaned as a deep arch appeared in the small of her back.

I suckled on that pink fucker until she yelped the first three letters in my name. I damned neared dislocated my shoulder trying to cover her mouth; there would be a time I would allow her to yodel my name. Yet, my dumb ass was still soaking her out.

Squirt Kelly's "All Night" blasted, making me one dangerous ass nigga. My woman had no idea how badly she had fucked up by not knowing my favorite sex jam would be the reason she would be close to getting us caught.

Like a snake wiggling across a grassy hill, I slithered up my woman's trembling body while ensuring my tool was in my hand. My tongue swept across her stomach until I arrived at her baby feeders. Sucking her nipple into my mouth, I graced the volcano-hot wetland and wasted no time dancing in her goodness. At the same time, I slid her hands above her head.

"Fuckamighty," she sexily hissed as I leaned to the left and interlocked our fingers.

"You fucked up, Nyomi," I softly voiced on her lips as I rocked one hip at a time. It gave the impression of me ascending stairs.

"How?" she moaned as I rolled my hips to the beat.

"One of my favorite songs," I answered, restarting the jam. She had the full effect of me. I needed her drunken off me while stumbling back to her sleeping quarters.

As her waterworks arrived, I rocked her G-Spot, dropped my nose on hers, and groaned, "You studied Morse Code, right?"

"I did," she whined, body violently shaking.

"Tell me what this message means," I chuckled, knowing I needed to cover her mouth.

Rising on my tiptoes, I went deep, leaned to the right, and rapidly hit it a few times. Her breathing became disastrous as her nails ate my back up. I didn't take a break because of the pain; I took it because it was needed for the code. After the three-second break, I hit her cumming twat six times. She showered me gloriously and peeled some skin from my back.

"Fuckamighty," I hissed, dropping my nose on hers. "Oou, baby, you hurt me with that one."

Removing my hand, she panted. "I'm sorry."

"No need to apologize. I had to let you know," I responded before sticking my tongue in her mouth, not kissing her. I used it as a gag while blitzing her non-stop. Her body begged me to demolish it.

Rapidly, Nyomi patted the center of my back. As I inhaled the spit from her mouth, her eyes grew big, she stopped patting me, and the suckling fucker became wetter. I marveled at her eye expression when I swallowed.

Baby, I'm nasty as fuck. All I had to do was find you, I thought, as "Clap Dem Cheeks" by Super Nard featuring Jr. Boss played.

Immediately and aggressively, an excited and hype Nyomi

shoved me on my back. With furrowed eyebrows, astonished and speechless, I stared at my thrilled woman who tapped the earbud in my ear twice. The song restarted as she hurried to my guy, gripped that motherfucka, put her lips to the head, and rapped. My eyes bucked as I couldn't believe what I witnessed.

"I got an ass on my back, but I ain't petite," she cutely rapped while clapping her cheeks.

I howled in laughter while my woman had a ball rapping on my shits and throwing ass. After the hook, she danced to the hard-on while rapping Jr. Boss's verse. I was no longer laughing; I was logged in to check out what her riding skills were like.

Once she lifted on her tiptoes, my baby turned into a lady thug while rapidly dropping down on him and rapping the verse.

"Shit!" I loudly moaned as her drenching sweetness sucked my tool. "Nut on it."

When her soft hands cuffed my neck, she gripped it, leaned forward, and bounced on me while clapping her ass. As she rapidly rotated her hips, I moaned, "Nyomi, you are a prisoner, baby."

"I know, and I'm going to fuck the shit out of the captain, so he can clap his feet," she cutely voiced before slowly rising. I couldn't laugh because Nyomi started tootsee rolling the chunky money she played with.

"Oh my God. You's a gotdamn freak," I groaned, eyeing

her rocking, rolling, and squirting on me. "I'm going to see if The Don can get us married."

Erotically giggling, Nyomi rose to the head, still playing with her clit, elevated her left leg, and rose onto the rest of her right toes; the leaking beast ate my head up. My eyelids fluttered, and my fingers twitched as I groaned her name while hitting her G-Spot.

The millisecond Super Nard's "CBFW" graced our ears, I stopped thrusting to comprehend what I saw. Delicately, she rode me while turning towards the wall. My toes curled at the suckling sensations. Whenever she dropped down, she one-cheek, two-cheek that ass, causing me to lowly grunt and admire the massive wave it created.

"Alright, now Nyomi," I groaned as the rapping woman planted her left foot on the bed and faced the bars. I was astonished at her never skipping a beat with giving me one spectacular performance and rendering my body amazing sensations.

"Baby," I horribly voiced, marveling at the sensational feel of her walls clenching and round, bottom plopping on my midsection.

The moment she leaned forward, using her pussy muscles extensively, my low moans rolled around the cell. Cutely giggling, she slid her pretty fingers across her ass. After spreading her ass cheeks, Nyomi jacked up her butt as if it was a tricked-out, hydraulic-having '64 Chevrolet Impala.

No longer using her muscles to please me, the beast slowly twerked. Tingles ran from my head to my feet as my stomach caved and toes spread before curling. I needed to touch her, but I desired to see her beautiful backside more.

Gripping, my stomach to keep my hands out of the way, I groaned, "Fuck me, Nyomi. Own me."

"Okay," she curtly voiced as another local artist's twerking jam blasted.

In that motherfucking prison cell, Nyomi put on a concert while fucking my mute ass off the bed. She didn't have to tell me where to go; the coochie directed me. When she busted a split and rapidly scooted the cat on me, she sexily hissed, "It's time to fuck me back, Richardo. You've been a blow-up doll long enough. Let's get nasty."

Slowly, I said, "You are an inmate, Nyomi. We can't get nasty."

"Tuh," she sassed, hopping off me.

"Nyomi. You can't cut up until I tell you to." I sighed as she looked at me nonchalantly while sopping my guy in her mouth.

"Oh God!" I loudly moaned as she violently gagged herself.

Tears flowed from her pleased eyes as she grabbed my balls and shook them bitches as if they were a bag of sunflower seeds. My moans, toe-curling, and finger-curling were never-ending when she started humming and quickly beating her throat.

"Beat his ass up. Let him know who owns his no manners-having ass," I groaned as tingles consumed my body.

"Mhm," she cooed while slowly dragging her mouth to the head while sexily gazing into my eyes.

After removing my dick, she mischievously grinned. "I never answered your Morse Code. I think I should give you your answer. Pay attention. Oh yeah, don't forget I'm in prison. You might want to cover your mouth, Captain Mets."

She didn't allow me to respond before suckling on the head. By the third ferocious suckle, I moaned, "Get from down there."

She shook her head while sucking six more times before taking a break. I was ready to toss her ass into the doggy-style position when she resumed suckling on the head. After three more sessions of her suckling and breaking, I was a limp noodle ready to explode in her mouth.

Dramatically removing him from her skillful mouth, Nyomi rose like a snake, extended her hand, and said, "It's time for you to fuck me from the back, honey. You've been a blow-up doll long enough now."

I looked at Nyomi as if she was crazy. She acted as if she didn't take my mobility and locked it inside her when we were on the bed. I was astonished at her thinking I could stand on my feet after she sent one hell of a Morse Code.

Stomping her foot, she rolled her neck while lowly and nastily barking, "Get your ass up, Richardo. I'm ready to be fucked, popped, hair pulled, bit … all that shit. I don't want to sex or make love to you, and I don't want to be sexed or made love to. I need to be fucked. Slutty style type of fucked. Treat this cat like you treated those bitches' slits you didn't want to sex or make love to."

Nice try, baby, but that's not enough to pull out who you want to see, I thought, laughing while getting off the floor.

"Alright. Bend the fuck over." I commanded, raising an eyebrow.

"My pleasure." She beautifully smiled, swirling and touching her toes. "Knock the lining out of this pussy, Richardo."

"Be careful what you ask for, Nyomi." I chuckled, spreading her ass cheeks.

"I always do," she stated, making her ass wobble in my hands.

Ooou, I have to say ... I don't think I'm up to par for her like this. I need a reason to be angry to give her what she wants. I just want to cruise in it. She wants me to beat this motherfucka up, I thought, gliding the wet tool up and down her moist slit.

Whipping her head around, she hissed, "Richardo, if you don't drop all that dick in me and treat me like a slut, I'm going to put on my clothes, grab your phone, and text C.O. Joseph to come get me. She will return to you with an answer of 'leave me the fuck alone because you can't provide as you said you would'. I have no problem dropping your fine ass for not fulfilling a gotdamn proposal you sang to my girl. What did you say? If she's not pleased, you won't have a chance with me? Yeah, that's what you said. I absolutely mother-fucking agree."

While she was heatedly speaking, she had no idea how angry I was by the end of her second statement. By the end of the fifth statement, I was annoyed with her voice. She sounded like my nagging-ass deceased grandmother and ex-wife. Two motherfuckas I loved stuffing shit into their mouths so I wouldn't hear them make a sound, including coughing.

Digging my nails into her ass, I rammed him into her juicy guts, bent my knees, and drilled it. Instantly, her body grew stiff as she lowly cooed my name.

"Shut the fuck up. I don't even want to hear that soft shit," I commanded, gripping her curly hair with both hands and digging deep inside her clenching walls. "You got a fucking mouth on you when it's not necessary. You think you want me to treat this pussy like I did them hoes. You are fucking wrong! I was a rude motherfucka in their fucking pussies before passing them bitches to Avery and Terry. I wasn't ready to fuck you because I'm tired of just fucking, Nyomi. I kept this dick to myself for three moth-erfucking years because I needed to motherfucking feel raw pussy. Pussy, that's for me! Not Everybody else! Don't comment. Just get your fucking nuts and moan in your gotdamn hands. I don't even want to hear it. You are a football head, so hike."

Instantly, the trembling, horny woman dropped into a squatting position. I played Whack-a-Mole gloriously as she tried to stifle her moans, coos, and whimpers. Glaring at the back of her head, I hissed, "The answer to your Morse Code question is the same as yours. Of course, it's yours. It'll always be yours. No need to respond."

Of all the songs that played, my brain registered Webbie featuring Bun B's "Give Me That". I chortled. "Drop on all fours."

After I snaked out of her goodness, she dropped like a fly that was sprayed with a bug repellant. With no time to play with an impatient woman, I gave her the unruly, angry dick while smacking her ass and pulling her head back. I couldn't marvel at the tantrum having coochie suckling my guy. I wasn't in the mood to dog her walls. There was always a time and place for it. Yet, not to lose her, I had to do what I had to, but she would know that I was upset.

Staring into her strained face, I hissed, "Cover your mouth. You need to moan."

Hurriedly, she placed her shaky hands over her mouth and yodeled my name. Unlike the other times, it didn't fuel my need to continue to hear it. Rapidly, I cuffed her neck and applied light pressure.

"Squeeze harder, Richardo," she erotically moaned in her hands as her body grew rigid.

Jesus, this woman you sent me ... that's all I have to say ... this woman you sent me, I thought, shaking my head, squeezing her neck tighter, and pounding the gushy goodness while rotating my hips.

Chapter 8

NYOMI

I can still feel his gentle to rough touches. The sincerity in his angry voice as he dug deep inside me, I can still hear and feel. Those succulent, tight lips on his handsome, strong face were enough to take my breath while it was being taken. I love how he pummeled my starved wetland, even though he didn't want to. Richardo. Richardo. Richardo. I am full-throttle into you all because you catered to me instead of yourself, I thought, trying to keep my smile from growing.

"Remove that smile from your face." C.O. Joseph lowly grinned as we neared the general population.

"It's hard to, but trust, I'm trying," I gleefully spoke as

Richardo called the friendly and loving correctional officer's name.

My heartbeat rapidly as my fingers twitched. Biting my bottom lip, butterflies floated in my stomach. At the same time, she turned on her heels and said, "Sir?"

It took everything in me not to face the ripped man who knew how to please a mind, body, and soul. As I felt his gentle hand on my wrist, he spoke to his friend, "I needed you to face this way so I could do this."

Quickly, he spun me around. My eyes bucked, and a coo ran from my voice box, floating into their ears before sticking to the walls. Gripping my throat, Richardo gently shoved me against the ivory-hued structure that needed a paint job.

"Oou," I lowly cooed, analyzing his blazing eyes. Richardo sexily bit his bottom lip as he spelled his name on my neck. When he finished writing the letter 's', his hand trembled.

"Richardo," I cooed, fingers curling into my white pants as I continued staring. I needed to slowly slip my fingers from his head to his veiny arm while rising on my tiptoes to run my tongue out of my mouth so it could escape into his.

After pressing his lips against mine, he passionately spoke, "You will marry me. You will have my second child. You are mine, Nyomi."

I didn't get a chance to respond because he shoveled his minty tongue into my mouth. Engaging in an erotic, gut-wrenching, and toe-curling kiss, my knees grew weak. The beautiful sounds from our lips and tongues gloriously clashing made me whimper as my pretty kitty awakened.

I was elated by the boldness of the captain but shocked at my reaction of slinging my arms around his neck. In the prison walls, he would be my knight in shining armor. When I became free, he would officially be my king. I wouldn't have it any other way.

"Captain, cut it off," C.O. Joseph lowly voiced.

Hissing, he slowly removed his tongue from my starving mouth. Observing my eyes, the attractive being nodded. "All mines."

I couldn't help but blush like a schoolgirl. I held and would always hold hostage the hottest man's demanding chestnut-hued eyes.

As he stepped from me, I quickly voiced, "All mine, Richardo."

His gorgeous face had the biggest and happiest grin when he said, "Good."

Just as quickly as he stepped from me, he rolled back on me, wrapping his arms around me and dropping kisses on my forehead. Deeply, I inhaled his scent and grinned. I needed the memory of my second time with the last guy I would ever sleep with etched into my memory. I didn't need to miss anything, especially how he smelled after catering to my mind and body.

After another slow and thoughtful kiss, Richardo walked opposite C.O. Joseph and me. Looking at me, the kind, short, petite, copper hued woman seriously said, "If you hurt him, I will beat your big, beautiful ass. If you make him angry, I will have to see what he did for you to piss him off. That will determine if I beat your ass."

"Good luck trying to beat this ass," I seriously voiced, even though I giggled, while staring into her captivating eyes. "Now, why would I hurt a man like that?"

"Some women do strange shit whenever they want," she uttered, giving me her undivided attention. "Richardo's a special kind of crazy. I know you let the beast out today. It took him seeing you cry for him to simmer. Simple, but not so simple things can make asshole come out."

Coming to a halt, I exhaled. "After what he displayed twenty minutes before calling you, tells me he's a damn good man. So, you don't have to worry about me hurting him. I would be a fucking fool to do that. Excuse my language. Now, The Don. Let's talk about that."

Stepping closer to me, she lowly said, "Richardo's paternal grandparents used to holler, snarl, and bark at them a lot when they were growing up. They treated their grandkids as if they were slaves, minus the beating, butt-breaking, and other demeaning shits. They were seldomly loving. One day, he snapped. He could no longer tolerate being hollered, snarled, or barked at. He put them in their places. Tied them up and put their old asses in the closet. He had to see a shrink. They said he didn't have any mental issues. Yet, you couldn't tell other people that. Minus us. We know what happens when he's about to have a fit. I'm not sure how much you know about The Don, so I can't really fully speak, but I know he's an asshole. He doesn't give a damn about shit. Boom, you are his and got nutted in. I'm sure you saw the signs of The Don before you got nutted in. His head jerks, eyelids rapidly flutter, and his stomach caves massively and repeatedly; his fingers twitch before they ball. All those movements are because he's fighting the images of his grandparents yelling in their faces. The wrong one comes about, and he's a gotdamn terrorist. We can't do anything with him. We just ride with him until he cools off. If he doesn't calm down after a week, I put his ass to sleep. At that point, I'm agitated, tired, and super musty, and horny. Seven days without my four peens, I'm on a rampage to concuss my best friend. We don't know which image causes the demon to come out. He won't tell us. When you notice his movements, and we aren't around, you need to stop it before shit gets out of hand."

If I wasn't stunned by anything in life, I was shocked at the pretty, loving woman who had me close to walking off on her. I wouldn't have pegged her to house that many dicks at once. She looked like a super good girl. Oddly, I asked, "How do I stop him from going crazy?"

"Be you. He's afraid of losing you," she helpfully spoke, causing me to nod and feel great about the captain and me.

"Well, alrighty then. Thanks for the deets. I will ensure to utilize," I responded, studying her eyes.

"You are welcome. Now, come on. Have to get you back to your area," she quickly spoke, taking a step forward.

When we arrived in my area, the ladies were louder than usual. Immediately, I focused on the ladies' thoughts about me being gone so long again. I wondered if they would see a change in me as opposed to earlier. I feared I glowed too much, or my eyes were brighter than they had been. I felt they would know I had great sex.

Nearing my cell, I prayed Dedricka, Hines, and Betterman weren't inside my resting place. I needed a few moments to ponder the lie I would tell them. As my knuckles graced the cold bars, C.O. Joseph lowly voiced, "Simply tell them to mind the business that pays them."

"How did you know I was worried about that?" I nervously giggled, looking at her.

"You have been nervous since arriving on this block," she spoke as Hines' loudmouth behind yodeled my name.

"Fuck. I don't want to be bothered," I whispered, causing C.O. Joseph to laugh.

After she bid me to have a good day, I skipped into my cell and eyed my bony-ass mattress. Halfway to my bed, Betterman loudly voiced, "Come hang out with us."

"No, ma'am. I want to be alone. I've hung out with y'all enough for today," I responded, sliding onto the decent enough mattress to get cozy.

Exhaling sharply, she calmly said, "Yes, for thirty minutes before you were whisked away like a damn princess."

More like a queen, I thought, forcing a smile to stay from my face.

"Betterman, I'm not in a talkative mood right now. I need time to myself. Can I get a raincheck on hanging out with y'all?" I calmly spoke, staring into her green eyes.

"Sure," she sweetly announced, slowly backing toward the iron gate.

"Thanks."

"You are welcome." Betterman faintly smiled, shaking her head.

Once she exited the cell, I faced the wall and closed my eyes. Before my eyelids were sealed, Dedricka ran into the cell. Nervously and lowly, she said, "Cell toss time."

Oh, my fucking goodness. How could I have forgotten about that? He did say some shit about them doing a search shortly after I arrived. He did mention this druggie broad may have stashed some shit in mine, I thought, hopping from the bed and playing the role of the nervous inmate.

"What I do?" I seriously asked while acting as if I was about to have a panic attack.

The nervous bitch didn't respond as she hurried to remove items from her mattress. Anger consumed me significantly at her carelessness. The principle of not fucking me over included having shit in our cell.

"What the fuck, Dedricka? Where we sleep," I lowly hissed, not acting. "Most importantly, where the fuck I sleep."

"Be quiet. Look innocent. If you don't, you will give me

away. The fucking captain is on the block. He's ordering for cells to be tossed," she whispered, staring at me and grabbing several things from her mattress.

With rapidly fluttering eyelids, I stammered, "Oh, shit."

"Right, oh, shit. Captain Mets is not to be fucked with, Nyomi. I'm in deep shit if I don't get rid of these drugs. Will you come help me?" she asked as her thin body shook terribly.

"Absolutely the fuck not. Shouldn't have brought that shit in this fucking shoebox. So, are you back to using again?" I lowly hissed, walking toward the bars, feeling lightheaded.

"That is not up for discussion," she quickly voiced as I approached the bars.

"It fucking needs to be," I shot back, looking at the antsy chick while my heart raced like I'd run a marathon.

My hands shook as I focused on the floor for my man and his crew. My eyes were all over the floor when I located Richardo stepping out of a cell six spots from the right of us, looking like he was close to spazzing out.

Is the asshole out? Or is this him standing on business, the right way? I thought, rushing my head toward our bunks to witness a shaky Dedricka flush the toilet.

"Move faster. Six cells away. From the right." I told her, hoping she hadn't betrayed me. I preferred her to be solid with me while I snuck around with Richardo versus her stabbing me in the back, getting her ass beat, and I had fifteen days secluded to be with Richardo.

While she scurried to her mattress, I focused on the voices

of the authorities speaking. Based on the sarcastic laughter, I knew they found contraband in someone's living area. Time seemed as if it slowed when Dedricka skipped toward me and rapidly tapped my arm.

"Time to step out," she quickly voiced, smoothing her hair.

"All of it is gone?" I asked lowly, studying her eyes.

"Yes." She nodded, eyes reflecting worry.

I semi-cared about the expression in her eyes. She should be boggled by that emotion. She had no business doing the stupid shit she had done. When the raid was over, and she hadn't put anything in my stuff, she would receive great words from me, but they would be nasty as fuck.

When Richardo, C.O. Daniels, C.O. Matthew, and Lieutenant Harris walked into our cell, I exhaled sharply and briefly looked into their nonchalant faces before focusing on Richardo's twitching right hand. I tried to keep from smiling at the buff man who damned near rocked my skeletal system loose.

Firm hands. Strong limbs. Built body. Stone cold facial expression. Juicy lips are wet with his pink flesh. Fingers uncontrollably twitching. He's aroused. Oh, the cell phone. I didn't get it from under the mattress. Gotdamn it. Dedricka is looking. She'll see it even if they will be sneaky trying to retrieve it, I thought while barely breathing as C.O. Daniels, C.O. Matthew, and Lieutenant Harris tossed our cell.

I had no idea how to tell him the phone was still under the mattress. When our thin bedding items were slammed on the floor, my heart dropped as they searched the mattresses well. Seeing nothing was in them, they skipped toward our little makeshift personal holders.

Now, what the hell? I didn't move the phone. Did he have one of them come get it? I thought as nothing was found in Dedricka's things.

When Lieutenant Harris opened my books and shook them like a cat shaking a mouse, a balloon and a few more things fell out. My breathing became erratic as my eyelids rapidly blinked. I prayed they had failed me, so I wouldn't have to tear into Dedricka's ass.

"Oh, wow. Captain Mets, come take a look at this," C.O. Daniels voiced, retrieving the items.

I'm going to see if this bitch will claim her shit, I thought, staring straight ahead as my jaws clenched.

"Well, damn, Richards. I didn't know you were moving like that. It's hard to believe you would since you've never had so much as a parking ticket. Nor do you have any visitors. Now, your roommate, on the other hand…" Captain Mets voiced, looking at me before planting his eyes on Dedricka. "Is this shit yours, Willis, or is it the one who hasn't even gotten into a fight during any of her school years? Not even a single disagreement."

Oh, wow. You are showing out with knowledge, I thought, trying to read him but praying Dedricka proved me wrong.

"It's not mine, sir. My nose is clean," the bitch confidently spoke, lying through her fucked-up teeth.

Richardo growled as I didn't let Dedricka's lips shut before the back of my right hand slammed into it.

"Oou, shit!" the ladies hollered as I noticed Richardo's head twitch as his jaws clenched.

"You's a treacherous, rotten mouth bitch," I barked as she wildly swung, but my left punch caught the center of the bitch's throat. "I looked you in your face and told you not to cross me. I told you I could be the sweetest bitch or the devil's granddaughter. You chose this side of me. Handle it, druggie bitch."

Her face was my punching bag. Blow after harsh blow, I ensured she received. I gave her an ass whooping that should've been rendered to a punching bag. All my frustration went into tearing Dedricka a new ass. I needed her in the infirmary for many days, just as I wished my father, the judge, the prosecution team, and the gotdamn jury could be in the hospital after I beat the fucking skin off them.

"Enough, Richards!" Lieutenant Harris hollered, apprehending me. I didn't resist, nor did I speak. I glared at the beat-up bitch with tears running from my pretty eyes.

Against the wall, shivering and bloody, Dedricka looked like a helpless child. C.O. Daniels kneeled before her and whispered, "It's not hers. It's yours. Someone dropped on you. We've been known. Get up, Willis. Game over."

As I was hauled away with several eyes on me, many tears dripped onto my chest as my head dropped just as my shoulders. I really hoped Dedricka would've been the good person I hoped she would be. If she crossed me, I felt it would be only a matter of time before Hines and Betterman did.

It's time to push all motherfuckers from around me, I thought, scanning the stunned faces staring into mine.

When we arrived at a door that led to quite a few places, C.O. Daniels whispered, "The fighting incident will not be in the report. It will be hearsay. It will be denied if anyone inquiries about it. Stop your tears. It's making him angry. You can't hear the growls, but I do. When he's angry, his wrath is off the charts. He becomes the asshole. Surely, everyone, including us. We will be musty for a week. That's when Ashley put his ass to sleep. Two things have him riled: Dedricka lying on you and what you had to say about your father. What you had to say has him overly pissed. That family just might be underneath a tent by next week. We will gladly assist him in ensuring whether that line has an open or closed casket funeral. As always, do not look at me or acknowledge me. Just continue to walk forward."

If they are under a tent, oh well. I'll be laid up in this bitch with my legs crossed and body filled with hickeys.

RICHARDO

Wednesday, May 4th

I had fallen deeper for the woman who needed the simple things in life. She believed in bringing more to the table other than her looks and pussy. Unlike my ex-wife, I would do anything to relieve any stress from her. So, I took advantage of using my power to make her as comfortable as possible while she was isolated.

Her beating the shit out of Dedricka was the best thing she could've done for us. As expected, gossip slithered through the prison about her predicament. The cell I felt would be best for us, Avery's round face ass outbid me for it. So, my woman was held in a semi-dank isolation cell for two more days.

I hated that our time of sneaking around would return. I liked how carefree and peaceful she looked, far from people and their thoughts. She glowed better when she was out of sight. I loved hearing her soft coos as I raked my fingers through her hair while she lay in my arms, gazing into my face and doodling on my chest.

Damn, I hate you are in here. You deserve to be in a house with me. We shouldn't be held up in this damn cell, I thought, massaging Nyomi's feet while we stared at each other.

"Captain Mets," the sexy beauty called.

"Yes, Richards."

"Why are you so quiet?" Nyomi cutely asked, placing her hands behind her head.

Rocking my neck from side to side, I exhaled. "Trying to find the best way for Glover and Dad to leave me alone about the family's land."

"Do you love what you do for the land?" she asked, removing her feet from my hands.

"I do. Being about business is my thing," I offered as she crawled toward me.

"So, what's the issue with you taking over the land?" she quizzed, descending before me, gripping my shoelaces.

"I'm laundering money through the company." I sighed, resting my head on the wall.

"Have you lost your fucking mind? You don't shit where

you lay. Everybody should know that," she lowly screeched, causing me to look at her disappointed face.

While she removed my shoes, I responded, "No, I haven't lost my mind, nor had I when I decided to do so. I didn't know we would be that big when we found that dope. We were only supposed to have done a simple drop to help Avery care for his sick uncle. We didn't know much about dealing with a paraplegic man and his needs. We were teens ourselves. Many years later, we had to get a then fifteen-year-old Lucas out of the shithole he was in with their druggie and alcoholic mother. Lucas and Avery are twenty-three years apart. We started to love what we did. By overseeing the finances, marketing, and other business stuff for the family land, I had access to wash the money."

"I'm going to assume you don't want to be in the firing pit because you love being the guy with two faces," she voiced, spreading my legs while climbing between them.

"Correct." I nodded as she unbuckled my belt with one hand and unzipped my pants with the other.

"Have you thought critically about doing both?" she asked, tapping on my waist for me to lift.

Lifting, I shook my head and said, "Nope."

"Maybe you should," she seriously voiced, removing my pants and underwear.

Searching her calming eyes and long, oval-shaped face, I sincerely breathed. "The only way I'll entertain it is if you be my wife the second you are released. It will seem as if I'm running the land full-time. It won't be anything like that. You will be the head honcho, and I will be your second set of eyes. My parents and Glover will push for you to sign a prenup. You will *not* sign one. I will say that shit again, Nyomi. You will *not* sign a prenup. They will try to chat with you individually to persuade you to sign. I don't give a fuck what they say. Do not sign it. You will have no rights to anything, down to what I bought for you, even if it's dirty money. If I was to die and you survived me, you would be on your ass. They have those prenups ironclad. I know; I'm the one who created it to where nothing leaves our family, nor can the spouse have a claim to run the fields."

Dropping her mouth, she oddly analyzed my eyes. She was stunned, and I loved that. It was the shine in her eyes, or it could've been I was everything she prayed for in a man. Rubbing her face, I softly chuckled. "What's on that mind of yours?"

"You want me to run your family's land, going against everything you stood for," she offered while gripping my sleeping dick.

"You've bitched at me all week about not wanting to be a housewife. You wanted to get back to the working world. So, why not place you on the higher end of the food chain? Why settle for a regular job when you can be much more than that?" I lovingly said, pulling her on top of me. "Leave that man alone for a while. I'll give him to you after I've held and talked to you a bit."

Scurrying her thick thighs around my waist, I ran my hands down her hickey-filled neck as she said, "That's the only way you will think about agreeing to be the boss on paper?"

"The only way," I admitted, dragging my short-trimmed nails toward her titties.

"How much time do I have to think about it?"

"Three days before you are released." I exhaled, massaging her neck as she unbuttoned my shirt.

"Well, you will have your answer three days before I'm back in the free world," she cutely responded, removing my work and undershirts. As the soft buzz from the lights in the hallways hummed, the soles of my people's shoes created soft patters on the polished floors.

"Sounds good." I nodded. "What kind of house and car do you want?"

"I've always wanted a house with a spiral staircase but quickly changed it once I saw the L-shaped, two-floored homes. As an adult, I'm fine with a one-floored home but must have a nice-sized front and backyard to show off my gardening skills. Screened in porches is a must. I don't have time to fight mosquitoes. A crossover or an SUV. Not sure which brand," she happily spoke, studying my eyes while massaging my neck while I groped her titties.

"I'm going to put my house on the market by fall or at the first of the year," I confessed, catching her eyes narrowing.

"Why?" she inquired, furrowing her eyebrows.

"No need to have my last wife in a home that I shared with someone I didn't want to be with, let alone live with," I admitted as Ashley's laughter could be heard from down the hallway. "It'll be time to make good memories in a home of your choosing."

Gliding her hands to my lips, Nyomi's eyes brightened as she adorably cooed, "These right here will keep you in trouble. Good trouble, though."

Lightly chuckling, I placed her on her back and grinned. "Good to know."

"When will Rayne and I reunite?" she probed as I rested my head on her chest.

"Valentine's Day."

"Why so long?" she inquired, rubbing my head and back.

"I've bought her spoiled ass any and everything she asked for. I can't think of anything better than to place the two of you face to face as a gift for V-Day."

"How will you pull that off?"

Resting my chin on her chest, I narrowed my eyes and asked, "Who am I?"

Blushing, she voiced, "The captain."

"Right."

"And who is the warden to the captain?"

"His uncle," she squeakily voiced, causing me to chuckle.

"Right. So, she has reasons to see her father and great-great uncle."

"Since I've gotten that out of you, what do you have

planned for our birthdays?" She grinned, repeatedly raising her eyebrows. Winking, I zipped my lips and laid back on the titties I couldn't wait to see our first child resting against them, making me jealous as fuck.

Silence overcame us as I wrote my name and social security number on her arms. After my fourth time doing so, she planted her mouth on my head and recited the numbers. "Richardo, what the hell are those numbers?"

"My social. Remember it."

"God, the man You have laying on me has been doing the most." She giggled as I wrote my license number on her soft palms.

Once again, after the fourth time, she recited the numbers and asked what they were. Looking into her eyes, I voiced, "My driver's license number. Of course, Alabama issued."

"For whatever reason, I'll remember those numbers," she sweetly voiced.

"Okay."

"I've waited patiently for you to speak about your darker person. I can no longer hold my tongue. Let's talk about it," she calmly commanded, dragging her nails around the crown of my head.

"My dad's parents were mean, judgmental fuckers with money. They weren't humble towards their family as opposed to those they fake smiled and chatted with. I hated them; my parents knew it. Momma hated them but loved their son, so she dealt with them. They weren't physically abusive, but mentally and emotionally, they were. Just fucking draining people. They made me angry a lot. Respect your elders always was Momma's favorite saying, so I did until that bitch of a grandmother whooped my then-four-year-old sister too hard. She had welts on her butt, legs, and arms. A few of them caused her skin to break. They were on her butt. That caused me to snap. I beat that bitch with her church shoe. The one with the kitten heel. I clucked that bitch like she slammed the very shoe on flies. I was in Boy Scouts, so I knew how to tie well. I tied her up and shoved her into the hallway closet. Granddad came home, and I clucked his ass unconscious with the shoe. I tied him up and shoved him in the closet with his ugly, pissy-ass wife. I picked up my crying sister, took her to the bathroom, and put a cold rag on her wounds. When our parents arrived to pick us up, my sister was sleeping in my arms, and I nastily told them where the fuck his parents were and why. That was the last time we ever saw them. They were fearful of me. I learned not only had I beat their asses and put them in time out, I pissed on them, shitted in my hands, and smeared it on their faces. While sticking my shitty hand in their nostril, I kept saying, 'The Don, I am now. They get shit done ruthlessly. Not Richardo'." I softly exhaled, slipping back to the day I gave no fucks about elders when they crossed a line.

"Whew, they had a shitty day. That's what their asses get," my woman seriously voiced, causing me to laugh. "What did your parents say about your behavior?"

"Momma's facial expression informed me I did right to cut up. Dad was disappointed I disrespected his parents. He fussed at me for what I did. I tuned him out until he started yelling, sounding like his parents and causing my sister to cry. I took off my belt and wrapped it around his neck. When the car swerved too hard and Momma politely told me to calm down, I released the belt and told him who I was. He shut the fuck up and drove home, ensuring the rearview mirror wasn't on me. The next day, I was in a shrink's face. A month later, I saw another one, and the month after that. All told them I was fine even though he ordered them to yell at me to catch my reaction. Momma returned and told them not to yell at me because I wasn't a dog."

"She saved them and you," Nyomi acknowledged, more to herself than me.

"Yep. I got my mind checked when I learned Rayne was due to enter the world, Nyomi. I told the shrink the truth. I promise nothing is mentally wrong with me. I have a short fuse when triggered by things my grandparents did. I don't like abuse of any kind. I will go batshit crazy. I don't like being belittled; I'll stomp a bitch to sleep. Glover got that side of me after our sister died. I damned near killed him. Her death fucked me up. I lost it badly, Nyomi when Momma called me and spoke about what happened to my kid sister. I couldn't talk; all I could do was hiss and growl. I could barely move. I didn't eat. I didn't hurt; I motherfucking ached behind Maysha leaving me. I wasn't allowed to view her body, go to her funeral, or burial. I couldn't see her obituary. My then-wife, Zella, Avery, Lee, and Palmer went in my place. Momma begged me to go away during my bereavement by confessing how bad it would hurt for her to lose two kids back-to-back. So, Ashley packed our bags for two months, and we visited her family in Idaho. I had no means of communication, nor was I allowed to be away from her. Avery, Palmer, Momma, Ashley, and Terry found a way to make me somewhat me again—they let me see my sister's obituary. When we returned, I wasn't the same. I was worse, and they knew it. Yet, they do what they always have done. Stuck by me."

I felt a tear drip onto my head. I didn't mean to dampen the mood; telling her what she needed to know about me felt good. I didn't need her to be surprised when I was okay one minute and rearranging someone's home the next.

Snaking my hand between her legs to change her mood, I said, "I didn't mean for your mood to change. I'm sorry."

"No need to be sorry. I'm a softy when it comes to people losing a loved one, especially when they are extremely close. Never shy from wanting to tell me something dear to you, regardless of how it may affect me. Okay?" She sniffled, lifting my head.

Sliding two fingers inside her, I observed her glossy eyes and nodded. "Okay."

"Ooou," she moaned as I slowly finger fucked her and rising farther onto her body.

"Earbud time," I said.

With my thighs resting against hers, I dropped my mouth onto lips I would have to occupy with my tongue once her waterworks arrived. "Time to press play."

Reaching underneath the pillow, my sweet woman produced our earbuds and my phone, which she could unlock. While she put an earbud into my ear, I attached my mouth to her neck. I wanted to leave her neck another hickey, but it took her body too long to get rid of the love bites. She was still rocking one from five days ago.

"Richardo," she whimpered, slowly fucking my fingers, putting an earbud into her ear, and pressing play on my sleek device.

As Ro James' "Rain" drifted into our eardrums, delicate, loving kisses graced a titty that would provide our child with the proper nutrients he or she needed. While my right hand was still employed between her legs, my left hand caressed her left titty, the one with the most hickeys.

"Richardo," she moaned as I suckled her nipple.

Through six songs, my mouth and fingers explored my woman's body as her soft coos and whimpers floated around the room. When the smooth beat of Trey Songz's "When We Make Love" sounded, my mouth ran from Nyomi's playland to her quivering lips. As I stuck my tongue into her mouth, I slowly slid him inside the hotness.

"Richardo," she moaned, back arching and nails digging into the small of my back.

Scooping the backbends of her legs in the crook of my

arms, I slowly thrust deeper into the clenching treasure land, ensuring to make him jump. As I deepened the spine-tingling kiss, a deep but hearty gasp jogged from her mouth, gliding down my throat. My sweet woman's playland clamped as her waterworks sloshed around my tool, making him harder while I craved more of her.

At a snail's pace, I removed my tongue from her mouth. Rubbing her soft face, I planted my nose on hers and swerved in it like I swerved on my motorcycle during bike weekend on the East Coast. Beautifully, she rained on me as her facial expression informed me she needed to let out her sex cries. I hated that she had to be quiet and how I felt placing my hand over her mouth.

Pathetically, I begged, "Let me hear your voice. Please."

Once her lips quivered, resting on my palm, I leaned to the right and beat it up. In seconds, a deep arch arrived, her eyelids flapped, and her beautiful, muffled erotic sounds arrived. I became a cocky fucker needing to hear my name repeatedly as she wet us tremendously. So, I did what I did best since I knew she loved it—gloriously and proudly fucked her.

When her breaths were trapped in her throat, I realized her arms and legs were pinned beside her head. Still, my hand firmly pressed her against her juicy lips as I stood up in the goodness, erotically and savagely dancing. With her body violently shaking and face close to being wetter than her pink monster, Nyomi removed my hand and stuttered, "Have your way with me, Richardo. The next song should make sure you do so."

Rubbing her chin and digging deeper into her goodness, I grunted, "Always be careful what you ask for, especially from me."

"Aren't you the captain, baby?" she whimpered as I gripped her waist before falling onto my back, bringing her along with me.

"Nih, I said have your damn way with me. Not have me number two-hundred and fifty-sixth into the Lord's line," she sassed, causing me to laugh.

With my body positioned as if I was about to perform sit-ups, I thrust into the pink monster while dancing to an old-school twerking jam. Studying the strained face woman, I gripped her throat and voiced, "Ride the bull, my captain."

"This bull is out of control," she moaned, rising on her tiptoes and leaning forward.

Deliciously stabbing her guts, I responded, "But this is what you wanted. Me to have my way with you. Be careful what you ask for, Nyomi, especially coming from me. Put your legs behind, not beside, but behind your head. Wrap your arms around those beautiful ankles. Do not let go, and do not sound off."

Once she was in the desired position, I smiled in her face while exiting the bed. A few inches from the bed, I stood tall —ensuring my feet wouldn't slip—and I had a damn good hold on her. Shortly afterward, I raised her off him. She shivered as her right eyelid fluttered and hot core tightened.

My jaws clenched as I rocked my hips and used Nyomi's body just as I used my hand to masturbate after taking my time with it—fast and reckless. The more her pretty cinnamon brown face turned another shade darker, the more I artistically, yet pleasurably, drilled it.

The intensity of my sexing her was too much for us, mostly her. With each drop downward, her muscles contracted, her pleasure noises would become louder, and my toes curled. When I slid her to the head, the monster nibbled it before vomiting on it. My stomach caved, my knees buckled, and my grip on her waist became tighter. Yet, I didn't stop; I needed to give her exactly what she requested.

Without notice, I rapidly squatted while moving from side to side. Nyomi's mouth opened wide as her head flopped backward. My heart raced as I knew she would yodel my name while her nectar covered me while steadily glided in and out of her. Thankfully, I didn't hear her sex noise, but our skin slapping was heard. They overpowered the music in my ear.

As I rolled in her body like rain tumbled down a windshield, Nyomi's toes curled, resulting in a few popping. Ogling her fat slit, I aimed my head toward her G-Spot. Lowly, she cooed, "My God."

"Cover your mouth with both hands, Nyomi."

She barely had time to complete her task before I destroyed

her sensitive spot while hungrily putting a nipple into my mouth. Too many pounds on the sensitive spot caused her to yodel my name. It was muffled, but it could be heard. I didn't focus on who could've heard her say my name. I focused on her going to sleep, smiling. Leaning backward, digging in her guts, I focused on her sweet, erotic moans and the tears cascading.

"I know you are weak, but bring my lips to me," I whispered, slowly grinding in the saturated goodness.

Assisting her in coming toward me, I analyzed her wet mouth. Finally entangled like snakes, I slithered my tongue across her bottom lip. Shivering, she cooed. A tear plopped onto my nose right as I sucked her bottom lip into my mouth and pushed deeper inside her.

Jeezy's featuring Plies' "Sexe" played, resulting in Nyomi showing me why she was my captain. After placing her arms around my neck and her legs on my shoulders, the sexy beast slowly twerked while leaning to the right. The pink monster cradled the hard-on, resulting in me slowly licking my lips. After three more long strokes, I admired my creamy pipe and her wildly shaking body.

Resting her nose on mine, Nyomi slid up the hardness, outstretched her legs, and slammed the cumming twat on me. After the seventeenth rapid drop, my knees buckled very hard, which caused my legs not to support us. She didn't make a sound as I fell on my ass.

Staring at her, I didn't bother to ask if she was okay. She

was still fucking the shit out of me and singing Giveon's "Heartbreak Anniversary".

"We will never have one of those," I moaned as my fingers dug into her waist. "I promise we won't."

"I'm going to hold you to that, baby. That I can promise you." She lovingly breathed before rushing her pink flesh into my mouth.

That kiss. Her soft body. Our tongues. My groans. That nasty, much-needed kiss, the thought of me having the best woman in all the land, and her pouring her heart and soul into pleasing me caused my sex tears to gather.

Once Yung Bleu featuring Baby B's "Slide Thru" glided into our ears, Nyomi left no crumbs on our lovemaking. She ate it up before sexily removed herself from the wet pipe. My eyes were locked on her as she looked at me. With her mouth hovering over my manhood, Nyomi wet her lips several times before opening her mouth wide. Seeing her saliva pool on her bottom lip made me anticipate the feel of her masterful mouth. Witnessing her tongue slowly roll from its resting place, I groaned as my toes and fingers balled.

Viewing her eyes leave mine as much saliva dripped on the head, I groaned, "Shit, Nyomi."

Slowly, she moved her head counterclockwise, drizzling her spit around my head. My right eyelid fluttered when she gripped the base tight, just like I liked. Bit by bit, she jacked up while ensuring her saliva blessed every inch of my stick. I think I blinked one too many times, or Small

Tyme Ballaz's "Dawg"—it wasn't supposed to have been in rotation to play—I missed her shoving him into her mouth. However, I didn't miss hearing and feeling my toes pop.

Through fast eyelid flutters, many stomach caves, and the inability to move my mouth, I watched Nyomi savagely suck me to the song's beat. Meanwhile, the fine woman rolled and popped her ass with the music's rhythm. I didn't know where to look, so my eyes worked overtime until she gagged and shook her head like a dog.

"Eat it up," I poorly voiced, wanting to grab her head.

"Grrrrrrrrrr," she sounded before making a suctioning noise while dragging her mouth up the shaft.

My lips balled tightly while watching her narrowed-eyed behind seal her mouth around the mushroom-shaped tip. The hungry suckles on my head and the softness of her palm gently fondling my balls caused me to mouth 'I love you'.

The ultra wetness from her mouth and the sexy neck movements grew my guy as I pleasurably held out. "Fuck."

"Mhm," she hummed while hurriedly shaking her head and gazing into my eyes.

"Ooou, shit, Nyomi," I moaned, slowly pumping in her mouth, chasing the vibrations.

With her saliva flooding me, Nyomi rolled her tongue around the middle of the hardened pipe. I thrust it farther down her throat while she jacked the inches not in her mouth, extended my balls, and aggressively shook her head. The sexy, dick-gobbling woman slung saliva onto my thighs and her titties.

"Shit, make it fucking nasty then," I coached, gripping the back of her head.

With a mass of her healthy hair entangled in my fingers, I enjoyed massaging her scalp and fucking her mouth as I saw fit. A massive euphoric sensation rippled from my feet to my head once I danced in my woman's talented mouth to a sex jam. Like the sex and dance goddess she was, the cooing woman spread her legs wider, popped her ass, seductively rocked her body back and forward.

"I love you," I passionately voiced as she delicately dragged her teeth from the middle of the shaft to the head.

Sloppily and rapidly, Nyomi flickered her tongue across the head. The prickling feeling ran from the one-eyed guy to my thumping heart. The sounds of her soul-nurturing, pipe-rising, mellow, but nasty, gobbling and slurping sprinted into my ears before running around the room.

"Mhm," she provocatively voiced, shaking my balls.

In between inhaling her spit, she aggressively shook her head and hummed a tune. Turning her head, Nyomi brushed her teeth before scrubbing her tongue. Several times, she brushed her teeth and tongue before rapidly and repeatedly sending him down the dark path of her throat. The sensation was so intense and fiery that I dug my nails into her scalp, gazed at her, and hissed, "Fuck it up."

Nyomi ruthlessly beat up her throat. The spit, her sex

noises, her body rolls, eye fucks, ball fondling, and her as a person lined up my cum. When my eyes lowered, she clamped her mouth tighter and hungrily sucked.

"Oh, my fucking God. Ah, shit. Shit. Shit. Fuckamighty," I loudly groaned as my stomach quivered repeatedly, my toes curled, and my fingers locked in her hair.

After several long and rapid sucks, massive tingles and heat consumed my body. The humming and head-shaking woman caught my boneless friends while lovingly looking into my eyes. Instantly, I tried not to say, 'I love you'. I tried not to tell her where her engagement ring rested in a house she would never live in. I fought not to tell her there was no me without her. I would've been too loud when sincerely expressing myself.

Once she sexily swallowed and removed her mouth, I pulled her farther onto me. I had hearts in my eyes when I softly and happily grinned. "Your engagement ring rests on your side of the bed. It only leaves when I have to put new bedding clothes on it. There's no me, this happy and satisfied me, without you. I am complete now. You made damn sure of that. I love you, Nyomi Richards."

Chapter 10

NYOMI

I was still high from my orgasm. My breathing was erratic, my pussy pulsated, and my ears were occupied by the sounds of the music and my rapidly beating heart. So, I wasn't sure I heard him correctly. With my shaky, sweaty hand, I removed the earbuds from our ears while oddly observing his content, shining eyes. Gently patting his chest, I said, "Come again?"

Skating his nails across my back, Richardo genuinely smiled. "You make it so easy to say I love you. I love you, Nyomi Richards."

Still, my breaths were rugged as my eyelids flickered rapidly. I didn't know how to respond, so I said nothing. Simply, I studied him while hoping he would change the subject.

"You are stunned, and I understand that tenfold. I don't expect you to say you love me until you feel it in your bones," he deeply voiced, sending chills running up my spine as he snaked his hands to my hips.

"I can't speak those words unless I mean them," I said, rubbing his bottom lip. "I do feel that you are speaking them too early. It does make me uncomfortable. We haven't gotten to that stage to think about being in love or full-throttle love the other."

Cuffing my chin, he searched my eyes a while before speaking. "If one feels they love someone, time shouldn't be a reason they don't say it. I know exactly how I feel, and it's not lust. I know that very well. That's why this dick is well known. I'll never withhold my feelings again. I made that mistake twenty-five years ago. I vowed never to do it again. So, I told you the truth. All of it."

Silence overcame us as he scooted toward the edge of the bed. We never stopped observing each other. So much was in his eyes. There was no denying he cared for me; a blind person could witness it.

The satisfied man smiled when he leaned forward, reaching for the wet wipes in his pants pocket. Like all the others, it was the biggest and brightest. My heart melted, and my stomach quivered at the sunny grin I loved when he presented it.

"A person knows who they need in their lives once that person runs across them, Nyomi. I knew immediately you were for me. I was certain I would have to jump through hoops to make you feel the same way about me. I've never jumped through hoops for a female. They gave me what I wanted on demand. I didn't woo any of them, including my ex-wife. I woo you. I didn't see more children from her as I do us. I see a gotdamn fleet coming up out of you," he sincerely admitted while placing me on my back.

"I don't know about a damn fleet now." I lightly giggled as he opened the cloth package.

"Shit, you catching hell now telling me to pull out." He chortled as I opened my legs for him to clean me. He would become anal if he didn't clean me. I loved how he was serious about taking care of a nutty kitty after he made it act like a fool. He was super sexy, cleaning me while talking.

As he carefully cleaned our cum from my kitty, I said, "Speaking of that, we need to use condoms, Richardo. Sucking down those morning-after pills isn't the thing to do."

"Okay." He exhaled before fake pouting. I laughed at the silly character I wished I could go home with.

After exhaling sharply, I rubbed the back of his hand and said, "On a serious note, you were an asshole in not expressing yourself to your ex-wife. I understand wanting to give your child something you had, but to hurt yourself and another being is not it. You didn't do the right thing by your ex-wife or Rayne. Your mind was made up when you asked your ex-wife to marry you; you would still be the same man toward her. She was the fool for accepting your hand, knowing how you felt. Doing the right thing was co-parenting and being there for your ex-wife emotionally after she'd given birth to Rayne."

"I know that now." He nodded, spreading my ass to wipe the excess fluids. "I was thinking about sliding back through when lights out. How do you feel about that?"

"I love it, but how much trouble would it be?" I asked as he dropped the used wet wipes onto the floor before lying backward.

"Not hard since all my players are in place. I had a few swap to different shifts to accommodate what we got going on," he admitted as I snatched four shea butter cloths from the package.

Cleaning him, I grinned. "Well, I'll be looking forward to sleeping with you tonight. Instead of us falling asleep on the phone."

"Good." He smiled, resting his hands behind his head. "Have you been thinking of baby names?"

I laughed into my hands until tears cascaded down my oval-shaped face.

"I'm serious, Nyomi. I have thirty names written down," he voiced, causing me to laugh harder while I poorly cleaned him.

"I know you are. That's why I'm so tickled." I giggled, cuffing my titties.

"You need to be adding to the name collection," he seriously spoke, raising an eyebrow.

"Can I be three weeks away from getting out of here before doing all that?" I sassily spoke, bucking my eyes as I cleaned him well for the final time.

"Nope. Do as I say, or I'm going to get angry, and the asshole will come out and make you give me those names. You will be loud as fuck too." He grinned, pulling me on top of him.

I rolled my eyes and said, "A boy will be a junior. That's all I have for now."

"Ah, was that so hard to do?" he sexily asked as I dropped my head on his chest.

"No," I responded, feeling his soft lips on my forehead as he wrapped his loving arms around me. "It's a small pizza party this evening for Zanning, right?"

"Fuck yes. A bunch of musty-ass kindergarteners in my house." He yawned, body relaxing.

As his phone vibrated in a different manner than the others, he lifted us and happily chuckled. "Rayne Lisa Mets."

I was a sucker for men loving on their daughters. To know I was on top of one who was a faithful, loving father had me stuck on him. Once he lowly answered the phone, our bodies' positions resumed. "Why I'm whispering is not of importance, Rayne. What's up?"

As I tried to capture her soft, sweet tone, Richardo sternly voiced, "Rayne, you know damn well you aren't allowed to drive my damn car. You bent all my gotdamn rims at once on Thanksgiving last year. I'm going to save your ass from getting a ticket this time. Dillion, I hope you are listening well. The next time you pull over my child in an expensive ass, customized, white Donk that's all mine, make sure you call me, so I can file a report about my shit being missing, so she can be arrested for grand theft auto. I'll see her ass every day right where I'm at as the fucking captain. Rayne, get my motherfucking car home."

Lord, I know Rayne did not call her father to get out of a ticket. He called the officer by his first name. Oh, yeah, I am dealing with a mighty man. A sexy, pussy-eating, dick-slinging, honest man of all men, powerful man, I thought while eyeing him.

♥♥♥♥♥♥

Lying on the bed with my legs crossed, I reflected on Richardo wanting me to run his family's land. I'd never dreamed of being a part of a thriving cotton farm. I would have to learn much about the cotton industry and receive the knowledge that Richardo knew to do as great a job as he had. In addition, I preferred to have his parents' and sibling's blessings instead of going behind their backs to run what has always been in their family. I didn't want to bring more problems between Richardo and Glover.

Being professional when need be wasn't and would never be a problem. I was a kindergarten teacher with strong clerical skills. I researched many things in my leisure time, so doing so wouldn't be an issue for the cotton farm. In honesty, I was the perfect person to aid the Mets.

"I'll be so glad when I'm free." I exhaled, closed my eyes, and rolled over.

"Me too," Richardo announced lowly, startling me as I awkwardly flopped onto my side to look into the area he spoke from.

"When did you come in? I didn't hear the lock or the door open." I smiled as my heart galloped while the man dripping in sex appeal in all-black regular clothing and gold jewelry walked toward me.

"I came in about ten minutes ago. You were deep in your thoughts. Why were you that deep into thinking?" he asked, kicking out of his black boots and dropping the black knapsack beside his shoes.

"Thinking about your offer of running the cotton farm and receiving your parents' approval by being myself," I answered, stuck to the decent mattress.

As he climbed out of his shirts, I was a trembling mess filled with excitement and horniness. Folding his shirts, he calmly breathed, "They will love you, but they won't love the fact you will be running the farm. That's why I said you won't be signing a prenup. No matter how much they love you, they will never go for it. You will have to deal with them not giving you their blessing. You will run it because I know you will do a great job. You are business material, just like me. So, is it safe to assume you will be beside me, rocking a badass two-piece suit, heels, hair curly and bushy, and got a mean ass rock on your left hand along with my wedding band?"

As he dropped his shirts on his boots, I blushed. "I think so."

Climbing between legs I had opened wider than the Mississippi River, Richardo sexily said, "I don't do 'I think so'. Yes or no, Nyomi?"

Yes, I thought, pulling him farther onto me while saying, "I'm not sure."

Rubbing the tip of his nose against mine, he whispered, "I have four hours with you. I will make all hours count so you can answer me with a 'yes'. What do you say about that?"

"I'll be looking forward to seeing how you will get me to say yes," I moaned as he dragged his hard, well-covered thang across my treasure chest.

"Good," he sultrily voiced, unbuckling his belt. "You know where your hands need to be."

"That I do," I responded, eyeing him while digging into his back pocket for his phone and our earbuds as he referenced them. "How was the party?"

"You are going to view it once we are naked," he

announced, removing my socks. "You will see the host doing the damn most. You will see my crew and me in our real skin."

Thrilled to see the best young lady in the world, I gleefully replied, "Hurry up and take off my clothes, please. I have our stuff."

"Eager ass." He chuckled, kissing my lips and grabbing the waistline of my panties.

"Did the party turn into an adult party?" I quizzed, unlocking his phone.

"Fuck yes. Avery's stupid ass is at fault for that. I'm surprised you don't smell alcohol running from my pores." He chortled as my shirt and bra were no longer on my body.

"Slide to the photo gallery. You'll see our foolery," he admitted, placing my items on the floor.

Seeing the earbuds were paired to his phone, I quickly placed one in our ears while opening the photo gallery. While he rested between my legs, slithering a finger inside me, I cooed, "Oh, wow. Just come right on in and start tickling the cat, huh?"

"Yep. Was thinking about it too much," he erotically spoke as I saw a sketchy video that possibly needed my attention.

Once I clicked the play button, he chuckled and fingered me faster. At the same time, my eyelids rapidly flapped from what I saw, felt, and heard.

"You stumbled across this video because your ass is nosey. You like how this sudsy dick look, Nyomi?" Richardo sexily spoke while washing his beautiful shaft.

"Why, yes, I do like how it looks," I moaned, nodding while rocking on his wet fingers.

The fucker between my legs chuckled as I slowly licked my lips and watched him make love to his palm while giving me pure hell.

"I can't wait until you get out. I'm… going … to … fold … your … ass … like some motherfucking towels," he spoke through gritted teeth while beating his dick faster.

"And fold me like a gotdamn folding chair. I don't give a damn," I whimpered as the chuckling man finger fucked me faster, making my stomach sink hard.

"I need you to do me a favor when I'm in your guts, Nyomi," he stated while bending and slowly pumping into his hand.

"And what is that, Captain Mets?" I whimpered, eyes glued to the damn phone as if he wasn't between my legs, causing a rainstorm.

"Bark. Snarl. Yell at me so The Don can come out and play, too." The foolish being laughed in the video and against my stomach. He had stopped fingering me.

I paused the video, turned on the flashlight, and aimed it at his silly ass. His face was beautiful as it was the happiest. While he planted his eyes on me, I lifted my head and asked, "Do you like having me with walls?"

"Nyomi shut up and finish the video." He laughed, rubbing my face.

"Answer me first," I responded, searching eyes that would always make me fold.

"Yes, I do."

"So, why the hell would I trigger you?"

"I need you to fall in love with that side, too," he seriously voiced, observing my eyes.

Nodding, I voiced, "Okay."

Resuming the video, my kitty cat, eyes, and ears received a lot of nastiness. By the tenth minute of the video, the naked beast stepped out of the shower, water running from his body—just as my sweetness tumbled out of me.

"Richardo," I moaned, thrusting my hips just as he served his fingers—cutthroat.

"So, I noticed you like pain during sex, Nyomi," he spoke, sitting before a computer in a well-decorated bedroom. "What do you think about us having a sex room?"

"I am with it. I am with it," I dramatically moaned as my back arched and toes curled.

"I think you like to have your ass plugged. Correct?" He chuckled as I nodded and came on his fingers. "I know exactly what I'm doing to you in real time, but I need you to answer me."

Turned the fuck on wasn't the correct phrase when my back arched, my waterworks started, and my voice box threw up, "Yes, in-motherfucking-deed."

"I have a feeling what your answer will be so exit this video. Get online and go to this website. I created an account just for us before I made this video. Your task will be simple. Put our sex room together. Whatever you want, get it," he spoke, showing the naughty website he was on.

Once the video ended, so did his finger play. While doing what he commanded, I asked, "When did you do this?"

"Two hours into that musty-ass party. Those kids had me thinking I was the one smelling like onions and shit. The main musty ringleader, Zanning, pissed me off by coming by me and flopping his arms and shit. One too many times, I gagged. I don't like to do that shit at all. So, I locked up badly. The fellas and Ashley had a time moving my big ass from the kitchen before the kids saw me," he seriously said, causing me to laugh. I couldn't look at the naughty website because he was continuing to talk about the excited, stinky kids and his best friends struggling to soothe him.

Tears rolled from my eyes as I asked, "What were you going to do to him?"

"Throw him and his stank ass friends in the pool and toss the bottle of Dawn at them," he voiced as I had to drop his phone to cover my mouth. "Maysha was the only one who could get away with being musty. She wouldn't be musty for long once she started sweating. She would hop in the tub. She had an overactive armpit sweat gland condition."

Rubbing his arm, I asked, "Do you think Maysha would've liked me?"

"Absolutely. Sometimes, I think she is Rayne," he lightly voiced.

"Why do you say that?"

"She does the same shit as Maysha. For instance, my Donk. Maysha used to always get my shit when I came over for dinner. She and Trina would joy ride in my shit, bend my rims, get noise ordinance and speeding tickets, and eat in my shit." He chuckled, rubbing my arm. "I would always do the same shit when I caught wind my car wasn't in the yard. Fuss. Threatened to press charges. Ask them if their asses needed anything. When they said no, I would still give them money. I would hang out with them for a few hours before going to fuck on somebody's daughter."

As if he was off in his thoughts, he happily said, "Maysha was my boss, and I was her protector. Rayne's my boss at times, and I'm her protector. Both make the oddest noises that drive me crazy, but I never lock up. Rayne never knew of those noises. She barely knew anything about Maysha until I started seeing my sister in her. Do you think my sister may be my daughter now?"

"Possibly." I shrugged, heavily believing in reincarnation. Yet, he wouldn't know. I didn't want any complications or his mind to trip.

"I need our first girl's name to be Maysha, Nyomi. Rayne's mother wouldn't go for it. So, I had to bite the bullet and let the bitch have it," he sadly voiced, looking up at me.

Gently tracing his lips, I nodded and smiled. "I would be honored to name our first girl Maysha."

"Thank you," he soothingly spoke.

"No thanks needed," I said, dropping my lips on his.

As our tongues clashed—causing fireworks to pop off in my head—I closed my eyes and wrapped my arm around his neck. His hold on me became tighter while rising farther on me and gently pushing my legs toward my chest.

"Mhm," I cooed as he slowly removed his tongue from my mouth.

"You'll pick out our sex room furniture and décor and view the party later. I need you to put my mind on right," he voiced, eyes filled with hurt and regret.

"Of course." I nodded, understanding what I saw in his eyes. I was still in his shoes.

Richardo suckled my toes into his mouth, creating a prickling sensation that didn't overpower the arousal stemming from his passionate sucks, licks, and French kisses.

"Oou," I lowly whimpered as he took his time tasting my toes.

When he swept his tongue across my ankle, Richardo glided farther onto my body until his chunky member rested on my stomach. Resting my legs on his broad shoulders, he rained kisses on my shaky thighs, causing me to purr and drag my hands down his forearms.

Bunching my stomach, the alluring man eyed me and genuinely said, "I must show her some love. She'll be the reason our child will be extra protected."

My heart melted from him loving on me splendidly. It was a beautiful sight to witness. Adoration seeped from his fingers as deep feelings crept from his eyes, lingering wherever he ogled. I would never get enough of how he showed me love with and without clothes.

"Richardo," I whimpered as he French kissed my stomach and inserted two fingers into my moist, prized treasure chest.

"Yes?" he answered, savagely attacking my G-Spot and toying with my erect nipples.

"Ahhoouuu," I moaned as my toes curled, fingers balled, and my back rose from the mattress.

"You are mine, Nyomi. All mine," he sexily yet lowly barked while dragging his mouth to my nipple. At the same time, he finger-fucked me faster and lifted my right breast. His warm, firm hand melted into my large baby feeder he loved sucking.

"I love how you please me, baby. I don't need it to ever stop," I lowly moaned, feeling the heat rising from the soles of my feet.

"Trust me, it won't," he passionately confessed against my nipple, sending chills jogging through my body.

In need of chasing all the euphoric feelings he gave me, I spread my legs wider to give him full access to his playland. Gloriously riding his fingers, my sweetness gushed out of me. Knowing what was to come, Richardo hurried his mouth to mine. As always, he swallowed my sex cries and pleas while continuing to make my body have a horrible tantrum.

Ready to have our tongues fucking, I ferociously suckled on his pink flesh. While granting me the most wonderful, sloppy, steamy kiss, I motioned for him to get on his back. Still kissing as his fingers were stuffed inside my tunnel of love, Richardo's back rested on the mattress. Once I removed his fingers from my pretty kitty, I slid down his mighty pole as if I were a stripper.

"Damn," he sexily hissed, turning me on.

While enjoying him packing out my drenching pretty kitty, I slowly rode the hardness. Lightly groaning, he gripped my waist and matched my rhythm. My wetness stirred, exciting me, but nothing like witnessing his serene, delighted facial expression. He was returning to a somewhat peaceful mind state.

Gazing into my eyes, he groaned, "You are everything, Nyomi."

"So are you," I cooed, running two fingers from his forehead to his navel. Meanwhile, I slowly rocked while leaning forward.

As if my favorite sex jam played, I put on a show for him while wetting and squeezing his pipe. Slithering my right hand into my hair, I tumbled my left hand from my neck to my stomach. Provocatively, I eyed him while rotating my hips, rising on my tiptoes, and pussy-popping on the head.

"Yes, Lawd. Do the damn thing," he sexily praised while I leaned to the right. I stopped bouncing to flex my muscles.

"Mhm," he loudly moaned, biting his bottom lip.

Resuming to bounce on the dick upright, I stimulated my clit while clapping my ass. After six hungry, circular rotation movements and several delicious G-Spot hits, my sweetness flooded him. I fought not to yodel his name while he beat in my goodness as I slammed it on him.

"I'll never let you go, Nyomi. Never. I'm yours. I'll never grow cold to you. I'll always be hot for you," he groaned, gripping my ass and slamming me on it.

"Ah, shit, Richardo," I whined, realizing I tilted too far onto the bed.

"I need you, Nyomi," he erotically confessed while milking me for all I had.

Once my face met the mattress, a few of my sex cries, moans, groans, and whimpers hopped into it. Quickly, Richardo lifted me from it, grabbed my neck, and fucked me as he had never done before. His demanding eyes were why I couldn't see our love organs connecting. Those eyes urged me to fall in love with him. Again, through his eyes, they showed me the happy future I would always have with him and what unconditional love looked and felt like. Immediately, I was at peace with finally having a man who stood on what he said.

With teary eyes, I gazed into his content peepers while grasping his neck. With no fucks giving, I made love to my man. Rubbing my cheek, Richardo worriedly asked, "The way you are moving suggests nothing is wrong. So, tell me what is right."

"Everything is perfect between us," I weakly confessed, studying his eyes and working out our love organs. "I wasn't big on sex before entering this place, but you had me masturbating and fantasizing about wetting him up. You had me close to asking how I could land my naked behind in your presence without getting into trouble. I wanted you from the first day. To know I do and will have someone in my corner satisfies me. Everything you have done for me has captivated me and would always hold me hostage."

Before the last word escaped my mouth well enough, I was on my back, staring up at him. I didn't want to be on my back. I needed to be on top of him, pouring my love onto him.

"Shit, Nyomi. You can't get on me in here and speak passionately like that. Your emotions seep well from your lips, but that thang does numbers when you are comfortable and spill your heart. You will have time to make me sing because God knows I was about to," he whispered, delicately gliding through my drenching hole. I had been told by a previous lover about my coochie's ability when I spoke passionately.

Richardo snaked his hands up my arms, sending tingles floating around my limbs. His rich voice melted my heart when he grabbed my left ring finger. Sexily, he sucked it and said, "As you know, I have your engagement ring. I bought it a few hours after you allowed me to make love to you. I can't let you see it because I need it on your finger. So, I took one of my little cousin's small scrunchies. You won't get into trouble for wearing your scrunchie engagement ring. It's pink, your favorite color. Nyomi Reanna Richards, will you do me the honor of wearing your pink scrunchie engagement ring?"

Filled with joy and giggles, I rapidly nodded and came

while eyeing the little girl's hair tie sliding onto my ring finger. Fucking me faster, Richardo grunted, "Gotdamn, this thang doing some shit while you are laughing."

"I love my beautiful temporary ring, honey," I sweetly voiced, lifting my hand toward the wall to better view the simple scrunchie.

"I'm pleased you love it. Take good care of it. It's a loaner. I have to return it to the kid with only a few strands of hair. I had to pay her baldheaded self three dollars for that thing." He chuckled against my neck while increasing his thrusts.

I had to slap my hands over my mouth to conceal the hearty laughter. That giggle caused Richardo to stand up in my pussy, spread my legs, and rock my body. I couldn't moan or coo; I was locked against the mattress, watching him rapidly enter and exit me. I gawked at the volume of fluids that rushed out of me, only to splash on him. Thrust after thrust, I doused the lowly growling man with a big heart and a complex dark side.

"Ooou, somebody's amazing wet-wet is having a fucking tantrum. Do I need to shove my tongue in your mouth, or can you continue to conceal your dick-rising sexual noise?" Richardo grinned, fixated on my eyes and banging the spot that had me erratically breathing and unable to respond.

Erotically, he chuckled. "Oooh, she can't respond. That's a great thing. That means I can access being at a waterpark and not worry about anyone hearing how much fun I'm having."

Richardo fucked me so well that I forgot to breathe. As his

body clashed with mine, the sounds of our skin slapping and my wetness stirring were louder than I would've liked it. Yet, it didn't make me tell him to slow down.

"Gotdamn, this pussy is life. Baby, wrap your legs around my waist," he whispered before hurrying his mouth to my neck.

After I did so, Richardo lifted me from the soggy mattress. As he stepped from the bed, my honey planted the tip of his nose on mine and sweetly spoke, "My woman."

"My man," I cooed, kissing his lips.

Placing us in the darkest corner of the cell, he whispered, "Hold on, baby. If you want to sing for me, stick your tongue into my mouth."

Before I could acknowledge, Richardo spread my ass cheeks. Wind crept around my hairless crack as he jackhammered my coochie. My back slammed into the wall as my abdomen trembled, and my mouth opened. I was thankful he paid attention to me. I would've informed all who was in me and how well he beat it up.

Our fiery, nasty kiss and his loving took me to another dimension. I was volcanic hot while our tongues beautifully collided, increasing my arousal and need for us.

While I moaned in his mouth, Richardo dropped into the squatting position. I screeched in his mouth, causing him to chuckle. The heart-pounding, fearful noise was the last sound I made until I came for the umpteenth time and he for the first.

Walking toward his clothes, the well-endowed sweetheart

of a man panted, "In my knapsack, there are two Gatorades. Please grab them."

"Sure." I yawned as he kissed my chin.

Arriving beside his items, I leaned toward the black bag. When I grabbed it, he eagerly said, "Now, it's time to discuss our wedding. I know your mom was all you had, even with family close. I'm family-oriented, as you know. I don't need you being uncomfortable on our union day. So, would you like a small ceremony?"

"It's your wedding day too. So, I say no to a small ceremony." I answered as he walked toward the bed.

While I opened one of the beverages, he responded, "Nyomi, I'm marrying you as soon as you are released. So, I'm going to ask again. Would you like a small ceremony?"

"You heard me the first time I spoke. Remember that," I said sassily, smiling.

The handsome one chuckled while nodding and placing me on the ground. Retrieving the orange beverage, he pulled me close and studied my eyes. "I sure did hear you the first time. We will have a big wedding unless you say no. Nyomi, to be clear, I don't care for a big wedding to show how much I love and adore you. I am showing that now and will continue with no problem."

Needing him to have his dream wedding as well, I happily smiled. "I know that Captain Mets, but you deserve to have your dream wedding since the first was an episode from a reality TV show."

"That was a good one." He chuckled as butterflies floated in the pit of my stomach.

Rubbing his face, I cooed. "You are everything, Captain Mets."

"Just as you are, Mrs. Captain Mets." He sexily breathed against my lips.

After I dropped a quick peck on his lips, he whispered, "Nyomi, get on that soggy ass bed, so I can clean you. You standing in my face while them damn kids tickle the top of my feet."

I howled in laughter while shaking my head. Meanwhile, Richardo chuckled. "Come on, woman. You still have two tasks to complete before it's time for us to rock each other again."

"Can we be real nasty?" I quizzed, raising an eyebrow.

"How nasty?" He laughed lowly.

"So nasty God will put us on the 'Do Not Enter' list." I grinned.

"I'm… motherfucking … with it." He smiled, doing the beat-it-up dance.

RICHARDO

Thanksgiving

Twisting my head from left to right, I rolled my tongue over the squirty slit I would be nutting in soon. I basked in the glistening pretty fucka, begging me to come back in it and show out. It wasn't time for me to dive back in; I needed to pay my woman's asshole a visit. Rapidly, I flipped Nyomi over like she was a flapjack.

"Nih, wait a motherfucking minute, Richardo. I haven't snarled at you. Why are you doing me this gotdamn way in this cell, knowing I can't moan, holler, or none of that shit? Who taught you how to flip a big girl like that? I thought I was in the gotdamn dryer," she comically yet fearfully spoke, looking back at me with bucked eyes.

"I need you to know your weight doesn't mean a mother-fucking thing to me. I'll fold your ass up while flipping you the fuck over. By the way, I'm sorry I scared you. I'll warn you next time." I laughed while dropping my face in her ass.

"We've been together for seven months. I know you can handle me," she cutely cooed.

"Just had to make sure you really knew," I sincerely breathed into her asshole as Steven G's "Handcuffs" sounded in our ears.

"Fuck," she lowly cooed, head and hands flopping onto the bed.

With the entirety of my wiggling tongue stuffed into her asshole, I spread her pussy lips. Slowly, I slid two fingers into her saturated hole. Shaking like the strippers in the A when they saw my crew and I walking through the door, she lowly moaned, "Eat your birthday cake up, baby. Take me to the king in this cell."

This woman of mine is wild with her mouth, I thought, rapidly tapping on her G-Spot. Immediately, Nyomi's toes curled as her soft body locked. Beautifully, she drowned my wrist. I wished I could've observed her sweetness flowing from her like a cascading fountain.

As I French kissed her asshole, my wonderful lady sweetly cried a bit too loud. It overpowered the music. It was officially time for her to receive a beautiful nap from Captain Dick Her Down Mets.

After slowly removing my tongue from her delicious asshole, I seriously voiced, "Baby, I'm ready to nut in you. Do you want me to put you on low tumble?"

"Absolutely the fuck not," she answered, slowly rolling over.

As I chuckled, scanning her sex-crazed face and holding my guy before her precious temple, Dreezy featuring T-Pain's "Close to You" satisfied my eardrum. While slithering inside her fortress, I questioned, "Ready for a little nap?"

"Yessss," she moaned as I slowly thrust into her gushy goodness.

"Good," I grunted, admiring the fantastic feeling of her cumming.

"Richardo, fuck me," she whimpered, thrusting faster.

"I will, but when the time is right. So, down. Patience, you need to learn, beautiful one. I want to feel you through making love, not fucking you," I groaned, pushing deeper inside her.

"Okay," she whimpered, sliding her tongue into my mouth.

She will fuck around and say that 'fuck me' shit one day, and her damn ovaries will barely be hanging on them damn fallopian tubes. They will be loose as fuck, once I shake her body the fuck up like a baby's bottle. She better chill with that shit. My stupid ass will lock up on her again, I thought, towering my mouth over hers while rocking her walls.

♥♥♥♥♥♥

"Gotdamn it! I'm behind door number one! I'm the best motherfucking prize, niggas and niggettes! And she got me!" my drunken ass hollered while grooving to the ending of LSG's "Door #1".

"Somebody tell Rayne to come get her daddy offa this table! He carryin' on nih!" Roq laughed loudly, causing an uproar of laughter to soar through my maternal family home.

"I love it when she is really nasty!" I hollered, gripping the waistline of my jeans and imagining fucking Nyomi from the back as I had earlier.

Boosie Badazz featuring Latto's "Nasty Nasty" was shut off before Momma calmly said, "Son, get your ass off my mother's table."

"Yes, ma'am." I chuckled, hopping from the oval-shaped, black table. "Can you cut the music back on, please?"

"That couldn't be Deborah Mets sayin' that." Roq chuckled, causing everybody, especially me, to laugh. "She would've kicked the legs offa that table while yellin' fo' me to get down. A nigga already on the floor, an' she would be screamin' fo' me to get down. Grandma, I got two thousand dollas to give to you if you holla at that nigga ret nih."

"Roqik, find you something to do!" Momma shouted, pointing at the silliest of her grandkids.

"That's how you need to holla at him. I got yo' funds,

Grandma," he continued, messing with the sweetest lady in the house.

"I don't need to see The Don right now, Grandma first-born," Momma seriously voiced before the nasty song resumed.

I was back on my feel-good shit since my fiancée made sure she tightened a nigga up well from eleven p.m. until four this morning. While grooving to the jam and drinking the potent lemonade moonshine, I smiled at the surprised woman who thought I wouldn't bring in our birthdays/Thanksgiving with her. She was my first meal, dessert, and birthday present, and she would be my last meal and dessert once I sobered up and left my folks' crib.

"Daddy, I heard you were in here cutting up!" Rayne shouted excitedly from behind me. At the same time, several grownups, Zanning, and a ton of kids flew by me. At once, all sorts of smells hit me, fucking up my dance steps to The Isley Brothers' "Between the Sheets".

Smoothly turning around, I stared at my daughter with the ugliest facial expression. Nervously, she looked at me as the music was cut. My idiotic nephew laughed. "Unc, you smell that?"

"I'm sick of you, Roqik! Leave my boy alone!" Momma hollered as I tried to find the musty person.

"Daddy, let's go walk outside," Rayne softly voiced, walking toward me. "You need some fresh air."

"Rayne, I am fine. I have not locked up. You looked at me

nervously, which meant you smelled that stench, too. I know damn well it's not Zanning because we discussed his armpits. Simply, I need to find the musty person to direct them to the bathroom. They need to baze," I seriously voiced as everyone howled in laughter.

Becoming upset because they thought the shit was a joke, I nastily hollered, "Ay, I'm trying to have a peaceful holiday! Whoever is musty, please go to the bathroom and baze!" I shouted, looking around the room. Roq fell to the ground, laughing, and Rayne slapped her face while shaking her head.

"Well, let me go fix me a few to-go plates. This nigga finna act up." One of my female cousins with a mountain of kids giggled.

"There is no fixing any to-go plates. We will eat shortly," Momma voiced, lighting a million incense.

Instantly, I gritted my teeth and said, "Ma, if you light all those incense at once, I will surely turn into a nut basket. All those strong scents at once, ain't it."

"Go outside, Son. Please," Momma sweetly voiced, even though she didn't want to.

"I always have to go outside. Why hasn't the funky person left yet?" I inquired, becoming angrier.

"The funky person, your grandson, just left from outside," Momma stated, putting her hands on her hip. The house erupted in laughter as I glared at Rayne.

Stepping closer to my laughing daughter, I pointed my

pinky at her and hissed, "Go baze·him. Now. Put deodorant on him, Rayne Lisa Mets."

"Daddy, I did. He's been playing hard." She giggled, shaking her head.

"Uh-huh! Zanning!" I hollered, walking off on my child.

"Sir?" he shouted from the kitchen.

"Bring the dish detergent! Bath time!" I hollered, walking down the hallway. "Rayne, bring me his clothes."

"Yes, sir!" they responded loudly as I stepped before the bathroom door.

Zit. Zit. Zit.

Walking into the cleaning area, I retrieved my device and stared at a number I was surprised to see. I simmered greatly while cheerily answering, "Well, well, well, birthday woman. What made you call me?"

"I'm missing you, and I needed to know if you were having fun," Nyomi announced as her background was noisy.

Plugging the tub, I turned on the water knobs and sincerely replied. "I was having a good time until a certain somebody brought his biracial musty ass in the house. Now, I will instruct him on how to baze properly and apply deodorant."

"Zanning, huh?" She laughed.

"Fuck yes." I chuckled as my grandson and daughter stepped into the bathroom.

"Baby, hold on for a minute," I told Nyomi as Rayne hurried to push the funky armpits kid into the bathroom. "Get naked and get in that tub. Squirt half of that Dawn into the tub."

"Yes, sir," he answered, extending his glasses to me.

"Jesus, honey." Nyomi laughed as my child outstretched behind the door, just like her auntie had outstretched behind my door when I talked a girl out of her underwear.

"It's needed. He might have two days of mustiness in those pits. Maysha used to take baths in Dawn to clean her armpits and remove the musty stench," I stated as Rayne smiled massively at me. At the same time, Zanning stripped from his shoes and clothes, and his mother and I turned away. He didn't like anyone looking at his lanky ass like we hadn't cleaned him before he could half-ass do something for himself.

"Ah, gotcha," Nyomi cooed, causing my dick to jump. "Well, I just wanted you to know I miss you and checking to see if you are enjoying family time. Get back to your family. I'll see you tomorrow. I love you, Richardo."

"Gotdamn it! She said it!" I excitedly hollered, hopping from the toilet, scaring my grandson but causing my daughter to smile. "There is no hanging up. I can't say much because my child is staring at me."

"Oh." She giggled, sounding like she was outstretched on her bed.

"To your comment about you seeing me tomorrow, Nawl, baby, you will see me at our usual time," I voiced as Zanning hopped into the tub, tossing water onto the ground. "Boy, I'mma beat yo' ass if you do that shit again! The last time you did that shit, I forgot about it and almost busted these nuts. I need them."

"I bet you were on the phone, smiling like you are now, which would explain how you forgot." Rayne's messy behind giggled.

At the same time, Nyomi cackled. "Granddaddy knows he can holler, but no one can holler at him."

"Exactly." I grinned, sitting on the toilet. Meanwhile, I looked into the tub and didn't see my grandson's face, but I saw his feet. His ass needed to submerge. The stench required to be carried away with the suds.

"Get out of that tub like that, Zanning Lucas Lee!" Rayne hollered, causing me to buck my eyes and point at the door. "I'm not leaving, Daddy. You are on the phone with my friend, who you have yet to let me see or talk to."

"Awe, listen to that beautiful heartbeat over there fussing like a momma bear," Nyomi said. "Um, is Zanning kin to Avery?"

"His uncle."

"We have been engaged for months now. Why am I just now knowing that?" She held out, astonished.

"Never crossed my mind to tell you. The father is on my shit list, honestly. Been on it for a while," I replied as Rayne removed snacks from her pocket.

"Why?" Nyomi calmly asked.

At the same time, a sudsy Zanning looked at me and

loudly said, "Granddaddy, Mommy and Daddy having another baby!"

As I whipped my head in her direction, I had never seen Rayne move so quickly to escape my presence. Meanwhile, Nyomi lowly squealed from excitement. I hopped from the toilet and shouted my child's name.

"She's grown, honey. She's in her own place. Take a breather while telling me why he's on your shit list and why you dislike them being together." Nyomi calmly breathed as I stepped into the hallway.

"She needs the same thing I need with you but with him. He doesn't want a commitment. He's fascinated with sleeping with Black women. He's not into Rayne as she's into him. He's a whoremonger junkie, just like his mother," I spoke, stomping closer to my laughing best friends as they socialized with my family.

"Wait, what?" she screeched as I stopped in the middle of the single-family living room, scanning the many faces.

"I keep tabs on my people. I know what everybody is doing. No one knows but me. I've known for a few days. Trying to figure out the best way to tell Avery. He might kill him," I voiced, unable to spot my child.

"Oh wow. They need to know immediately, especially Rayne, Richardo," the sweet-talking woman voiced.

"Hold on for a minute, baby," I quickly voiced as the bastard I didn't need to see strolled into the house as if he was the man of the hour.

"What's the issue?" my crew asked as Lucas' face was red and eyes glossy.

"At the moment, Avery, your fucking brother's facial expression is my gotdamn issue. Why is he looking like that?" I probed, analyzing the urban-dressed fucker rocking a slick, short mohawk and tapered sides.

"Rayne isn't biting his bullshit anymore. She tossed his ass to the streets last month after giving him the business. Now, he's looking like a death row inmate after being executed." Avery chuckled, telling me something I didn't know.

"It takes a little time for us to see shit really stinks," my woman voiced as Lucas arrived before us.

"It shouldn't when we put y'all up on game," I responded as Lucas stared at me. "What's the issue?"

"She left me alone for good this time. She … um … called it quits a month ago. Every time she sees me, she shows me whose daughter she is. I'm sure you understand that," he voiced, tears gliding from his face.

Proud and smiling, I observed the six-foot-four, overly tattooed and fit individual. "I do. What did she do to you?"

"Why does it sound like you are smiling, Richardo?" Nyomi giggled.

"I am." I grinned as he exhaled sharply and shook his head.

"Your child is a man-beater. My apartment looks like an F-5 tornado hit it since she picked the lock to get into my apartment. She took my belt and destroyed my back with it before choking me with her hands. A few minutes ago, she palmed my face and punched me in the chest. She doesn't give a damn that she's two months pregnant. She won't answer my calls or texts. She makes me talk and see Zanning through the window like I'm in prison. Now, she is on social media talking about accepting applications for a stepdaddy of two biracial kids. Motherfuckas at my job wants her and our kids. I love Rayne, Richardo. I always have. I love her enough to make her wait so I can be right. She's so gotdamn impatient that she doesn't see that I'm a broken-ass man. I need time to heal," he confessed as I tried to hold in my laughter.

"Heal from what? Motherfucka, you haven't been in shit since I received custody of you. We took damn good care of you. Suppose you had to heal or whatever the fuck you telling yourself, why would you have gotten her pregnant twice, idiot?" Avery hissed, shaking his head.

"If I didn't, idiot number two, another fucker who was sniffing her gotdamn thong harder than me, would've gotten her. Married her. So, I knocked Rayne's ass up twice, big brother," the red face fucker snarled, staring at his sibling.

"What do you expect my position in this mess that should've never been?" I asked as furniture was turned over, and the quads hollered my daughter's name.

"Yes, bitch, I lured your stupid ass here. Had you thinking I didn't have a clue about shit. I'm beating your mother-fucking ass, hoe, for playing underneath me. I don't give a fuck about Lucas like that, for real. I fucks on him and keep it moving. I like my cat visitor's low. So, please don't think I'm dragging you over Lucas. It's you playing under me that got you this shit, bitch," my child nastily voiced as I stared at Lucas.

"Who's the bitch my pregnant ass child is beating?" I spat through clenched teeth.

"Loreal," he sadly announced as Avery popped his brother in the mouth.

And the fights began. I looked around, smiling and laughing, as children hurried into the hallway. Meanwhile, Nyomi screeched, "What the hell is going on over there?"

"Everybody fighting somebody minus Terry, Ashley, Palmer, and me." I chuckled, proud that I wasn't the one who fucked up another holiday gathering. I held the fight starter for twenty-something years. I had passed the torch to Rayne.

"Ahh, we have officially gotten old, partner." Palmer chortled as I eyed my child, dropping blows on her supposed friend's face.

"Beat her ass, Grandma! Beat her motherfuckin' ass!" Roq hollered while hopping on the banister. "Beat her ass, Grandma!"

"What the fuck?" Ashley, Terry, Palmer, and I surprisingly yelled, running from the front room.

"You better tell me what you see, Richardo." My nosey fiancée giggled.

"Folks getting their asses torn up, but I think Momma

fighting somebody," I quickly announced, stepping into the chaotic kitchen.

"Gotdamn it!" my friends and I shouted as we witnessed Momma holding her neighbor's throat and whacking her with a meat tenderizer.

As I ran and laughed at the shit going on around me, Momma nastily shouted, "His thang has always belonged to me, bitch! Always! I signed a prenup for that thang. So, you know I love it and him. I knew your ugly, big booty ass had been scouting who belongs to me! I've been waiting all day for some shit to happen, so I can tenderize your motherfucking head!"

"Oh, my God, Richardo, is your mother speaking like that?" Nyomi squealed.

"Yep," I loudly voiced because dishes and backs were cracked on tables and walls. "Ma! Turn that lady loose before you kill her! Terry, go find Dad!"

As I wrapped my arms around Momma from the right of me in the corner, Dad said, "Son, I'm right here. I'm not coming out into this fucking madhouse. It's a gotdamn brawl. I'm too old for this shit. Your mother had been wanting to fight since she woke up. She dropped to her knees and prayed someone pissed you off, which would trigger a brawl. She prayed to God for a fight, Son. Her bones are too old for this shit. She's done enough of fighting when we were younger. My God, she still has her hood ways. She's beating Mae like she beat the steaks last night. Get your momma off that woman before you oversee her instead of her overseeing y'all. Y'all, as in you and The Don."

As Nyomi cracked up, I had a horrible grip on Momma, who was still talking nasty to her neighbor of thirty-plus years. Terry, Palmer, and a red-faced Avery helped me get my strong mother off the beat-up woman who flopped to the ground, holding her head.

"Boy, this Thanksgiving lit, and we aren't the ones who started it!" Terry laughed as we lifted Momma while stepping over numerous beat-up persons.

"I said what the fuck I said, bitch!" Rayne defensively, yet nastily, shouted, causing my jaws to clench and my right eyelid to flutter. My hold on Momma became tighter because my fingers twitched.

"I feel you, Son. Let him out. It's not a holiday if The Don doesn't come out and play," Momma voiced, looking up at me.

"Did she really just say that?" Nyomi squealed as we entered the living room to witness Rayne backhanding Lucas.

"Yes, she did. He's not going to come out. Rayne's feelings are hurt. I'm going to get my child and grandson home before I lose my best friend because I murdered his brother while Terry and Palmer hold him back to make sure I don't kill him, too. Momma, I need you to get Zanning from the bathroom. His things are in there. Bring him outside. I have to get Rayne out of here. My baby is in love, and her feelings are hurt. I don't like that," I spoke, eyeing my child work out her children's father's face before shoving him into the entertainment center.

"That's enough, Rayne Lisa Mets!" I bellowed as she raised her foot to kick Lucas in the face.

"Fuck this wanna-be nigga!" she snarled, turning to look at me.

"Put your fucking foot down! Now!" we hollered as she looked at me and brought her foot down.

"Fuck nawl, guh! I ain't finna let you get down like that! I told yo' ass to leave that fuck ass dude alone! Nih, yo' gotdamn soul achin' 'cause he fucked a supposed friend! This is yo' fault! You knew he wasn't shit! Unc told you that dude wasn't shit! Unc Avery told you his own brother wasn't shit, but you upped the idiot yo' exclusive ass pussy an' heart! You take this motherfuckin' L, Rayne! Good niggas in these streets wants you! That damn social media post doing gotdamn numbers! Motherfuckas in my inbox askin' where they can sign up to be at all doc appointments fo' boffum! Get yo' fuckin' mine right!" Req, the third of the quads, angrily screamed as he scooped my furious daughter into his arms.

I was thankful he carefully snatched her from the ground. Her angle and attitude would've killed Lucas. She was officially fed up with loving someone who couldn't give her the same love.

"Baby, I lied to you when I said I would come see you tonight. I can't. My first heartbeat needs her dad," I confessed as my third nephew carried my crying child out of the house.

"No, you didn't lie, sweetheart. Our daughter needs her dad, but it would be great for her to hear my voice." She softly exhaled, causing me to run out of the house.

"Seems she will hear you earlier than I planned," I genuinely said as the fourth quad, Raq, chuckled and shook his head.

"Unc, she been beatin' that dude's ass since he pulled up. I almost felt sorry fo' him. She hurtin', Unc, so don't be too hard on her. He's her first everything. You don't know how it feels to be hurt by yo' first everything. My brothers an' I do. That's why we let her rock his fuckin' head every time she sees him," he confessed, making me stop and look at him oddly.

"Raq, how long has she been beating on Lucas?" I inquired as my partners slipped out the door with the beat-up character.

"About three months after she lost her virginity to him." He chuckled, firing a blunt.

"Raq, she was pregnant with Zanning," I oddly voiced, searching his eyes.

"And been rockin' his motherfuckin' head since. She bought this sex kennel thing an' be tossin' his ass in there." He laughed, causing Nyomi to howl in laughter. "Man, the guh put a cover off the cage like the bitch a real dog. That guh rough ass fuck when she's mad an' hurt. Also, um, you might wanna talk to her. I'm sure what Zella had to say to her got her fired the fuck up too."

God, don't let Zella do what she promised years ago, I thought, stuttering, "What the fuck did that bitch say to my kid and when? Details."

"We was in the grocery sto' last week. Zella told her that she was yo' mistake baby an' that you didn't love her fo' real. You just did the honorable thing since the condom broke. Told her she didn't want to be bothered wit' Rayne or be a grandmother to Zanning. She remind her of you, a man she really loves an' always will. Rayne turned aisle two out once she popped that bitch in the face wit' a pack of noodles. Oodle noodles went everywhere. She whooped her momma into aisle three. She had that bitch playin' dodge the cans before bustin' her in the mouth wit' one. She was unconscious after that. The police came, an' Rayne clearly said these words, 'I'm The Don's daughter, bitch. Back off.' An' they backed the fuck off. Unc, why is people afraid of The Don? Family included, especially Granddaddy," he seriously questioned, observing me.

"Nephew, that dark side gets shit done by any means. My head isn't in the present. It's in the past, stuck on a moment that hurt me deeply. I'm dangerous when that particular moment is vivid." I exhaled as Nyomi requested to speak to Rayne.

Seeing his mouth open, I had to walk off. My daughter needed me, and my love required to chat with our child. While marching toward the end of the driveway, Glover noncon-frontationally hollered my name from my left.

Looking in his direction, I voiced, "Not now, Glover. I need to get to Rayne."

"Brother, we really need to talk now. It's about the fields," he hurriedly spoke, walking toward me.

"Glover, not now," I calmly stated, walking toward Req and Rayne.

"Then when? You are yet to teach me the things I need to know. It's always something that comes up that keeps you from helping me," he spoke, running next to me.

Looking at him, I exhaled. "Glover, I don't like to repeat myself. You heard me the first time. There was a gotdamn brawl inside the family home. For the first time, it wasn't my squad and me who started it. It was Rayne. Momma beat the fuck out Mae with a gotdamn meat tenderizer while Dad stood in the corner, sounding like his fragile ass was trembling and pissing on himself. The house is disastrous. Bodies, dishes, and food are everywhere. I am not in the mood to deal with business talk. It's family time. I suggest you make yourself useful by checking on our father."

"Do you want the fucking company for yourself?" he hollered, causing my head to oddly rock as I spun on my heels.

Through gritted teeth, I slithered up to him, dropped my nose on his, and hissed, "I don't want the fucking cotton farm. I prefer to be in the background. However, you are too fucking lazy and dumb to oversee it. It's always 'Richardo, I need' or

'Richardo, I want'. It's never 'Richardo, what do you think about this?' You want me to do the entire fucking job while you have the title. Fuck that. If I'm going to do all the damn work and you don't put in shit, I might as well oversee it. So, now you have your fucking answer. I am going to oversee our cotton farm, Glover. Now, leave me the fuck alone. Unlike you, I am a damn great father and grandfather. My babies need me."

I left him with an open mouth and glossy eyes. Applauds sounded in my ear as Nyomi gleefully voiced, "Ah, you handled that beautifully. What stopped The Don from coming out?"

"Rayne's hurting," I offered, nearing my nephews and daughter.

Reaching into my pocket for the other earbud, I stepped before the chatty crew, loving on their favorite cousin. Extending the earbud to my disappointed child, I said, "Put that in your ear, and let's walk down the road."

"Yes, sir." She nodded, retrieving the black item as I extended my hand. "It's noisy."

"Yes, it is, beautiful one. The perks of being in prison." Nyomi softly giggled as my kid's knees buckled.

"Nyomi?" Rayne sweetly voiced as she stopped walking and looked at me with teary eyes.

"It's me. I'm not going to ask how you are. I heard it all. I have another message for you. One, I need you to hug your dad tight. Right now," she lovingly confessed before my child ran into my arms as she had every time she fell off her bike, scooter, or skates.

"Are you in those loving, big arms?" Nyomi softly voiced as I rubbed my kid's back.

"I am." Rayne choked up.

"Close your eyes and breathe in and then breathe out. While you are doing so, I'll talk to you. Is that okay?" my fiancée lovingly announced.

"It is." Rayne nodded.

"You've been hurt, and it's okay to show it. What is not okay is you taking a person back who keeps hurting you. That is not healthy for you, Zanning, the pregnancy, and most importantly, your father. Let the bullshit go. That's Lucas. If a person truly wants to heal, they will not involve anyone in their lives as Lucas has done you. He would've been your friend and would've kept his dick to himself. Now, this is what will happen, and I stand on this shit. Your father and I will be your and no more than three other crumb snatchers' best parents. I'm not going to keep pushing out all those damn kids for him. He can kiss my ass on that tip. Whew, sorry, got off the topic. We will be the best grandparents to Zanning and the new baby. You and I will have a lot of girl time. I need you beside me on April 7. That's the day I will officially become Mrs. Richardo Vincent Mets. No need to respond. I'll give you a few minutes to reflect on what I've said," she calmly said as I kissed Rayne's head.

Looking up at me, she calmly yet oddly asked, "So, you are going to have your happily ever after, Daddy?"

"I am." I happily breathed, observing her eyes. She was no longer upset, but she wasn't happy either. My child was sad.

"Good, because you deserve it," she stated, rocking her head. "Momma said you don't love me for real. She said I was your mistake baby since the condom broke. She said you were outraged that she had gotten pregnant. Is any of that true?"

Slowly, I licked my lips and said, "No and yes."

Instantly, I knew the shitstorm Zella promised me had landed. Slowly backing from me with cold eyes, Rayne choked up. "Well, thanks for being honest. I'll talk to you later. I need to get Zanning home. Nyomi, it was good hearing your voice. Congratulations on your nuptials. I won't be present, but I will send y'all a gift. He's getting married to his real love, which pushes the unwanted kid out of the way. You and y'all's kids will be happy. That I can assure you."

"You better explain shit to her now, Richardo! Now! You shouldn't have waited to explain shit to her! You should've dropped the rest in her lap when you answered!" Nyomi nastily hollered as Rayne hurried to toss the earbud at my chest. I never wanted to tell her the naked truth for a reason.

As I grabbed my child's arm, she yanked it back and said, "We are good, Dad. I'm tired. Talk to you later."

"Don't you fucking move, Rayne Lisa Mets!" I shouted, eyeing her wet face.

While I reached for her hand, Rayne walked off. Her reaction hurt me. I never saw her pulling away from me or looking at me as if she didn't believe or know me. Walking behind her, I shouted for her to stop moving. When she didn't, I grabbed the neckline of her T-shirt and gently pulled her to me.

"Tell her, honey!" Nyomi hissed.

After exhaling a few times, I searched my kid's teary, hurt eyes and finally confessed. "I didn't love Zella. We were just messing around for years. The condom broke. Yes, I was pissed. She told me she was pregnant; yes, I was angry as fuck. I never called you a mistake baby nor did I view you as one. You were simply my baby. I never asked her to have an abortion. It never came across my mind. What did? Me giving you a two-parent home as I have. Something she never had. I was on board with being your dad, Rayne. I promise. I saw your little body on that ultrasound machine and fell in love with my kid. I couldn't stop smiling at my creation. I heard your heartbeat, and everything made sense to me. I was attached to Zella because of you. I showed her more affection than I had ever shown her. I needed you, Rayne, not her! I loved you, not her! You are my fucking world, something she could never be! You helped me more than your uncles and auntie! I was in a very dark place when you were conceived and born! I was hurting like a motherfucka over my sister! I would look at you, and my world was bearable! If you walk away from me, I will fight for you! I hopped into a loveless marriage for you! I move the way I do for you! I need you unfuckwithable, Rayne Lisa Mets! I love you! You are not, and was never, not wanted! The situation of being with the wrong person was unwanted! I didn't want Zella to tell you how we were! I needed you to believe that we were happy because you deserved a two-parent home, just as I had one! Don't walk away from me! You will have no idea what that will do to me! I love you too fucking much! I love you more than she ever could. More, Rayne. Please don't walk away from me. I need you, Zanning, and Nyomi."

She rose on her tiptoes, kissed my cheek, and exhaled sharply. Stepping from me, she nodded. "Enough has been done and said on this holiday here. Many mistakes have been made, and we have to live with them. We live, and we learn. We trust, and we love. We get fucked over, and we go batshit crazy. Life is very comical, especially when you are genuine and loving. Everything really does start at home, Daddy. I needed Zanning to have a two-parent home like I had. Excuse my language, but I no longer give a fuck about my kids having a two-parent home. They are fine with one responsible parent, who is a go-getter. Your situation would've been mine, and I would've been Zella, minus not loving my kids. I'm done stepping on bitches' backs, and I'm done hollering 'I'm The Don's daughter' just to make sure I walk out wherever I've torn up. I'm going to move at the first of the year, but I won't be in this raggedy ass state. As you stated, it's time for me to live my life for me, not you. Again, as you stated, you will be fine. I'll text when I make it home. No need to pop up. I don't want any visitors. After all, I am The Don's daughter. I will always bounce back after being in solitude. Goodnight. I love you."

My eyelids fluttered as I poorly saw my heartbeat walk away from me. My head felt heavy as it dropped. I loudly asked, "What does that speech mean, Rayne?"

"Time to start fresh. Away from family and everything I'm familiar with."

"Away from me?" I questioned as tears ran down my face.

"Like I said, Daddy, you have finally found your first true love. I can go. There's no need for me to stay anymore. You will be fine," she spoke.

"Stop beating around the gotdamn bush with me, Rayne! What the fuck are you saying?" I hollered, heart aching.

"I don't want to be jealous of a kid who you will look at utterly different than me! Just like Zella looks at her other kids with Flex! So, I'm taking myself out of the fucking equation before you hurt me like you hurt Zella, and she hurt me!" she angrily yelled, staring at me. "Yeah, I'm yelling at you! Pull out The Don so I can put his ass on his fucking back! I got fucking time tonight! I'm emotional, and I'm all over the fucking place!"

"She's angry with her mother, Richardo, not you. Just hear her tone, and you'll hear it. She's running away from her mother. Her mother got into her head by telling her a truth you should've been broken down to her." Nyomi softly exhaled as I strolled toward my angry kid.

"Come here, Rayne," I softly voiced as she backed away.

"I'm going home, Richardo," she hastily spoke as all moved from us.

"What the fuck you called me?" I nastily voiced, running up to her as my hands twitched.

"Richardo! That is your name, isn't it?" she spat, just as my grandmother had done numerous times to my sister and me.

My stomach caved as my knees buckled. My right eyelid twitched harder than my fingers when I neared my wet-faced child. I cuffed her chin and struggled to speak. I closed my eyes to gather my shits and to cease my mind from thinking about the worst verbally abusive grandparents.

"Rayne, I love you, but I advise you not to call me by my government name because I was never a deadbeat dad. No matter what side was present, I was always there for you. Do you think I could easily forget my first heartbeat? Do you really think I can push you out of my life as if you never existed? Rayne, I was with you since that bitch pissed on the stick, and it came back positive. I never missed anything concerning you. Not your first tooth, crawl, or walk. I'm the one who changed your pamper first. I bathed you first. I did everything first, not her. I made damn sure I did everything first. I made damn sure I loved you hard as fuck because a father's love goes a long way in my eyes. Do you think I will let you leave my life like you haven't impacted it for the great? I'm The motherfucking Don, Rayne. I'll crush your dreams of wanting to move out of the state. I'll make it hard as fuck for you to cross the gotdamn state line. Get your mother's words out of your head! They are her words, not mine! I am telling you I need you in my life. Richardo Vincent Mets, The Don, is fucking death row! Ain't no fucking walking away from me! Even in death, ain't no fucking walking away from me! Maysha's all over my home! Her pictures are in my wallet! Her obituary and numerous pictures are on my dresser! I got my sister's pictures in both my cars! Ain't no fucking leaving me! You are mine! These nuts created you! You were on my gotdamn chest all the time! Fuck that bitch! Fuck her and her words, Rayne! I'll knock that bitch off the map for hurting you with her words! With that being said, go home! When you see me sitting in your kitchen, shit has become real, and you better never speak or act like you are going to walk out of my fucking life like I'm a deadbeat ass nigga!"

"Richardo," Nyomi worriedly voiced as I turned on my heels and looked at Ashley, her four sisters, Terry, Avery, and Palmer.

"My house. Suit up. Two black trucks only," I responded before retrieving my phone.

"Copy that," they replied as we walked in separate directions.

While we stomped towards our vehicles, I slowly licked my lips and wiped my face. Meanwhile, Nyomi continued calling my name. Once I hopped into my truck, I spoke through trembling lips. "I know what you are thinking, but you don't understand how I feel. You don't see me. No one knows Zella's promise she made when I handed her the divorce papers. She promised she would hurt me one day when I least expected it. I am suffering because she hurt my baby just to hurt me. I don't like to be hurt, Nyomi. I like to do the hurting or have someone do it for me, so I will have it done for me. Keep your phone on. I'll call you when I'm settled. Don't stress. I'll be okay. I'll always be okay. I love you, Nyomi Reanna, soon-to-be Mets."

Chapter 12

NYOMI

Valentine's Day 2023

"Wow, Richardo. This is nice. I love it. When did y'all have time to do this? We parted ways three hours ago," I lowly voiced in awe as I ogled the middle of the isolation cell, romantically set for two. At the same time, he removed my shoes.

"They did this before leaving yesterday. The food was brought in two minutes before you arrived. So, let's have a good breakfast before we have to part ways. Today's one busy day once noon arrives," he admitted, removing his shoes incorrectly while lifting me from the ground.

I wrapped my arms around his neck as he walked toward several thin blankets filled with fake red rose petals. Eyeing the four serving trays with four different juices resting behind them, I fake pouted. "So, our time is a quick one, huh?"

"Yes, but I'll be back at my usual time. I'll make up for this quickie I'm about to deliver. I promise," he confessed, kissing the tip of my nose while stepping into our seating area that housed four pillows.

Placing me on the blanket, I gazed into his eyes and said, "I'll be looking forward to seeing you at our usual time."

"As you should, beautiful one," he sweetly voiced, sitting beside me. "Time to eat."

"Yes, it is," I genuinely voiced, eager to feed him as I had two nights ago.

"I love you, Nyomi," he genuinely responded, gazing into my eyes while interlocking our fingers.

"I love you," I sincerely responded, rubbing his chin.

"Everything folding out beautifully as I had hoped." He smiled, bringing his head closer to mine.

"Yes, it is." I grinned, overflooded with happiness. "I do hate that Rayne couldn't come to see me today. It would've been great to see her."

Sexily, he leaned against me and wickedly grinned. "Who said my precious one isn't coming? Who do you think delivered this food? Who do you think will deliver lunch? Oh, my baby is coming through for her daddy. She loves him just that much."

"She's back?" I gleefully questioned, covering my mouth as happy tears fell.

"Yes, my baby came back this morning. Big belly ass was in my bed sleeping." He happily smiled as his eyes had become teary.

"I told you she needed time to herself. She would know where home was once she received a breather from every-thing," I whispered against his lips while wiping his tears and gently rubbing the tip of my nose across his.

"That you did. Thank you for talking me out of putting a leash around her neck," he lovingly said, searching my eyes.

"You are welcome. Everything is surely back on track, right?" I questioned, analyzing his eyes.

"After we terrorized Zella and Flex, they have been scared to breathe. I've issued the order to have their doors kicked in ASAP. Time for them to move far away from my child. Won't a fucking soul make her feel unwanted. No one," he spoke, gliding his hand down my face.

"Gotdamn, I'm glad you are mine." I rushed to say before suckling his bottom lip into my mouth.

Instantly, he gripped my thighs, causing me to coo. He placed me on his lap as I rested my hands on his neck. The slow tasting of our pink flesh continued as the soft patter of shoes sounded from the hallway. His hands traveled from my romp to my neck as he deepened the kiss, sending shivers running faster than lightning.

"Ooh," I moaned, loving his hands massaging the neck that I had worked out well before he left me three hours ago.

Slowly removing his tongue from my mouth, Richardo glided his nose across mine and tenderly spoke, "All mine."

"All yours," I acknowledged, reaching behind me for our food.

"I told my parents about you and that you aren't signing a prenup. They are excited to meet you, and there was no bickering about the prenup. Then, again, Dad probably knew not to go back and forth with me would be useless. So, when the day comes for you to get out, he might try to talk you into signing one. Again, you won't," he passionately confessed as I removed the top from one of the circular trays.

"Copy that." I softly smiled, staring into his captivating eyes.

"We are almost at the finish line, Nyomi," he calmly spoke, squeezing my butt.

"Yes, we are." I nodded, grabbing a beautifully scrabbled cheesy egg.

As I brought the fluffy item to his mouth, he asked, "What kind of car do you want?"

I wasn't expecting that question, so I oddly stared at him. He went above and beyond to make me fit into society easily on my first day out.

Seriously, he voiced, "Stop looking at me like that. You will need a vehicle, Nyomi. I'm sure you had a car in mind."

"Hyundai Palisade," I responded as he finally accepted the egg.

"Any particular color?" He chewed, grabbing the spoon and shoving it into the maple and brown sugar oatmeal with small, diced strawberries.

"Any standard color is fine," I answered.

"While we are eating, you will search for your car. I'll start setting it in motion to retrieve it. Grab my phone and unlock it," he sexily ordered, sliding the plastic fork filled with one of my favorite breakfast foods to my mouth. It had been a long time since I had the delicious goodness swirling around my mouth before it met its fate.

"Okay." I nodded.

I closed my eyes and savored the sweet and soft texture of the oats. It was cooked just as Momma had prepared mine before I started cooking—with milk and butter instead of water and butter. It felt like home to me. In a split second, I returned to three days before the accident that changed my life. Momma and I had dined on our favorite breakfast food for dinner.

It was the best last dinner I had with her. We laughed, held hands, and never broke eye contact while enjoying each other's company. Her sparkling eyes were brighter and more loving than the other times we shared meals. I should've known something horrible would come our way.

"What's wrong?" Richardo softly asked, rubbing my cheek.

Opening my eyes, I confessed, "I remembered the last meal I had with my mother."

"Tell me about it." He smiled, grabbing a piece of crispy bacon as I grabbed a round sausage.

Running the sausage to his mouth, I studied his eyes and said, "We were eating a similar meal. Way more food. The vibe had always been great between us. That time, it was perfect. No life lessons did she give. Only love, extra hugs, kisses, and holding of hands. It was as if she knew her time would expire within a few days. There wasn't a moment of silence from the time I arrived. It was like a holiday for us. Just being appreciative and loving toward the other."

"That's how your life will always be with me. Your eyes will dazzle just as they did when you spoke about that moment. I'll make your mom proud; I'm sure I'm already doing it. We will pay her grave a visit when you are released. I need to be introduced," he heartily stated, making me fall more for him.

"It'll be my pleasure to finally introduce her to my man," I cooed before savagely wrapping my tongue around the crispy bacon before it met its fate.

"It'll be my pleasure to be presented to her as your man," he confessed before biting the sausage. "Your mom gave you a beautiful happy ending despite the horrible accident. From here on out, I need you to reflect on y'all's last dinner more than the accident. Okay?"

"Okay." I nodded, watching him enjoy the rest of his sausage while eyeing me.

Sexily, he devoured it just as he did me. I was no longer hungry watching him eat. His chews turned me on, and I wanted to tease him. Leaning toward his semi-greasy, succulent lips, I observed the twinkle in his peepers while skating my tongue across the bottom of his lip.

"Mm," I moaned, snaking my hand underneath his shirt and continuing to taste the lips that would forever be mine.

"Yeah, I see what type of breakfast you are trying to have," he growled before taking over the kiss and setting the spoon on the tray.

Quickly, I stopped him and said, "Pick up the spoon and feed me. You are so quick to get things on and popping. Let's take it slow and build up the steaminess. It'll be so much better."

"Look who's talking. The queen of rushing." He chuckled, unbuckling his belt. "It's hard waiting when I have you close or have access to get to you after light's out. I want you morning, noon, and night, Nyomi. But I can try to wait."

Dipping my finger into the oatmeal, I cooed, "Let me see if I can turn that 'I can try' to a 'yes'."

"Let's see," he groaned, reclining on the pillows as I ran the oatmeal from his forehead to his lips.

Rising farther on his body, I licked and suckled the thick, brown concoction from his lips and stopped at the center of his forehead. Occasionally, I sprinkled in a coo or moan while massaging his neck and chest.

The handsome being moaned, "You are making this hard."

"No, honey, you are making it hard by being impatient. I am at fault for that. I'll own it," I voiced while raining kisses on his face and unbuttoning his shirt. "I'm releasing any tension you may have. I'm intensifying your need for me. I'm ensuring you will always know that I will focus on you. I don't need you to get used to or me getting used to us."

"I'll never get used to us, and I damn sure won't let you get used to me," he calmly responded.

"Good. Time to be quiet and focus on me, focusing on you," I whispered, pulling him forward so I could remove his uniform top and undershirt.

Obediently, he kept his mouth sealed as I removed his clothes, including his socks. I had never seen his feet. I thought they were ugly since he kept them hidden. I was mistaken when I viewed them; they were long and wide but pretty and soft. I could tell he kept his pedicure appointments regularly. Grabbing his large feet, I massaged them. I noticed his dick grew harder the more I applied pressure to the bottom of his feet.

"Mhm," he groaned, closing his eyes.

Skating my hands up his strong, tattooed legs, I ensured significant pressure was applied to his calf muscles. The more I rolled my fingers around the well-crafted muscles, the more Richardo relaxed. As the hustle and bustle of the hallway sounded, he didn't open his eyes. It seemed he was in his happy place. Thankful for him being there, I suckled his head into my mouth.

"Well shit," he lowly groaned as I swirled my tongue around the head.

Moving my head from left to right while the tip of my tongue visited the hole, I gently hummed. He grunted, "Well, blow in that flute then."

"Be quiet, Captain Mets." I giggled before French kissing the sensitive spot that allowed his sperm to grace my exclusive pussy faithfully.

As he sweetly sang how much he loved me, I slammed my throat on the veiny goodness while quickly shaking my head. While admiring my saliva rushing out my mouth, plopping at the base, his manly sexual noises turned me into a dick-suckling gobbling. I inhaled my saliva, ensuring the suctioning noise graced his ears.

"Well, alright now, Nyomi," he groaned as I gazed into his eyes and slowly slid my teeth up the shaft. "We have to do a quickie now. Don't get carried awa—"

Without a moment's notice, I hummed while gently scrubbing my teeth. After ensuring my teeth was dick clean, I cooed while rubbing the head around my gums as if it was cocaine. I needed to make sure it was pure dope. To ensure I didn't have any breakfast residue on my cheeks, I moaned while rapidly tapping the head against my jaws, like a car owner knocking on a dying starter. Needing to get my throat swabbed, I whimpered while slowly gliding my mouth farther on it. Gagging, I slowly moved my head in a circular motion.

"Nyomi. Christ now," he erotically moaned as I initiated a throat-to-dick domestic violence case.

My mouth beat up his pipe so severely that he struggled to breathe. While Richardo tried to push my head back, I latched on to the mighty fine pipe and barked on the bitch as if I was a Great Dane.

"Unhand me. I have shit to do today, Nyomi," he loudly moaned with a trembling body as tears flowed from his eyes.

"Grrrr," I sounded, ferociously shaking my head while sloppily sucking and aggressively gripping his balls.

"Come rock me, baby. I have shit to do today," he grunted as his toes popped.

"Baby, come rock me," the serene, happy, and in-love man moaned. Seeing him at peace granted me pleasure.

Stopping my antics, I narrowed my eyes and said, "Not now. Be patient."

"We have to do a quickie." He exhaled heavily, searching my eyes.

"I heard you the first time, honey." I sighed sharply, climbing on top of him.

"I see your face, and I'm sorry. I don't need you on top of me anymore. I need to be on top of you, clearing your mind as you've done mine." He sincerely breathed against my lips while gripping my waist.

"Okay." I exhaled, not removing my clothes. I had

become spoiled when I was around him. Plus, I loved feeling his fingertips gracing my warm, silky skin, sending chills hopping through my body before settling into my bones.

"You are amazing," he graciously stated, hand on my neckline.

"So are you," I erratically stated, anticipating his loving touches towering over my body many hours after he'd stopped touching me.

"I tried to show you how the build-up is better," he acknowledged, finally removing my shirt and bra.

"Yes, you did, but I needed my spine realigned, though," I moaned as he rubbed my titties.

"Quiet time," he whispered against my left nipple before suckling it into his warm, wet mouth.

My toes curled as he kneeled, pulling down my pants and underwear. The heat from his fingers and the rapid tongue flickers against my baby feeder set my soul ablaze while relaxing my frame. My back arched as tingles rushed through my body like a ball inside of a pinball machine.

Richardo placed my left leg on his shoulder while skating his mouth downward. I softly cooed his name as my legs trembled at the tingling sensations. With his warm palms resting on my butt, his wide fingers kneaded the ass that desperately needed a grand rubbing.

Within a blink of an eye, his skillful mouth graced my ladylove. Passionately, yet hungrily, his tongue skated across, around, inside it. His intentional deep breaths towered over my pink tunnel of love, making me tremble.

"Mhm," I moaned, gripping his shoulders and thrusting my hips.

"Drown me." He breathed in my coochie, sending euphoric vibrations running into my womb.

Richardo became a savage while rapidly flickering his tongue on my clit and finger-fighting my G-Spot. I brought the throat-to-dick violence to him, and he brought the finger-to-G-Spot battle to me. I lost quickly and horribly when I covered my mouth and yodeled my fiancé's name.

"Give me the dick, baby. I need it in my guts. Knocking on my stomach. Taking my breath away. Making me want to be careless with my mouth," I whimpered into my hand as the constant suckling on my sensitive bud made my stomach sink repeatedly as the heat from my feet rapidly rose to my knees.

Tightly holding my mouth, my breathing became pathetic as my body violently shook. Immediately, I braced for my body to give him exactly what he needed. As it did so, I softly wept as it seemed a million black bugs were before my eyes.

"Richardooo," I lowly whimpered as his tongue disrespectfully drove my clit insane, just as his finger did against my G-Spot. I wanted to grip my hair and howl his name. I wanted all to know who he gave dope loving to and for how long.

The erotic sounds of him ferociously suckling and slurping my sweetness demanded me to focus on him and nothing else.

His loving stares captured me more than his masterful tongue. Those longing stares were why I fucked his pink flesh. The sparkle in his eyes informed me he was happy for me to join his party. The sloppy French kisses caused my voice box to disobey him. My trembling hands flopped onto the blankets as I was thankful, my low sex cries could only be heard by us.

After many more long tongue strokes, lips nibbles, and clit sucks, he aided me from the floor and whispered, "Bend over, baby."

Standing on wobbly legs, I put the perfect arch in my back to receive him. I cuffed my ankles because he was indeed to make me topple over. The spreading of my ass cheeks caused me to tilt my head and quickly utter, "Oou."

With his twisty tongue sliding into my asshole, my soul left me as my eyes crossed. I saw many galaxies as my slender fingers rendered a death grip on my ankles. When he passionately French kissed my asshole, his hands went into overtime, working my coochie, and massaging my titties.

Richardo didn't stop feasting on my body until I crashed on my knees. The sex god shoved the pillow next to my head before gripping my waist and slowly throwing his delicious clogger into my suckling monster. As if he was in a slow grind dance competition, Richardo slowly rotated his hips, ensuring he went on a grand journey.

"Babyyy," I sang into the pillow as he slipped a thumb in my butt. My body shook harder than a building in an 8.5 earthquake.

Throwing my goodness on his pipe and looking back at him was the worst thing I could've done for us, yet it was motherfucking worth it. I saw tears rolling into his mouth as he stared at me. I witnessed him repeatedly mouthing 'I love you'. I saw my wavy ass plopping on his stomach. I viewed a man pushing up his queen's ass and ruthlessly fucking his strained-faced woman.

Never tearing his eyes from me nor stopping how he delivered his loving, he whispered, "I tried not to get you in this position again. I don't know how to act from the back, Nyomi. Getting my dick sucked by your phenomenal pussy, seeing the waves in this gorgeously dimpled-out ass, and knowing who I am behind and always will be … will always have me acting a fool. I can't be in this position anymore until you are free. So, when you feel that I'm about to put you in the doggy-style position or I ask you to get in it, you need to stop me. We will be fucking singing, and I can't have that … not here."

"Richardoooo," I cooed into the pillow as he slammed his saturated head onto my G-Spot.

"I can't wait until you are released. I don't like being restricted during sex, Nyomi. I don't like not hearing you. It makes me feel like I'm not doing a good job," he confessed, drilling my precious treasure chest. "I'm trying not to remove that pillow from your mouth. I need to hear your sexy pleasure noise. I'm trying my best to behave, but you making shit very hard for me."

"Richardoooo," I squealed as several things happened at

once: my stomach massively caved, my body grew rigid, and my waterworks appeared.

"Yeah. I need allathat sweet shit on me," he enthusiastically groaned, having a wonderful time in my playland.

While looking back at the calm man no longer talking proper, my right eyelid quivered at the sight of his lips balled. The rotation of his hips and the scooping of his tool into my slit drove my arousal to another higher level. The narrowing of his eyes as he spoke in slang made my nipples harder. My muffled purrs slithered into his ears as the gut-wrenching growl he rendered while fucking me faster caused my beautiful waterwork show to surface as I descended.

"My motherfuckin' pussy, Nyomi. Never fuckin' forget it," he hissed, narrowing his eyes.

"I would never," I moaned, body still locked.

"Then, tell me who the fuck this pussy belongs to," he spoke through gritted teeth, causing me to buck my eyes.

What has pissed him off? I thought as he carved into my stuff as if it was a pumpkin.

"It belongs to you," I whimpered, feeling the blanket on my shoulder. My ass was toppling over like sprinkles on an ice cream cone.

"I can't fuckin' hear you. Whose fuckin' pussy is this I'm motherfuckin' in, Nyomi?" he barked, gazing at me.

"Yours, baby. It's your kitty cat," I screeched into the pillow as he gripped my hair and beat my guts up. The dick was knocking, and my head was rocking.

"Don't ever make me bark that shit again!" he hissed, placing his sweaty body on mine.

"I promise I won't," I cried from pure bliss as my private area resembled a fire hydrant on full blast.

"As the fuck it should be," he growled, leaning to the left and banging my saturated treasure chest. "I told yo' ass I had shit to do today. It's a lot of shit on my plate that has me very angry. You sealed the fuckin' deal when this pussy leakin' like this an' you can't sound off. That fucks wit' my pride. I need to hear you hollerin' in this bitch, but you can't. I ain't got no motherfuckin' business doing allathis shit in the current mindset I'm in, Nyomi. The fuckin' warden is here. I gotta see his ugly, nasty ass fo' whatever gotdamn reason. Avery is extra gotdamn chipper, an' ain't opened his gotdamn mouth 'bout he found Lucas wit' a fuckin' needle in his arm last night. He's hurtin' behind that, an' he didn't come to me. I'm furious wit' his ass fo' that action. Ashley's fuckin' an' suckin' the shit out of my quad nephews. She spinnin' them niggas in rotation, an' they all know she runnin' through them. I'm at my fuckin' wits end wit' the shit my private investigator sent me. To top all that shit off, I can't hear yo' amazin' ass sex noises. I'm 'bout to fuckin' explode in this bitch," he growled, slamming his pulsating member into my vomiting playland.

"Ahhhooouuu!" I loudly moaned into the pillow as he rested his head on me. I hated it when he let stuff build and build; that caused him to be a ticking time bomb.

Hurtfully, he said, "I'm sorry fo' not tellin' you what I got going on befo' nih. I gotta go play like I ain't 'bout to crash out."

"It's okay, but don't do that again. If you can come back at our usual time, we will not have sex. We are going to lay up and talk. You need to get everything off your chest. What affects you affects me. Remember that. I hope all is well with Lucas. Do not crash out on Avery. I'm sure he has a good reason for not telling you about how he found his brother. Now, Ashley's ass, I don't know what to say. Most importantly, honey, you don't get too far into the angry land that you must do much to bounce back. I love you. Be safe. Be mindful. Be humble. Go handle your business," I soothingly spoke through erratic breathing while needing to pray that the warden didn't ask me to step into his office.

Chapter 13

RICHARDO

Damn, I can't wait until April 7th. Just like that, she stopped me from being upset with Avery, disappointed with Lucas, annoyed with Ashley's fuckery, and disgusted with my great-uncle's bullshit. My woman has a healing voice and eyes. She will save a lot of idiots from me. The survivable idiots better be thankful when the time comes for me to let them slide on a final warning, I thought, walking down the empty hallway smiling.

I can still taste her sweetness. The softness of her body as mine slowly clashed with hers, I can still feel. Her soft whimpers while I dug deeper inside her clenching walls, still dangling in the middle of my ear. I need more of her after all business and a little personal time with Rayne has concluded, I thought as a chipper Avery professionally called my name.

You better tell me about Lucas, Avery. One band, one sound, I thought, turning to face him as I said, "Yes?"

"Warden Rawlinson's in your office," he announced, walking toward me.

"I know." I nodded, causing my friend to look at me oddly.

"Besides the prison, is there a reason he's requested all of us?" he lowly asked, arriving beside me.

"Not that I can think of," I answered as we strolled toward my office.

"Are you sure he doesn't know about my endeavors with Lockley?" he whispered, observing me.

"Nope. What could he say if he did when he sees these?" I voiced, extending a brown envelope I quickly retrieved from my vehicle after leaving my woman.

Opening the package, Avery asked, "What's in here?"

"Just look in there, man." I sighed as we turned left. Immediately, the fool played Hopscotch while laughing at the images.

"What the fuck is this shit?" he mocked Dad's stunned voice while looking at the photos.

"Dear old uncle likes to get spanked, not by his wife or any woman. I don't think he knows he's getting tossed around by an XY individual," I responded as Palmer, Ashley, and Terry called our names.

"I hope I'm in the office when this shit is dropped in his ashy ass hands," Avery excitedly voiced as we turned to face our crew.

They hustled down the hallway as Avery asked, "How did you get this?"

"The same way I get everything else," I offered, hoping he would tell me about Lucas before I had to up what I knew.

"Um, do you really not keep tabs on us?" he oddly inquired as the others landed in our presence.

I threw my head back, eyed him, and grinned. "Should I keep tabs on y'all?"

"That isn't what I asked, dude," he worriedly voiced, searching my eyes.

Lightly popping his chest, I lowly chuckled. "I promise I won't tell anyone exactly where you will be on Monday, Wednesday, and Saturdays, precisely from two a.m. until four a.m."

"Gotdamn," the fool screeched, turning around multiple times before lowly barking. "I knew you kept tabs on us."

If I didn't, I wouldn't know you are hurting massively right now. You are great at not letting your eyes tell on you, I thought, needing to burst his bubble.

At the same time, our friends stared at me oddly and voiced, "What the hell?"

"I wouldn't say keep tabs, just a close eye. Y'all relax," I stated as the trio curiously looked at me.

"Why? You don't trust us?" Ashley heatedly asked, raising an eyebrow and touching her petite hips.

"The opposite. I need to know y'all safe at all times. I need to know if a motherfucka think he or she can fuck with y'all just because they don't see my face. Plus, I wouldn't be the head honcho if I didn't make sure my people were okay," I seriously admitted, causing the trio to nod.

"Gotcha," they replied.

"Why does Donovan need us in your office?" Ashley inquired, searching my eyes.

"Only one way to find out, so let's go do that," I announced, slowly rocking my neck from side to side. "Let them see what you have, Avery. Y'all hurry and study that shit before we step into my office."

"Do you think anyone has his dick pressed against a glass?" Palmer questioned as Avery and I looked at each other and howled in laughter.

"What the fuck is going on with this shit?" Terry screeched, studying the images through wide eyes.

"Time to see what he wants," I responded, turning on my heels.

Walking to my office, the trio made comical noises while observing the many photos.

"Ooou, this nigga got on a pink tutu and rocking a gag ball. He better not sit next to me in church Sunday. I will not act right," Terry oddly voiced, causing us to laugh as the brown envelope returned to me.

"Bruh held open his cheeks while having a candle above his back. I'll never see him the same again." Avery laughed, causing Ashley to squeal and push him.

"Y'all chill." I chuckled, three doors from my office.

"How after seeing that disturbing shit?" Palmer inquired seriously.

"The best way you can," I voiced, looking over my shoulder as we closed my door. I saw a hickey on Ashley's neck that I swore I wouldn't mention anything about when I first saw it yesterday. Yet, the look in her eyes caused my tongue to tap against my teeth. I badly wanted to speak about her whereabouts, which she possibly assumed I didn't know about.

Stopping, I looked at the ceiling and exhaled several times. Leaning toward me, they asked, "What's wrong?"

"Ashley." I sighed heavily, turning to face her.

"What's up?" she cutely asked, removing a few bite-sized Snickers from her pocket.

"Will you please stop spinning my nephews into rotation? You have been fucking the shit out of them since Christmas. Stop it," I lowly voiced, observing her eyes as she smiled massively.

"Now, wait. What?" the fellas squealed, sliding from our friend while shockingly analyzing her.

"Whew, actually, it's been longer than that." She giggled

as Avery covered his mouth and flopped like a fish.

Whipping my head in his direction, I hissed, "Bitch, stop that. Before I get on your case."

"Howww?" he oddly voiced, pointing at our friend. "She's smashing the quads. I need details now. Fuck Donovan. Also, how can you get on my case? You already know where I will be on certain days."

"I know more than you think," I quickly voiced before slowly focusing on Ashley.

"Ashley, um, what hoe award are you trying to accomplish? Richardo got them all," Palmer awkwardly voiced, causing me to laugh.

Staring at me, she grinned. "No, he doesn't have them all. I got them all when I fucked Raq, Riq, Roq, and Req. In that order. They weren't aware at first. Two days after Thanksgiving, I gave myself another award when they placed themselves on certain days to be with me. Now, that's a badass, toxic hoe bitch. Another award will be given when I give each brother a baby. One down and three to go. Now, let's go, fellas. Talk time over."

Avery hollered in his hands while we watched our quiet but slutty friend sashay to my door. Palmer and Terry looked at me through bucked eyes and asked, "What the fuck, man? She's never wanted kids. Why the hell does she want them now? We are close to being over the hill. Will her body support kids?"

Looking at my friend, I exhaled. "Ashley has always

been an odd fucka. Since the beginning of the year, my nephews have been in my ear about having a kid. I would assume she's rewarding them for allowing her to fuck on them knowingly."

"Gotdamn, I love your family and us. It's like *The Little House on the Prairie* mixed in with the soap opera *Passion* type of shit." Avery chuckled as we looked at him with furrowed eyebrows before walking off, shaking our heads.

"Why is he our friend again?" Palmer laughed as Ashley opened the door.

"We wouldn't be complete without him," she sincerely voiced as we entered my office and witnessed my uncle standing tall at the window.

"Well, about time, my favorite five people and I have a nice chat," the bald man announced, looking out the window. Barely through the door, Avery withered to the ground, covering his mouth. Terry and Palmer stopped walking, dropped their aggressively shaking heads, and covered their mouths.

"What's the purpose of this visit, Warden Rawlinson?" I asked, looking at the ceiling and praying the silently laughing fuckers didn't have an outburst.

"Warden, I love you to pieces. Through and through, but um, that chocolatey pink thong in your pocket needs to be pushed in if you want us to take you seriously," Ashley seriously announced, causing Terry, Palmer, and Avery to violently cough. All I could do was stare at my only female best friend and laugh.

"Ah, well, seems I know why most looked at me crazy when I strolled down the hallway," he nervously voiced, avoiding looking at us. "I have a problem that only The Don and his best friends can handle."

"What's the problem?" I asked, walking toward the front of my desk. Instantly, the fellas were ready to conduct business.

"I believe someone is following me, taking pictures," he admitted, looking into my eyes. "I am trying to get on the senate board. I don't need any issues."

Knowing he was trying to move higher than I ever thought, I placed my hands together and smiled. "Then, you surely are talking to the right person. How do you know someone is following you?"

"I feel like I'm constantly being watched."

"Ah, tell me, what's in it for us?" I grinned, seeing dollar signs and unlimited power in his eyes.

"Whatever you seek, I will provide," he confessed before exhaling sharply.

"Don't say whatever we seek; when we start seeking, you can't provide. You are well aware of what I did to Dad when he thought he could yell at me for chastising his raggedy ass parents, right?"

"Oh, I'm well aware. You rattled my sister's nerve so badly that day." He chuckled. "But I was proud. You wouldn't be a pussy like Glover. No disrespect, Richardo, your father's line is weak as fuck. He's a good man, but he's pussy."

"Ah, shit," my crew lowly voiced, staring at me.

I didn't like anyone talking about my dad, so I chuckled while walking from my desk. "I'm the nigga that has motherfuckas watching you. I would tread lightly with how you speak on my dad, nigga. I'll have these photos spread across the fucking news before you leave here. Now, this is how you are going to keep these photos and more shit from the public, our family, and your wife's family's eyes…"

❤❤❤❤❤❤

SINCE CHATTING with my great uncle, I had become an even bolder motherfucka. I had him request a chat with Nyomi in his office. She wasn't retrieved by my people. I needed it to look like an ordinary visit with the warden. It was officially time for him to meet my wife and for her to know how powerful I had become.

She was a gorgeous, nervous mess, just as my great uncle was an ugly mess while sitting behind his polished desk. Meanwhile, my people and I stood at his window, eyeing the pair. Comical Avery had much to snicker about as Terry and Ashley continued to nudge him.

After ten minutes of Nyomi and Great Uncle Donovan oddly staring at each other, he sighed, wiped his forehead, and looked at the corner of his desk. Aggressively wiping his mouth, he turned a photo around. Nyomi stared at the image while sliding closer toward the edge of the black sofa. Her mouth twitched, which caused us to lock into the pair.

As I jetted my eyes to my uncle, to witness his calm but happy facial expression was priceless. Yet, it was valuable. So, I walked closer to see what I could use to blackball him more.

Through the biggest smile on his long, oval-shaped face, he boasted. "I'm the one who took this picture. I was thrilled that day and ten days after. I thought you were mine, Nyomi."

"Shit, now!" I hollered, stunned, stopping in the center of his office. I was no longer willing to use any information to shove him further into a hole.

"On the tenth day of being happy, I became miserable. The DNA test came back stating you weren't mine but belonged to the asshole of all assholes. My college buddy, now federal judge, Willington Mac. I would've been in your and her life openly, but too much had been said and done by him, which made her feel low about loving me. I was there the day you buried her alone. You just didn't see me. Nyomi, I tried my best not to have you here. The least I could do for you was ensure the family didn't sue you. They were going to. I paid them off. Your time would've been lengthy because, let's face it, the justice system isn't built for us even when we acciden-tally harm one of them. I'm in a compromising position to get you that light sentence. I am sorry you are here, but I knew you would be okay. My nephew's hell, but he's the best type of hell for women in a place like this. I'm proud to say he has you in his life, and you have him. You will never want for a thing, and I think he and I will go head-to-head at times because I need to be in your life. I am all for him destroying me if he can't allow me to love you as a man who prayed you were his daughter instead of the undeserving fucker you do belong to."

"Shit just got sticky as fuck," Terry voiced as Nyomi stood and pointed at him.

"If you weren't the warden, I would slap the fuck out of you for giving up so damn easily to a fucking nothing. I read your letters to her and me. All of them, the day I buried her. I knew you were there also. I saw you; I acted like I didn't. For what it is worth, Donovan Rawlinson, you are just as fucked up as him!" she hurtfully spoke, head wobbling as tears rolled from her eyes.

I became angry as he hopped from his desk. Slowly rubbing his palms together, through a crackly tone, he said, "He could've blackballed me, Nyomi. I had to visibly walk away. I didn't want to. I know you saw that in the letter. I did make sure you went on spring break and summer vacations. I made sure you got everything you wanted on your birthdays and Christmases. I did more for you than I did for my kids. When you learned how to drive, I was tailing y'all. I gave her the money to buy your first car. I gave her the money to buy your high school and college graduation stuff. I didn't need you to spend your money. That was a father's job, Nyomi. I know you hate me, but I need you to know I love you and your mother. I have always loved the two of you. I made damn sure y'all never went without anything! Motherfucking nothing! My wife knew who had my heart; it wasn't her or our kids. It was you and your mother!"

Is that why my cousins don't respect y'all? I thought, simmering as Ashley rubbed my hand and soothingly said, "No need to spaz. She's getting hurt off her chest by a person I'm sure she had been begging to find the will to go off on. He loves her dearly, friend. I see it. I feel it."

"Agree," Terry, Avery, and Palmer lowly acknowledged, walking up to me.

"I know. I see, hear, and feel it too," I confessed, slowly nodding and thankful she did have someone loving her other than her mother.

After fifteen minutes of the pair staring at each other's wet faces, Donovan looked at me. When he deeply exhaled, it seemed a significant burden had been lifted from him. Pointing his crooked pinky finger at me, he grinned. "I'll forever owe you, great nephew, for loving her. I don't have to tell you I'll go toe-to-toe with you over her. I saw you when a tear slipped from her eyes. It has always hurt me to see her mother cry. Imagine me seeing Nyomi cry for the first time in her life. My soul ached, and I never wanted to hear her cry again. I don't have to tell you to treasure her. I know they are making mountains move, so you can move freely to be with her. If I know you, I know she's about to have a name change within a few months."

"Correct." I grinned, walking toward my woman and wiping her face.

"Momma never told me why her siblings and parents stopped talking to her. Do you know, and if you do, will you tell me?" Nyomi softly questioned, eyeing the man sitting on his desk's edge.

Searching her eyes, he confidently said, "I'm a man with a particular taste, Nyomi. Your maternal family didn't like that. They didn't like your mother deeply caring for a man with a particular taste. They didn't like that she cared for two good friends. They felt she was a jezebel. She was far from that. So, when she couldn't pinpoint which one of us fathered you, they put her on her ass and disowned the two of you. Willington didn't care about the cutest, sweetest seventeen-year-old in the world having no one. I did. My parents helped her out. They let her live in the guest house. My sister, Donna, Richardo's mother, your soon-to-be mother-in-law, and your mother became best friends. I could barely rub her stomach because my sister was always hogging her. My sister loves you too, Nyomi. Willington made it hard for her to do for and see you. So, she had to cut ties with your mother and you. You will be welcomed once she sees Nyomi Richards, soon-to-be Nyomi Mets. My family, the Rawlinsons, loves you. The Mets will love you unconditionally, too. You have a family now, and gotdamn they are rowdy as shit. You will be marrying the ringleader. Oh, yeah, you have one feisty ass stepdaughter, but she has the heart of a saint, the hands of a boxer, and a mouth like a sailor when she's pissed off. I hope I answered all of your questions and cleared every concern."

As I rubbed the back of her hand, she nodded. "You did. Thank you, Donovan, for everything. She wrote you a letter. I hate to say this, but I did read it. It was beautiful. The most expressive letter I've ever read. I will give it to you when I'm released, along with some other things I'm sure you would want to have. She loved you."

"And I thought she didn't write me anything before she left us." He choked up.

"It's too emotional in this motherfucka. May I be excused?" Avery voiced, causing us to look at him. Rapidly, he wiped his eyes just as the others were.

"We will be leaving shortly anyway. Rayne should be here with lunch soon," I admitted as Nyomi interlocked our hands.

"Nyomi, may I be in your life?" Donovan lovingly inquired.

"Aren't I marrying your great nephew?" She smiled beautifully, causing him to grin massively.

"You are, but you know exactly what I'm asking," he spoke, walking from his desk.

"Of course."

"Am I reaching too high for you to call me Dad?"

Before she could open her mouth, I loudly voiced, "Hell

yeah, you are climbing higher than a motherfucka. I don't need a soul to think I'm marrying my cousin."

"Jesus Christ, Richardo." Nyomi giggled, looking up at me.

"Just saying. That's a disaster," I seriously voiced as we moved toward the door.

"How about if we are vibing good, and if it slips out, it just slips out?" Nyomi sweetly voiced to him, causing me to tilt my head and oddly look at her.

"That'll work perfectly," my great-uncle happily articulated as they embraced each other in a loving hug. "Nephew, don't worry about what people may think or say. My wife will make damn sure all know she's not my daughter. You might have to pay her and my kids a visit. They aren't too keen on Nyomi because of my honesty about where my heart lies first and then second."

Slamming his palm on the desk, Avery lowly screeched, "Uncle Donovan, why the fuck would you tell that idiot that? I'm trying to get my thang sucked from the back tonight. I don't have time to put anybody in a chest and leave them on the porch. It's Valentine's Day, man. I need to be romanced and do some romancing. I need to see somebody in what you got in your pocket."

"Oh, wow," Nyomi oddly voiced, covering her mouth as Terry, Ashley, and Palmer laughed hard.

"Please get the fuck out of my office, Avery," Donovan

seriously voiced as I snatched Avery by the collar of his uniform shirt.

Shaking my head, I thoughtfully stated, "Some things are best left unsaid, best friend number three. While some things you should freely say. Instead of making me bring it up to you."

Walking on his tiptoes, he laughed. "I told the naked, thongy, tied-up, and spanked truth."

My crew laughed as I released the collar of his shirt. I was close to dropping the dime on his fraudulent ass when Nyomi sternly cleared her throat. As we looked in her direction, she held a severe Poker face while motioning me to approach her. Nodding, I softly exhaled and strolled towards her.

She planted her soft palm on my face when I landed before her. Sweetly, she whispered, "Some things are best spoken when one is comfortable enough to express their feelings. Some things are best spoken when one can wrap their head around what they found. Some things are hard to comprehend when they can't place themselves in someone else's shoes. Give him a moment to collect his bearings, just as he did for you when Maysha passed away."

"Yes, ma'am." I softly exhaled, dropping my nose on hers while pulling her close. "You will be in my office next. It's time for you to see your daughter. Then, you will unofficially meet your parole officer. Followed by us having a few moments of alone time before I become mad because I have to part ways with you. See you in a bit. Okay?"

"Okay," she cutely replied before planting a juicy kiss on my lips, causing me to shiver.

"Do it again," I groaned, studying her eyes while wrapping my arms around her waist.

She sexily puckered her lips, rose on her tiptoes, and dropped the hot, kid-friendly kiss onto lips, starving to cover hers. Massaging the small of her back, I nodded and whispered. "I'm going to get a little coochie on my desk, won't I?"

"Just a little bit. You need to be humbled and quickly." She blushed, pointing at the door. "You have somewhere to be. I think you should head that way."

Dick growing, I gripped it and nodded. "Yes, ma'am."

Like the bosses we were, my best friends and I saluted the warden before dashing out of his office in the order of our friendship and team. I was first. Behind me was my primary muscle and observer, Terry. Avery was my muscle but the primary shooter. The third muscle, negotiator, and planner was Ashley. Palmer was my fourth muscle and investigator.

While we walked down the hallway, Avery said, "A lot of shit is fucking with me, Richardo. I'm unsure which one you know is messing with me the most. So, I'll drop the one that's the least problematic. My son will be born next week, and she doesn't want anything to do with him. That's good, right?"

Thankful he was opening up to me, I looked at him and smiled. "That's excellent. She will be back here once she's released in September. Please tell me you have a name picked out for my godson?"

"Not yet. I think I need to see him first," he voiced, sounding proud, just as I hoped he would be.

"Sounds good. I'm proud of you, man," I acknowledged, observing his blue eyes.

"I'm proud of me too. I … um … I need you to make Lucas leave the city," he spoke, causing the others and me to stop moving.

"Why?" I asked, searching his teary eyes as if I didn't know.

"He's been hanging out with the wrong crowd. I was late to work this morning because I hadn't heard from him in a few days. Go to his crib; he got a needle in his arm. I don't know how long he has been on the dope, but I took him to rehab. I don't need my goddaughter and nephew to witness him if he goes off the rails. I need my brother clean, Richardo," he confessed as a tear dripped.

As his best friend and faithful brother, I wiped his tears and sincerely voiced, "I know what happened when you learned. When you found him, we should've known about it. What affects you will always affect us. One band, one sound. Remember?"

"I remember. Just didn't want to put y'all through that again. Especially seeing a teen I had to receive custody of when he was fifteen. I didn't need you to reflect on anything," he responded through quivering lips.

"My reflection is on me. Never worry about my mind. Go home. Take a few days off. When I get off, I'm headed straight to you. No pit stops. Okay?" I commanded, causing him to nod.

"Palmer, go with him. Find out all you can about who Lucas has been dealing with. Check with the rehab facility and gather as much information as you can. If you need to dip into the bribing money, do so. You already know what to do once you have to dish out money. Ashley and Terry, no overtime today. Ashley, tell your sisters Palmer will be seeking them shortly. They need to be available, so if they are sucking or riding a dick, they need to catch that nut later. You and Terry will leave at y'all's regular time and be at Avery's house within a respectable time after coming off these grounds. Any remarks?"

"None," they responded as Palmer wrapped his lanky arm around Avery's neck.

"Come on, dude. Time to blow this joint," he comfortingly voiced as I agreed.

When we split ways and I finally arrived in my office, my head was heavier than it had been on the day Maysha died. Walking toward the window, I focused on the beautiful sky with pretty differently shaped clouds. The sun shined brightly, causing me to ogle the day I wished I could hop in my Donk with Nyomi and let the wind run wildly through her curly hair.

I would rush her to my mother. I would love to see her facial expression when she learned precisely whose daughter had me head over heels in love with her. I was glad I didn't tell my parents Nyomi's name. The surprise in my mother's eyes would be the highlight of my day. She would be reunited with a woman she had loved and cared for before she was stripped away.

Federal Judge Willington Mac, you will see me, bitch. Be prepared. I'm coming, and I'm sure you won't like what I will say before I do me. That's a promise, I thought, feeling movement on my arm.

Snapped from my thoughts, I smiled and looked at my beautiful, glowing daughter. All senses returned to me. I smelled greatness from within my office as my daughter's eyes captured me. She was happy and at peace.

It was brighter than the sun beaming through my office when she grinned. It had been a long time since I saw Rayne smile as hard as she did. It satisfied me more than she would ever know. I lived to make my child comfortable and happy.

"Hey, Daddy. We delivered the food as promised. I did act right in the Donk. I didn't speed, but I worked that trunk out," she cutely voiced as my granddaughter cut up in her stomach.

Planting my hand on her round belly, I smiled. "I wouldn't have expected anything less. You picked out a car yet?"

"I did. A crossover vehicle. It's at the house." She exhaled sharply and stretched. "She has been very active today. I wish she would take a nap."

I laughed and wrapped my arm around her neck. "She is going to be bad as fuck."

"That she is." She giggled, lovingly staring into my eyes.

A few knocks sounded on my door, making us look in that direction. "Come in."

"Ah, I finally get to see her," my child happily and lowly voiced as the door opened.

"Yes, you do." I grinned as Ashley escorted a smiling and teary-eyed Nyomi into our presence.

Once Ashley hugged and rubbed her goddaughter's belly, she left us. The atmosphere in my office was phenomenal. The happy stares between Nyomi and Rayne were incredible to witness as Rayne ran into Nyomi's loving arms. Love poured from them, slamming into the other before sinking into my bones.

I found my baby and future babies a great mother. I finally created the perfect family, I thought as Nyomi gently rubbed my child's face.

Sweetly and softly, Nyomi said, "Hey you."

"Hi, you." Rayne choked up as they still clung to each other.

Two queens, a musty prince, and a princess-in-the-making are in my life. God, look at You, my boy. I give You much praise, but I am not going to step inside a church, I thought, smiling as the two slowly separated but still held hands.

"How much do you know about your father and me?" Nyomi asked sweetly.

"Seeing that pink scrunchie and knowing who was bragged about receiving three dollars for it, I know it all. I must admit, that's a bad engagement ring, Nyomi. It's too fancy for me." Rayne giggled, pointing at my woman's ring finger.

Cheesing and wiggling her ring finger, she said, "Isn't it?"

Laughing, we sat on the sofa. I couldn't start any topic because the two stared at each other. While I analyzed them, my phone vibrated. Removing my device, I saw Palmer's name. On the fourth vibration, I answered.

"Lucas bang heavy with Dedricka Willis' people, especially Roderick's sons." He exhaled sharply, causing me to lowly growl.

"Find out if that's a personal hit. If it is, all-black. All four trucks come out. Packed to capacity," I hissed as the ladies looked at me.

"On it."

"Make sure Avery packs those trucks out."

"Most definitely. I'm out."

"Okay," I aggressively voiced before we ended the call.

"What's wrong?" the worried women inquired, studying me.

I didn't want to ruin their reunion or the meaning of today, so I sat in their faces and lied. "Nothing."

Pointing a finger at me, Nyomi snarled, "Don't you ever lie to me when you can't even fix your damn face or eyes to reflect the damn answer. That's a quick way for me to pull this gotdamn scrunchie off. Do I make myself clear?"

"Crystal," I answered, nodding and grabbing her hand.

"I'm sorry. I won't do it again. Something wrong. I can't speak about it until I know just how bad it is."

"That's all you had to say the first damn time," my woman sassed as a smiling Rayne sat back in the chair and crossed her legs.

"My goodness. She can snarl, talk rough to you, and ask a question. Somebody is deeply in love." My messy-ass child grinned.

"Shut up." I chuckled, hoping the news of Lucas wouldn't disturb her peace.

"So, when are y'all getting married?"

"The day I'm released."

"Do you have your dress, shoes, and hairstyle picked out?" my child inquired as I kissed the back of Nyomi's hand before walking toward the window. I needed to escape their conversation to think and put plays into motion in case Lucas was an intended target of a crew I despised.

"What are the colors? What do I need to do? Where will it be? What time? Where's the reception? Are you able to travel out of the country for y'all's honeymoon? If so, where are y'all going?" Rayne eagerly asked, causing me to chuckle. She was the only person I dealt with who immediately fired many questions.

When I rested my head on the window, my beautiful fiancée giggled. "I'm wearing an ivory-hued dress and clear heels. Yes, they are already purchased. They are at his house. He's wearing the same hue tuxedo with a coral handkerchief and cognac-hued shoes. Of course, he's already purchased them. We are getting married at the courthouse. A few weeks ago, I decided not to have a big ceremony. There will be no reception. We will go to Hilton Head for our honeymoon. Next year, we will do it big. I'll be more comfortable. I want to tie my money into it. Not have him do everything."

"Sounds good, Nyomi. I'm truly happy for you. I hate you are here," Rayne spoke sincerely.

"Thank you. So, tell me, how's school going?" my lovely fiancée inquired as I couldn't dip into my thoughts as I needed to. I adored them talking. I loved knowing I gave Rayne a mother figure even though they were thirteen years apart.

"It's hellish with this little one. It's too much to remember while I have this little cutie acting like she's in a trampoline park. So much studying when I'm tired and struggling to breathe. Maybe you could help a sister out with studying when you are released," Rayne sweetly voiced.

"Of course, I will help you. I will tell you this. I'm very strict regarding learning," Nyomi cutely announced.

"I need it. I'm willing to obey," my kind and thoughtful child responded, causing me to smile widely. "Is there anything you need me to do? Such as keeping an eye open for jobs, helping him redecorate the house—it's so manly—or stocking it with your favorite bathing items. Stuff like that."

"Ah, you are really a sweetie. I see it would please you to help him. So, I'll say yes, minus the job hunting," Nyomi's emotional ass stated, causing me to look at her. She was smiling and wiping her tears. It amazed me how she could curse someone out one minute and be filled with joy the next. That's something I could never do. Once I was on my rampage, I was on it for a while.

"So, I saw the way you were dressed that night. Is that your style?" Rayne inquired as I tried to get my mind right.

"Rayne, I got that covered. I know how she rocks," I hurried to say, resting my head on the window. "Don't take what I'm about to say hard, Rayne. One day, you will thank Lucas for not marrying you. You would've been miserable like I was with Zella. You would've done the same thing as she, and he would've done the same thing as I did to her to you. In time, you will get everything you desire. Focus on Zanning, the most active unborn child I'd ever encountered, and school. Trust, the right man for you is getting himself together because he sees you. He's coming. Be patient, sweetie. I'm proud of you and love you more than words can express. You are my first best creation. Never forget that."

"I won't forget," she calmly said. "So, are y'all pregnant?"

"No. Too early. Next month, it's on and popping." I grinned.

My ghetto, but could be classy and professional, daughter loudly screeched. "Geek!"

"Give us a hug and get your ass out of my office with that foolishness, Rayne Lisa Mets," I spoke through clenched teeth. That noise and word always drove me insane. Yet, I lived to hear it come from her mouth. She spoke it in the same manner as Maysha.

"Yes, sir." She giggled as I turned to witness her wobbling to Nyomi with outstretched arms.

Pointing at them, I lovingly admitted, "This is my second-best creation. A real family. Something I have needed for a long time."

When they separated, Rayne sweetly voiced, "I'm excited for you to be near me, Nyomi. I won't have to worry about you because you'll be with the best man God could've ever made."

"Oou, honey, you are something else with welcoming me into your family." Nyomi choked up, causing me to focus on her. "Thank you. I'm grateful for having a familiar face as I navigate my new journey."

"Don't thank me. It's unnecessary," the happy young woman eagerly stated, slipping from Nyomi.

"Okay." My fiancée grinned, placing her forefingers underneath her eyes.

"I love you, Dad," Rayne wholeheartedly said, searching my eyes while closing into me.

"You're a father's dream daughter, Rayne. I'm sorry if I don't tell you enough how proud of you I am. You are every-thing to me and always will be. Never forget that." I told her as she initiated the most tender and caring hug she could've ever given me. With my heart, mind, and soul at peace with our bond and love, I kissed my child's forehead while holding tightly to her.

"Dad, I can't forget how proud of me you are. You tell me every day. Too many times a day at that." She softly exhaled, breaking our embrace.

"I need to make sure you know." I sincerely breathed as she kissed my jaw.

"I'll always know. It's lunchtime, old man. The two of you should eat now. I'll see you when you get off. Please do not give Zanning any candy while I'm studying, Daddy. If I feel he has a morsel of sugar in his body, his spend-the-night bag stays in my vehicle," she seriously voiced like a true mother.

"Um, about that. When I leave here, I have to link up with your godparents." I exhaled sharply, trying my best to continue looking into her eyes.

"Something's wrong if you are taking a raincheck on spending time with Zanning. What's the issue, Daddy?" she worriedly voiced, observing me.

"I can't say at the moment. I promise I will when I know more," I earnestly announced while walking her toward the door.

"I'm going to hold you to that if you continue to skip on spending time with someone you've only done that to twice in his life," Rayne stated while waving at Nyomi.

"Okay," I responded as we walked out of my office. "I hope you aren't looking for anywhere to stay."

"I am. Y'all will need y'all's space," she acknowledged as I draped my arm around her neck.

"Everyone thought I bought Zella that house. I didn't. I bought my daughter her house. Damn, I'm a leech ass nigga, living off his daughter. I have to do better. In two months, I will be living in my wife's house. I can't believe I'm a whole ass bum nigga in these streets," I jokingly spoke, looking at my smiling kid.

"In my book, you are the best bum ass nigga in these streets." She cheesed, causing me to laugh.

"Would you like to go house hunting with me? I do need it to have at least eight bedrooms," I offered as we made a right turn.

"Um, why will there be so many bedrooms?" she oddly asked, furrowing her eyebrows.

"Master bedroom belongs to parents. Your room. Her painting room. Zanning's room. Baby girl's room. Nyomi's and my baby's room. Parents secured room." I grinned, causing Rayne to laugh loudly.

"One, my kids and I will have our own house. Two, you could've kept the last room to yourself. Three, we will be fine, Daddy. There's no need for y'all to have that big space to incorporate my kids and me. We know you love us. I won't be jealous of my siblings. I'll have my own terror to keep me very occupied." She sincerely breathed, looking up at me.

"I need at least eight bedrooms, Rayne Lisa Mets. The

final house I purchase will be our family house," I genuinely spoke, observing her eyes.

"I'll be happy to sit in the passenger seat while we find our family home." She smiled as we neared the entrance.

"I told you many times, and I'll tell you again. I'll never let you go. Even when I walk you down the aisle to a deserving man, I still won't let you go. You will always be my little girl rocking pigtails, Rayne," I announced, understanding what she was doing.

"Still, it's okay to let me go a little bit. I'll always need my dad, but you need a real life, too. Push back a little. For me," she sweetly voiced as a tear slithered down her face.

"I'll think about it," I lied before kissing her forehead again.

After telling her to be safe and text me when she arrived home safely, I didn't move from the door as I watched her enter my car. Softly smiling, I lowly said, "You have me wrapped around your finger, Rayne. How could I let the leash go? You, Nyomi, Zanning, and the new baby complete me. No leash removal. Bigger house. Daddy will always have a room for you and my grandkids. Y'all may be on the other side of the house since I will need to hear my wife moan while I talk nasty to her, but y'all will have a family home."

Chapter 14

NYOMI

Friday, April 7th

Ah, shit! Fuck me, baby! Yesss, fuck me like the dirty slut I am for you! I thought, rolling my tongue around the white gag ball while my soon-to-be husband ravished me from the back and held onto my hair.

"My motherfucking pussy," Richardo groaned while slinging his rod into me like an experienced bowler tossed a bowling ball into the pins.

Yes, it issss, I thought, cumming while clutching the decent mattress my body would no longer be on once the sun set high in the sky.

"I can't wait to come back here, and you are dressed in clothes you love against your smooth skin. I'm looking forward to driving, glancing at you, and wondering how loud you will be for the rest of our lives." He sexily breathed against my back while scooping his pipe into my saturated goodness.

Fuck my spot, baby. I know you feel this snatch suckling, I thought, moaning as my stomach graced the wet blanket.

Jackhammering my spot, Richardo rested his lips on the center of my back, causing me to shiver. As I came, my toes balled tightly. Erotically, he voiced, "We aren't going to visit our sex room when we change clothes. We won't get married today if we do so. I need you as my wife, so it'll be somewhat of an in-and-out kind of thing. I'm going to carry you inside your new house. I'm going to put you on the table, spread your legs, and eat the very pussy I'm anal when you tell me I can't have it right away. I won't stop eating until you peel the skin off my shoulders, and I bark for you to stop that shit because the asshole is about to come out. I really wouldn't want you to stop, so I'll go back to sucking on the cat while savagely fingering it. She'll throw up on me, splashing on the table. While slowly dragging my tongue from the bottom of the pussy to the top, you'll watch me sop your sweetness as I gaze into your eyes. I'm going to go back to eating the fat fucka ruthlessly again. You will summon asshole because I'll be demolishing you on our kitchen table. We are going to fuck you for all the air you have in your lungs just so we can blow it back into you while we are passionately kissing and cumming together."

"Oooouuuuu!" I yodeled, thankful the gag ball was in place to catch my pleasure noise.

"I love it when you make us sloppy wet," he growled, dancing in the beautiful tantrum-having cat.

I love you, Richardo, I thought, losing the mobility of my limbs as my head descended.

"I love you, Nyomi," he lovingly announced, beating my G-Spot as if it were a punching bag. "God, how do I love you. I will always treat you right. No one can have me. I'm all yours."

I know, I thought, eyelids rapidly wavering as I grew extremely hot.

"Ooou, shit," he hissed, gripping my waist and drilling my erogenous spot.

"Umph," I moaned, muffled, as my back arched and my toes curled harder.

Someone is bound to hear the delicious sounds of our skins slapping. Richardo is holding nothing back as he promised he wouldn't, I thought, grasping the covers with all my might while letting my pleasure noises run wild into the gag ball.

Long dicking me, Richardo used the tip of his tongue to spell his name on my back and dragged his hands to my thighs. Against my back, with the tip of his tongue, he wrote his name; on my thighs, he softly signed his name. I shivered at the delicate touches his pink flesh and fingers created.

Emotionally, mentally, physically, and sexually satisfied, I came and smiled.

"I must come out of this thang, Nyomi. I need to make sure I'm well rested for the first day our lives are to start, freely, that is," he lovingly voiced, sliding up my body, ensuring all of himself was in my saturated pretty kitty.

I don't want you to leave yet, I thought, whimpering once he slipped a thumb in my butt.

While slinging his tongue to the nape of my neck, fucking the sobs from my voice box, and delivering powerful asshole finger fucks, he announced, "Yet, I can't go until you fall asleep on this dick."

Yessss! I thought as my body started to tremble.

Much time rolled by of him making me feel phenomenal while I was locked against the soaking mattress. Once he unlocked my body, I was able to joyfully please him. I was a horny woman, so I took rolling and slamming my twat on the tool to another level. I clapped my ass on his midsection like a devoted, proud, and smiling grandmother standing and applauding the pastor's word on the first Sunday. My eager hands worked overtime against my clit and his balls.

"Alright now, Nyomi," Richardo lowly groaned as my pretty kitty doused him.

After the tenth gentle pulling of his balls and rapid strokes, Richardo gripped my throat and pulled my head back. I smiled as his nasty yet low bark glided into my ear. "This the shit I be talkin' 'bout, Nyomi. You always doing shit that make a nigga wanna get filthy."

The Don. Well, hello there, sir. I haven't seen you since yesterday. Now, I know exactly what causes you to come to the party, I thought, thankful Richardo couldn't see my grin. He would fuck me for dear life while I reached for whatever was nearby.

While I increased my thrusts, Richardo stood on his tiptoes, jacked my ass in the air, and shoved the rest of his thumb into my asshole. Handsomely, he chuckled. "Oh, you want it like that? I have no problem providin'."

"Ah," I whimpered, body flopping on the bed as he slowly danced and rocked from side to side.

Yes, baby, that's how I need my dick, I thought, sexily purring, amping up my man.

Richardo's dick head tore up everything it touched. Courtesy of his thumb, my asshole lining received a workout as I came and moaned until my throat ached. My body was officially sent into the center of a tornado.

"Fuck this shit. You ain't makin' enough noise fo' me," he growled, hurrying to remove his thumb from my asshole.

As he aggressively removed me from the bed, I rapidly shook my head and screeched, "Eeek!"

Richardo had me bent over in the middle of the cell; that wasn't good. He knew that was a disaster. Last month, he was so loud that Ashley had to intervene and create just as much noise. The following day, she cursed him out so badly that I felt horrible for him.

As I continuously tapped his legs and wrote 'no bend over' on his legs, my fiancé removed the gag ball and hissed, "Fuck this place. You's a free woman today. Sound off fo' me."

I didn't have time to react or buck my eyes at his demand. Quickly, he embedded his hand into my hair and drilled me. Promptly, my sweetness splashed out of me, hopping onto his midsection before cascading to his shaft.

"I feel that monkey. You better say som' before I fold yo' ass up, Nyomi," he growled, carving into me as if it was a pumpkin.

I couldn't speak, not from fear but because his loving was too good and nasty. I didn't want to hear my voice, just his and the beautiful noise of our skin slapping. Yet, the constant muscle clenches as my pretty kitty rained on him had me ready to risk it all. One look at my pink hair tie, and I decided to continue patiently waiting until we arrived home.

"Oh, so you ain't gon' give me what I want? Bet," he barked, rapidly pulling out of me. "Get on that floor, on yo' back. Fold them legs like a gotdamn pretzel. Selfish woman."

I giggled horribly yet whispered, "I am not selfish. You can't make me sound off in this place, Richardo. You better wait until I'm released to get what you want."

"Nuh-uh. I'm finna get it now," he told me as I landed on my back, brought my legs to my chest, and folded them.

"I bet yo' motherfuckin' ass gon' sing fo' me like a snitch

somewhere is doing right now." He chortled while descending and pushing my legs into my chest.

My eyes widened when I realized my breathing would become a problem. The pressure from his hand, hunger for me to yodel, and love and thirst for me were in his handsome eyes.

"Oh, shit," I lowly voiced as he slithered into his home. "Richardo, you can't have that right now. You need to learn patience. We are very close to the finish line."

"Shut up talkin' to me, selfish fine ass," he whispered, gliding farther inside my suckling tunnel of love.

"I love you too, dark one," I cooed, thinking that would simmer him.

I was fucking wrong! Richardo struck me like a smoker with one match in a matchbox. The growling beast fucked me into another galaxy and into different timelines. Pinned to the floor, getting fucked gloriously, I felt like Loki when Hulk got ahold of him in *The Avengers*. I was motherfucking done.

"Lookatcha, underneath me, justa motherfuckin' wheezin'." The fine fucker chuckled while resting on the soles of his feet and whacking my pussy. "Good. That's what yo' ass get."

Dropping his nose on mine, Richardo sucked my bottom lip and gazed into my eyes. His firm hands were no longer pinning my legs onto my chest; they were on my soft thighs, caressing them. A weak coo escaped my voice box as he tenderly served me his loving.

As he parted my lips with his thick tongue, I whimpered, "Richardo, I'm deeply in love with you."

Slowly rotating his hips, slinging hardness through my pink tunnel, he gripped my thighs and lovingly replied, "As I'm deeply in love wit' you."

Delicately, French kissing me, my man dug deeper into my constantly tantrum-having pussy, causing me to lowly and passionately moan. "Ooouaaahhhh."

"There's that beautiful voice," he sweetly voiced as my wetness stirred tremendously. It directed him where he needed to be, just as I knew where my soft coos and pleas had to do— run into his eardrum.

"Richardooo," I whimpered, feeling like I was on the highest cloud in the sky.

"What, gorgeous one?" he whispered, slinging dick into every corner.

Ah, the dark one has left the building, I thought as my back arched and eyelids flapped.

"I need you. I love you. Nut in your pussy, baby. We do have a big day today," I sincerely cooed.

"I need you. I love you. It'll be an honor to nut in you," he happily voiced, eyeing me while steadily making me feel fantastic.

Shoving his tongue into my mouth while standing in the pussy, Richardo quickly stroked me while wrapping my shaky legs around his waist. I tightened them while matching his fast thrusts and ferociously suckling his tongue.

When we came, I was sure some heard our muffled sex noises. As opposed to the other times, I didn't care because a beautiful tear from his eyes plopped onto my face. Meanwhile, he struggled to say, 'I love you'.

While carrying me to the bed on weak legs, I rubbed the back of his head as he rubbed my neck while we Eskimo kissed. Our eyes never tore when he placed me away from the wetness. After kissing my lips, Richardo placed the dry blanket over my body. Immediately, I yawned and rubbed my cheek.

Running his hand down my face, he beautifully said, "I'll see you at noon, which isn't coming fast enough. You'll hear me before you see me. I love you, baby."

"I love you too," I cooed, wrapping my arms around his neck and shoving my tongue into his mouth. I needed him to think about the erotic kiss on his way home.

When he broke it, he winked and said, "I will think about that kiss. See you later, baby."

"See you later. Be safe on the way home." I yawned, snuggling into the bed I would never sleep on again.

After another series of juicy kisses were planted on my forehead, nose, and lips, the sexy man quickly dressed before quietly exiting the cell.

God, make the next few hours go by quickly. I'm ready to be beside my king.

♥♥♥♥♥♥

PROUDLY, with the biggest smile on my beautiful face, I stomped through the prison, eager to step into society as a partially free woman. With each prance I made in the ripped denim jeans, classy, ivory-hued blouse, and tan ankle boots, it felt damned good to have on regular clothes. It felt amazing to be back in a skin I missed terribly.

My hopes, goals, and dreams had been achieved. I was proud of myself for not losing my mind or sinking farther into a sinkhole. I gained everything I thought I would never have. I had a life that would never be dull or lonely. I had a fleet of people rooting for me and one gorgeous woman in Heaven smiling down on me.

As I neared the door, Pastor Troy featuring Ralph's "Dope Boy" blasted. I rehashed Richardo's words, 'You'll hear me before you see me'. Instantly, my teeth were all the prison workers could see. I hated they couldn't see love flowing through my veins for their captain. I was confident they would know when he returned to work in a few weeks, rocking a wedding band and his desk housing a photo of us.

When the doors opened for me, the gentle breeze blew my curly hair, but it shoved the song deeper into a place I would never return. Thankful for the ivory-hued headband, I marched into the beautiful, sunny day to witness Richardo sitting on the hood of an ivory-hued with gold flakes drop top Donk sitting on gold rims.

"No wonder he fussed at Rayne." I giggled as the dressed like me man hopped from his vehicle, smiling as I was.

My heart sprinted as my coochie purred. My throat was ready to be clogged before it spilled everything I had whispered. My clothes felt heavy when Richardo neared me. I needed them off and him inside of me.

"My fiancée is free. Happy Release Day." He grinned, flashing a smile I damned near died from. He sported a gold bottom grill.

"Yes, God, I'm free, and thank you," I cooed, panties close to incinerating.

"We have some stops, gorgeous one, but before we get on our journey…." he said, dropping onto one knee and producing a gray ring box.

"Oooooweeee." I cheesed, eager to see the finest man God could've ever created place a meaningful ring onto a finger it would never leave.

Kneeling, ensuring not to let his knee touch the ground, Richardo lovingly gazed into my eyes and happily spoke, "I've never met anyone as interesting as you. You are the humblest person I've ever met. You are many gold bricks. Priceless. Always valuable. It is a must-have. I would've been a fool to ignore how attracted I was to you. I would've been stupid not to do everything I have done for you. I would be a fool not to ask … will you marry me, Nyomi? Will you be my wife forever and ever and ever?"

"Fuck, yes, I'll marry you, Richardo! I'm going to love you forever and ever and ever!" I eagerly sang as happy tears pooled.

"Thank you for everything," he sincerely announced, removing the hair tie before quickly placing my gorgeous gold ring in its final resting place.

Sliding his hands up my thighs, ensuring his face ran across my stomach, Richardo eyed my belly and said, "In many weeks from now, you better speak up. I'm anxious as fuck to know if we are giving Rayne a sibling. By the way, it's the good anxious."

Smiling massively, I stared into his eyes and cradled his neck with one arm. Gently, he lifted me from the ground before walking to his car. Our eye contact nor smiles never broke. We were indeed in our happy place.

Upon his opening the door, I grinned. "I'm glad when I can give you the news you deserve to hear."

"Me too," he cheerfully expressed against my lips. Instead of putting me in the car, the joyful man danced and rained kisses on my exposed chest. Feeling like a queen, I did.

Afterward, we were inside his decked-out vehicle, holding hands and speeding through the parking lot. While the rippling wind whipped through my curls, I exhaled sharply, smiled brightly, and welcomed my new beginning with my new family and a fantastic man.

While Richardo cruised out of Elmore County and landed in Montgomery County, the speakers weren't loud when he briefly looked at me. Calmly, he voiced, "Are you ready to be my wife?"

"Yes," I cheerily broadcasted, nodding.

"Are you ready for a wild and nasty night?"

Aggressively nodding and cocking my eyes, I whimpered, "Oh, fuck yes. My throat needs to vomit pleasure noises."

"Are you ready to meet your new family?" he quizzed, stopping at the traffic light.

"Nervous a bit, but I am," I responded, studying his face.

"Good. Donovan got on his best damn suit." He chuckled. "Oh, we aren't getting married at the courthouse, but we have to stop by to handle our business with the marriage license. Don't ask any questions. You'll see what has been changed when we arrive."

"Oh, Lord." I nervously giggled, catching wind of another favorite twerking song, Gorilla Zoe featuring Yung Joc's "Juice Box". Immediately, I rolled and rocked in the seat.

Richardo gripped himself and groaned, "Shid, something will have to wait if you keep on moving like that. I hadn't been in you since a few hours ago. He hungry, and I'm thirsty."

Restarting the song, I increased the volume and put on a seductive show. As the light turned green, he skirted off. While unbuckling the tan seat belt, I rapidly unzipped my jeans. I kept my eye on the man whose jaws clenched as the bulge in his pants rose.

"I need that," I voiced, sticking two of his fingers into my hot goodness.

While he fingered me and I fucked his fingers, I had the mighty assault rifle out, enjoying the fresh breeze. To the song's beat, I beat the gut's plunger and sexed his fingers. I ensured to scoop my pussy, so his fingers could slam into my G-Spot. When he noticed what I was doing, he laughed while beating it up. With a massively sinking stomach, my toes and fingers curled, and my waterwork show started.

Stuck against the white leather seats, no longer jacking him, I stared at the man sitting upright and zooming through traffic. I wickedly grinned, knowing he was about to get off in my guts like he had never before.

"Oh, shit. I'm wetting up my clothes," I oddly voiced as Richardo rapidly swerved into a familiar side of town that let people know the residents were well off.

"Richardooooo!" I yodeled as my body shook. He couldn't hear me for the bass. The wind would've carried my pleasure noise away even if it wasn't blasting.

While he zipped this way and that way, an unfamiliar song by a well-known artist blasted. Sexily, he rocked his head and sang. I observed the stern-faced man as he hurried to make a right turn. I didn't have the will to brace before damned near toppling over onto him. At the same time, fear and getting my body pleased caused the best orgasm to surface.

Once he swerved into the driveway of a beautiful home with black shutters, he gunned for the opening black garage that held the vehicle I had picked out weeks ago. My heart fluttered, but I wasn't sure of the exact cause. As the garage doors closed, Richardo shut off the bass and turned down the radio. The hunger in his eyes when he stared at me had given me the will to control my limbs.

Starvingly, I climbed out of my clothes and shoes, saying, "Right here. Right now."

"You motherfucking right!" he sexily hissed, opening the door while kicking off his shoes and removing his shirt.

Before I could open the door and turn my body so he could have easy access to remove me, Richardo stood before me with fire running from his eyes. I knew there would be no moving from the car as I suspected he wanted to fuck me on the trunk or hood.

Simply, I spread my legs, rubbed my ladylove, and cooed, "Your playland has arrived, baby. Get her as you see fit."

"And I'm fucking going to," he growled before kneeling and rushing his hands underneath my ass.

As I lovingly stared at my man gazing at me while driving his tongue to my twat, my body jerked. He chuckled until he arrived at the hairless, spoiled bitch. Slowly, he licked my coochie from the bottom to the top. I shivered and whined, "Yesss, God!"

While he massaged my legs and skated his tongue across

my folds, I rubbed his shoulders, thrust my hips, and loudly whimpered, "My God."

"Ooou, that noise of yours," he groaned before rapidly stimulating my clit with the tip of his tongue.

"Ahhhooouuuu, Richardo!" I passionately shouted.

When the oral sex god stopped scribbling a unique and heartfelt love letter on my clit, he latched onto it and made me sing for him. It wasn't long before I cried out from pleasure. My fiancé made me beg him never to stop loving on me. The slipping of his experienced tongue into my treasure box, granted me to cuff the back of his neck and fuck his mouth while talking nasty to him.

"Oooh, you had no idea how much of a freak you are about to marry after you paint my face like you are an artist. You have no idea how nasty I am, Richardo Vincent Mets, but you will before we say, 'I do'." I grinned, staring at his astonished face.

Quickly sliding my pretty kitty on his tongue and rolling my hips to the song playing, I hissed. "Yeah, I'm a big freak, but only to my man. I couldn't show you much of this side because of where I resided. Now, you will see just how nasty and loving I can be at the same time. When I'm done allowing you to catch my six nuts, please bring my one-eyed man to my face! Hover over me! I motherfucking miss him."

"As you wish," he handsomely grunted before sloppily eating me, staring into my eyes, and stuffing a thumb into my asshole.

"Yessss! Thumb fuck that asshole! Own it! Bust it open so when my dick blesses it … the virgin bitch will know who the fuck owns it!" I yodeled as he was fixated on sucking the pinkness off my clit.

"My God," I whimpered, body locking. "Suck on your pacifier, honey! Suck on it!"

After six glorious orgasms, my soon-to-be-husband hovered over my face with his guy in his hand. Hungrily, I suckled the veiny pipe into my starved mouth. I had a ball showing him what my throat could do while I looked into his eyes. I wasted no time making him remember that I would always relax and make him upset during our lovemaking.

"Gotdamn it!" he hollered erotically as I repeatedly rammed my mouth on it. Saliva spilled onto my titties, resulting in me scooping the drool before rubbing it on his balls as if it was lotion.

After ten songs, I was sick of giving the mighty member my attention. I had to show his balls some love, so I sopped them into my mouth like gnocchi. As I gobbled them, Richardo gripped the back of my head and moaned, "I love you, baby. Everything about you I love and will never fall out of love with."

Spitting his balls out of my mouth like I spat out a piece of pumpkin pie, I voiced, "I know. We will always be locked in."

"You fucking right," he stuttered; I was back to suckling, dirt biking, and fondling his balls. "I don't want my nut to be on your face. I need to fertilize your womb."

"Okay, honey," I spoke while sucking.

"Nyomiiii!" he growled, looking down at me. The astonishment on his gorgeous, flawless face was everything. It was apparent he had never had a woman talk on the stick. It wasn't hard to do if you knew how much to have in your mouth.

"What?" I asked, no longer sucking, but it was still in my mouth.

"Say my name," he stated, eyelids wavering from the sensations I rendered him.

"Richardo Vincent Mets."

"Get my dick out of your mouth. I need my body on yours," he spoke through clenched teeth.

"As you wish," I slowly announced, still massaging his balls and beating his pipe.

Slowly, I slid my teeth from the middle of the shaft toward the head. When I arrived at the fat tip, I clamped my mouth and rammed my throat to the base. His body jerked as his head flopped backward. A series of curse words left his mouth. I loved hearing and seeing him as he had me on the floor in the wee hours of every morning—helpless but filled with pleasure.

I continued to lovingly attack his member until he came into my mouth. He was mad, but I would make up for it later. I wasn't in the mood anymore to have my snatch pummeled. I didn't want to say Richardo while cumming. I needed to say, 'My husband'. Someone I felt I would never have.

Lifting me from the seat, he breathlessly voiced, "You were not supposed to have done that."

"I know, but I needed to see my wedding set gliding across your chest as I moan, whimper, and coo your official title. I need us to make love as man and wife," I honestly voiced as he opened the door many feet from his idling vehicle.

"I can't tell by how you fucked my face and talked to me before eating up my dick," he disappointedly voiced.

"I'm sorry you are displeased, honey," I calmly spoke, eyeing him. "I thought I wouldn't make it to this stage with someone's son. I'm thirty-nine, Richardo. You know I've only been in three serious relationships. You also know why I tossed them to the streets. Me having sex with you as man and wife is a big deal for me."

"Why the fuck am I just now knowing about that, Nyomi?" he asked, no longer walking through the high ceiling, beautifully decorated home. Our home. *Our family home.*

"I wasn't supposed to have said that," I announced, shrugging.

Rubbing his nose against mine, he sweetly voiced, "Since it's like that, I will wait to tear your ass up. Let me go make your fine ass my wife."

"As you should." I grinned as he walked off.

"Welcome home, baby. I hate I'm rushing you through your place for the first time. I'll make it up as soon as I can."

"That you will," I softly said, rubbing his neck as we entered a lavish, large bedroom.

My eyes widen, causing him to richly voice, "I see you like."

"Like it is such a lame word. I love it," I spoke in awe, unable to tear my eyes from the master bedroom that didn't look manly. "Rayne has done her thing tremendously."

"Absolutely not. I did this myself." He smiled, happiness soaring through his eyes.

"What?" I screeched, oddly looking at him.

"You heard me," he replied against my lips while walking into the jaw-dropping bathroom with a garden tub. "After our honeymoon, we will explore the Freak 'em Room. We will spend the night there once I'm done with you."

"My, my, my," I moaned as he turned on the water.

Flashing his handsome smile, he chuckled. "That's what you will mostly say."

An hour and ten minutes later, we were fully dressed in our wedding attire, leaving the courthouse, making it possible for the next step: to say, 'I do'. Twenty minutes later and still clueless about where we would tie the knot, we pulled into a gorgeous community on the city's outskirts.

I eyed the numerous cars lining the perfectly manicured grass. Bodies after bodies, I viewed dressed in their best attire. My heart thumped rapidly when I spotted Donovan. As Richardo stated, he was dressed in his finest suit.

Parking before the large, two-floored house with a wrap-around porch, Richardo looked at me lovingly and asked, "Are you ready, beautiful one?"

"I am. Um, whose place is this?"

"You'll find out in a minute. Do you want Donovan to give you away?" he questioned as the smiling man neared my honey's truck.

"I do," I genuinely voiced, nodding. Donovan and I had significantly bonded since Valentine's Day. I learned a lot about the man who was deeply in love with my mother and had never gotten over not being my father.

"As you wish, beautiful one." Richardo smiled, cuffing my chin as Donovan opened the door. "I'll see you soon."

"I'll see you soon." I grinned, becoming overwhelmed.

"Ah, how do I wish she was here in the flesh to see you. You are beautiful, Nyomi." Donovan choked up as he aided me out of the car.

"Thank you. You don't look so bad yourself, old man." I softly grinned, looking around the place. "Whose estate is this?"

"Yours," he spoke with a straight face.

"Come again?" I asked, rapidly blinking.

Briefly, he looked at the beautiful sky. Handsomely, he chuckled while focusing on me. "Some weeks back, someone kicked in that door. A door that belonged to Willington and his wife. A door that they walked out of many times while raising four children. Once someone kicked that door in, a fleet of all-black, tactical-dressed, grenade and assault rifle-toting individuals marched in. That someone went batshit crazy to make sure you own this land and the house it sits on. Someone got so damn crazy that the third person who walks behind him had to knock his buff ass out just to get him out of the house after everything was signed over to you. They said that someone shitted in his hands, tossed it at those people, and rubbed shit into that man's nose before doing the same to the wife and their grown kids. They said that someone drank a lot of water, stood behind, whistled, and pissed all over them folks. They said that someone ate so much food just so he could throw up in those folks' mouths. They said that someone…."

Weak to my stomach and could barely see, I laughed. "That's enough, Donovan. My God. That's enough."

"Damn, I was getting to the good part." He chortled.

Damn, I love my man and those who put up with him.

"Willington and his raggedy ass family, thank y'all for coming out dressed in your finest clothes and shit. I needed all present from y'all sorry ass line to see whose estate this belongs to. My baby's land and house are gorgeous, aren't they? Now, Willington, you know who did all those beautiful things many weeks ago!" Richardo loudly and excitedly voiced, causing me to see him shirtless while standing behind Willington.

"What the hell is he up to now? It is always something with his ass." Donovan exhaled a moment too early. That damn man of mine kicked the tall and lean federal judge down the steps. As laughter roared from the porch, another body was tossed from the porch.

"My God. He's like Hercules, just hurling motherfuckers

onto that hard ass ground," Donovan oddly spoke as I giggled and eyed the grand show Richardo put on for me.

Thrilled, Richardo pointed at the main bitch who turned her nose up at me. Flashing his handsome smile, he happily said, "You, old lady with the gray wig. Come on here and bring your teeth case. Your turn. Hold on tightly to them. It's my baby's and my wedding day. Come on. Stop all that twitching. Your baldheaded ass knew about her and didn't make him do the right thing. I don't give a damn your legs can't handle that ground. Come here now. I'm getting angry. I told your ass three motherfucking times to—"

"Fuck all that talking to her! Kick or toss the bitch like you did the others!" Ashley sassed, shoving the old lady down the stairs. She tumbled as if she was in the dryer on low. I covered my mouth and hurried to look away. I didn't want to laugh.

"My God." Donovan laughed as the old woman made odd noises.

Gently, I nudged him. "That's not nice."

"Fuck those people." He chortled as I focused on Richardo, oddly staring at his only female best friend.

"She's old as fuck, Ash. I wasn't going to push her. I was going to sit her on the steps and gently push her down it," Richardo seriously voiced, causing me to laugh as Donovan and I continued walking toward the crowded porch.

Angrily, she stood next to him and loudly voiced, "You have a fleet of motherfuckas to kick down steps they deemed wasn't good enough for Nyomi to walk up! That old, bare-mouth bitch was the fucking ringleader! She should've been shoved off the gotdamn roof! You better be glad I didn't have the patience to drag her diaper-wearing ass up the stairs to do so! It's hotter than piss out here! I'm hungry! I'm horny! And the nephew of yours, whose day is today … to get this knocked-up cat, has pissed me off! Get this show on the road before I start slinging bullets into her useless ass family!"

"Wait. What did she say?" Donovan awkwardly asked as four identical males tossed my paternal family from the porch.

I stopped walking to look at the shit before me. Richardo and his best friends didn't move, but Ashley did. When she plopped in a chair, Donovan said, stunned, "The quads and Ashley? There's no way. Come on, sweetie. They have some explaining to do."

As Donovan ran, dragging me along, we had to play hopscotch over the moaning and groaning people on the ground. When we landed on the porch, a striking woman dressed in a cute, loosely fitted pantsuit waltzed through the front door. Bodies stopped flying from the porch as all became quiet.

Through narrowed eyes, the familiar voice woman slowly nodded. "I didn't think it was strange when you didn't give us your fiancée's name. I didn't think it was strange when you stated you couldn't give me the details of the venue until the day of the wedding. It wasn't until I arrived on this land that I had an inkling who could be your wife. His other daughters are beneath you. I heard your voice from the kitchen, and I was certain who was to become your wife. To think about it, my brother has been extraordinarily happy since Valentine's Day. His eyes sparkled more. His tone was hopeful. His being around me has been different too. He smiles in my face as if he has something to tell me, but he never speaks. I question his behavior, and he doesn't open his damn mouth. If I know you as I swear I do, you purposely hid the one person, Nyomi Reanna Richards, I thought would always know me, just to surprise me. Am I correct?"

"Very much so." He grinned as his mother's teary eyes finally landed on me.

"Ah," the gorgeous, tall woman sweetly exhaled before lovingly snatching me into her arms. Immediately, she rained kisses on my forehead as her love blanketed my bones.

"I almost pushed you off this porch, Donna Mets. You were a little too rough with my woman," Richardo seriously voiced, causing all to laugh, especially me.

"Hey, sweetie. Welcome back to these arms. Arms you will never leave again," she lovingly spoke as my honey smothered us.

As I basked in her sincere tone and tender embrace, she shoved him out of the way. Nastily, he growled, causing Terry and Avery to laugh the loudest. Ashley hissed for Richardo to shut up and stop being selfish with me.

While I felt tears sliding from my eyes, only to plop onto Donna's neck, my hold on her tightened. At the same time, Richardo barked, "Raq, Riq, Req, and Roq, I wish y'all would get y'all's old lady! She's working my nerves with that bossy mess!"

"It would be nice for someone to explain that to me," Donovan stated as Donna slowly pulled from me, gazing into my eyes and wiping my tears.

"Ha! Not now! Time for my woman and me to say, 'I do'. They better write a book explaining that chaos," my honey seriously announced, grabbing my hand. "All the trash has been tossed out. Ready to get married on your estate, beautiful one?"

"Oh, yes." I grinned, interlocking our hands and winking at his mother.

"I got it from here, Vesta. I got our girl from here, and I have a lot of making up to do," Donna beautifully stated before her son left me in the care of the siblings.

An hour and fifteen minutes later, we were pronounced man and wife before his happily clapping family and friends. As my husband's mouth towered over mine, I tasted my tears and the sweetness of his tongue. My chest rapidly rose and fell as my stomach caved as our family happily shouted, "Congratulations!"

Christmas of 2021, I lost my only family. Today, I gained a large, welcoming family, all thanks to the man who looked at me as if he needed to fuck me senseless against his office door. Most importantly, today, I returned to another person who loved me just as Momma did. A beautiful woman who couldn't stop smiling at me, just as my Momma had.

"You are forever mine as I am forever yours. I am elated to have you as my wife. I will treasure you. No other can get in my vision. You will forever be my endgame. I love you, Nyomi Mets," Richardo genuinely spoke as I stared into his glossy eyes.

Holding his face, tears running onto my top lip, I choked up while grinning. "I love you, Richardo Mets. Life with you will surely be one great rollercoaster, and I'm looking forward to it all. Especially since I know how to summon The Don."

As the laughing and head-shaking man walked toward three rows of people dressed in formal server attire, he whispered, "Don't summon him until we get to the Freak 'Em Down Room."

"As you wish." I giggled, gently running my nails across his neck.

Chapter 15

RICHARDO

Ten Months Later

I gave up the captain title a week after being Nyomi's husband. Quickly, I settled into the cotton farm as the secondary runner. Palmer became the captain of the women's correctional facility. Terry and Ashley continued being correctional officers. A calm Avery became the lieutenant. He transformed a lot since Avery Richardo Lee had his hands full.

Nyomi settled beautifully as the leading runner of my family's land and a great family member. She brought unconditional love into our lives, and no one ran away as I felt they would. We loved witnessing love floating around our home before slamming into our bones, unwilling to leave because love herself, Nyomi, wouldn't let it. She had us in love when she passionately talked about never wanting to lose my interest or her falling out of love with me because it would hurt her.

My parents became more affectionate. Glover's observant eye on us caused his dying marriage to turn around for the better. The things they tolerated from my knuckle-headed nephews were no longer. He started cracking the sillies' backs. They ceased making him repeat himself. I thought Glover would be a significant hater and try to sabotage us, but he never did. He gave us the green light for Nyomi to stand beside me as we ran the cotton farm. Also, he embraced a look he never saw from me: peace. Many times, he thanked Nyomi for allowing me into her life. Like always, she was all smiles while hugging him and telling him how welcome he was.

Uncle Donovan's wife and their daughters hadn't been around us since Ashley had to put me to sleep on Christmas, two weeks after Richardo Junior was born. Their nasty behavior and unnecessary dick-suckers pushed out words that weren't nice. That caused me to snatch Nyomi from Donovan's table before I flipped it over, trapping his daughters and wife. With the table on their bodies, I choked them until their eyes closed.

When my eyes finally opened, vision blurry, I knew Nyomi would knock my ass sideways for not controlling my beast. That beautiful fucker stood over me, smiling, and said,

"Next time, let me handle that, but thanks for showing me exactly how to correctly flip over a table to pin people under it. I must say that was remarkable. Anywho, sit up so we can go home. I'm a little bit horny. Nothing major, though."

Her recently emptied womb ass was more than a little bit horny. I shot her fucking club up throughout our stay in the Freak'em Down Room. We were back on the pregnancy train.

It was the month of love, and it was another pretty Saturday. My magnificent wife, sassy freak in the sheets, and the captain of my heart decided to continue hosting the love theme late lunch at our home. Eager to be a part of the gathering, my ugly ass family showed up two hours early, interrupting me soaking out my wife while she fed our son.

Her soothing tone was why I didn't act out about them stepping across the door, jumping into setting up our back patio, and finishing the last of her food preparations. Her massive smile and the bright glow in her eyes as she looked at our eager family put me in my place. After all, I lived to see her happy and passionately involved in a conversation with the ladies: Ashley, Momma, Deborah, and Rayne.

Ding. Dong.

Lucas ass. He's the only invited person not here, I thought, slipping from my son's nursery and rubbing his back.

"I'm coming!" my cheery wife eagerly shouted while zooming from the kitchen, not looking my way.

"Son, she on the go," I whispered against his forehead as I stopped to hear what Lucas and Nyomi would discuss. They had been clingy since I had a strong feeling of pulling up at Avery's house a few hours after marrying Nyomi.

"Hey, Nyomi," a saddened Lucas voiced, stepping inside our warm home.

"Hey, you. How are you?" she asked the ten-month clean-nosed man who was chronically beaten by his brother on Nyomi and my wedding day.

As they walked farther into the spacious front room, the unhappy man exhaled sharply. "I'm horrible, but my therapist said I need to find someone I trust to talk to. That person is you. Is it okay if I do it now?"

"Of course," she spoke sweetly and lovingly, causing my heart to flutter at how kind and loving she was.

"I hate seeing Rayne with someone else. I hate not being next to her and our kids. I hate this arrangement of spending time with them here. I miss my girl, Nyomi. I hate that I had promised Richardo I would stay away from her on a sexual or serious relationship stance just so he wouldn't tell her about my slip-up with drugs. I can't breathe without her. I've been a lowkey addict since a teen. She doesn't know. I never wanted her to look at me as if I was scum. Honestly, Nyomi, I was surprised I slipped by my brother, Richardo, Terry, Palmer, and Ashley for so long, given who they are," he stated as I narrowed my eyes.

You pulled a good one over our eyes, bitch, I thought as he continued, "She made me not want to sniff coke, pop pills, or shove a needle in my arm. Being off the drugs and not having

Rayne is eating me up. I know I'll never find anyone as adventurous, always smiling, cheerful, and a handful when she's pissed. I won't find another her because she's one of a kind. She's a full house that I need, not the next man. I love my brother's goddaughter. I have loved her since the first time I placed my eyes on her. She has always made me feel comfortable, just like you. I cheated once because I was stupid and thought it was the thing to do, even though I knew she was a good woman. I was on drugs when I messed around with her supposed friend. Hell, we were doing them together."

You and Rayne getting back together is not going to happen, I thought, gently rubbing my son's legs as Lucas exhaled. "I need my family back, but I need to get myself back first. I can't lose her because I had a dark cloud over me. It's been over me since they left me, a lost teenager, alone with Avery and my paraplegic uncle as if I could really take care of his needs while dealing with my own issues. They were always rushing to jet from the stable but lonely environment. I needed them, but they were so busy that I didn't open my mouth when they came to drop off money and food."

My knees buckled as I feared clearing my throat would raise awareness of my snooping. Something I hated I did. Lucas was about to bring forth something we all should have realized.

Hurtfully, he announced, "For them to toss me to the side and leave me, they left me to deal with my thoughts the best way I knew how. I wasn't used to being alone and acting like an adult as a teenager. They used to talk to me, spend time with me, and ask me if I was okay. I would tell them when I wasn't. When they stopped being there for me in a way that really mattered, I didn't answer when they did ask. I take ownership of not opening my mouth to them when needed. I take ownership of hurting the only one I can ever love."

As he sobbed how he hated we left him, I felt horrible as tears poured from my eyes. My head and heart became heavy because he didn't tell any lies. We were caught up in the dope game, me losing Maysha, and my revenge against the fucker who supplied the high schoolers with drugs. We thought we were doing good by Lucas and their uncle because we were financially able. We forgot him, and that hurt me most because I was supposed to have caught that shit and corrected it.

As I took a step to right my wrongs, my woman's trembling tone slithered through our home as she said, "First thing first, today not tomorrow, you need to chat with my husband, your brother, Terry, Ashley, and Palmer down. They need to see you telling them how their mistake of not seeing you but seeing you affected them. They need to hear you take ownership of not opening your mouth about your feelings. I'm certain if you would've opened your mouth to them, they would've ceased it all for you."

Meanwhile, my knees were slowly crashing on me as my heart squeezed. Sincerely, Nyomi continued. "Always remember you are stronger than you know. Find that backbone that's deep in you. When you have it, hold on tightly to it.

Never let it go. Another thing, your past trauma of dealing with an addict as a mother needs to be talked about in detail with your therapist. Get your past off you, Lucas, and you may have a shot at being Rayne's husband. I'm going to say shit for what it is. You aren't doing enough to make my husband recant anything. You are just dragging your dick across the ground, hoping things will go back to the way they were. They won't. Richardo's not having that shit. It has to be better than before, Lucas. Show him you are willing to go above and beyond to be deemed worthy to have his firstborn. Make all of them see who you are. You weren't born an addict, Lucas. Your environment created an addict. Give them a reason to lift all bans about the one person they will start a war over."

As I couldn't stop thinking about how often he needed to say something but never did, I wiped my face and thought, *fuck, I saw it, but I didn't see it.*

He hopefully stated, "I'll do just that."

"Good. Now, come on. You were last to show up for our family lunch date," she cutely sassed as I hurried to duck into the guest bathroom.

"Is Bryant here?" Lucas questioned, sounding as if they were in the kitchen.

"No."

"I'm surprised," he eagerly spoke about Rayne's boyfriend of three months.

"Between you and me, Rayne didn't want to make you

uncomfortable, so she broke up with him two days ago," Nyomi stated, stunning me.

"So, there's hope, huh?" he eagerly voiced as if he smiled.

"Seems so. If I were her, I wouldn't have cared about your feelings," she sassed.

"So cutthroat." He lightly chuckled.

And always on point, I thought, nodding as she asked, "It has been helping you this far, right?"

"That and how badly my crying brother did what I begged him to do," he exhaled, which caused me to shiver and briefly reflect on that horrific scene. Seeing a crying Avery rapidly kick the bloodied face and weak Lucas in the face caused me to become stuck for a few seconds before springing into action.

"Dad!" Zanning eagerly shouted as the love jams played from a nice listening decibel from the back porch.

"My boy," the happy man announced as I couldn't stop my tears from flowing from the guy who was a damn great dad. "How y'all doing?"

"Good," everyone cheerily voiced as I heard nothing else. The sliding door had been closed.

Resting my chin on my son's head, tears poured as I owned the truth that we had failed Lucas. I slid down the wall and retrieved my device to open my best friends and my group chat. A simple '9-1-1' message had them hustling and bustling inside the fine house Nyomi and I really turned into a home.

"What's wrong?" Ashley asked as they neared me.

Slowly, I looked at them through blurry vision. I struggled to move my trembling lips to speak, "We failed Lucas. We overlooked him because of the other shit we had going on. We financially took care of him, but we forgot the fact he was still a gotdamn fifteen-year-old, recently separated from a fucking drug addict that I made sure didn't breathe again. He took ownership of everything. Now, we have to do the same. We have to fix what we fixed up and then broke. Him. He loves my child, his only friend. She loves him, and I can't get in the way if I'm not doing my part. I put him in a junkie category instead of where he belonged. In the fucking center of us. That's where we had him before we were pulled into a million fucking directions, leaving him alone to deal with his thoughts, a paraplegic man, and loneliness."

After helping me off the ground, all had wobbling heads, twitching mouths, and wet faces. When we stepped onto the patio, looking at Lucas, there were no more conversations, only concerned and worried facial expressions. Weakly, I pointed at us and hurtfully spoke, "We failed you, and I am sorry. We saw money and better living arrangements for you. You should've never had to turn to drugs. You shouldn't have had the need to look like you needed to talk to us. We were the adults. We should've fucking seen it. I did, but I didn't. So much was going on. I am taking responsibility for my actions of making you be something you were never meant to be. You have to come back to the center of us. My child loves you. You love her. I love you but put you in a category I shouldn't have. I am sorry, Lucas. I'm not allowing the outside world to further destroy you, and I'm coming back into your life as I was before becoming too big. Will you forgive me?"

Nodding, he happily said, "Yes, I do."

"Thank you," I responded, unable to move due to Avery dropping his head.

My beautiful wife hurried to me as Ashley sincerely apologized to Lucas. Handing my second precious cargo to his fantastic mother, Lucas verbally accepted and forgave Ashley. My tears were unlimited as Terry spoke. The more he talked, the more I felt less of a leader.

"I accept your apology, Terry, and I forgive you." Lucas choked up, nearing us.

Palmer sincerely followed Terry's apology while holding tightly to Lucas. That broke Avery. It was tough to watch Avery snatch his brother to him and beg him to forgive him. Everyone at the table learned who almost killed Lucas and why. It was earth-shattering to watch Rayne unravel at the table. I didn't have time to get to her because the brothers withered to the ground as Lucas had forgiven his brother.

"I promise I'm going to do right, Avery. Seeing Rayne with another man isn't it. I love my family I made with her. I give myself a year and two months, and y'all will see me like y'all never had before. That's the day I'm coming to y'all to ask if I can turn Rayne Mets into Rayne Lee," he cried, lifting his brother's face to stare into his eyes.

"My wife and I will be waiting on that day." I nodded as Lucas helped his brother from the ground.

"It was hard to see you like that. I hated I did that to you, but I saw your eyes. They looked like hers. I never wanted to do that to you, but I rather … I preferred it to be me. I am your keeper, and I failed in the biggest way. I will never fail you again. I promise, Lucas." Avery sobbed, placing his hand on the back of his brother's neck.

"I'm going to hold you to that." Lucas softly smiled, walking toward me.

As he stood before me, I saw him as the timid, skinny White boy with the saddest blue eyes. I gently placed my forehead on his as I had many times before and said, "I love you, Lucas. I won't let us leave you again. You are forever back in the center of our circle. Go be open with Rayne. I didn't because you begged me not to. Always tell her the truth, even if you feel it will scare her off. Nothing can scare off The Don's daughter. You know this. Hell, he's scared of her at times."

"Okay." He lightly chuckled, as did the others. I was thankful my truth simmered the sadness.

"You have one hell of an amazing wife, Richardo," Lucas praised, staring at my smiling woman.

Lightly tapping his chest, I smiled. "That's why we, the ones who surround you, put in overtime and pulled plays, so I could sneak around my old place of employment to be with her. I knew who was to land in there before she got there! I was already scouting for that monkey to be mine forever! Ha! Look at her five weeks and a few days pregnant ass over there wearing *my* ring. I'm going to repeat it! *My* ring!"

The hoots and hollers started as Nyomi bucked her eyes and smiled. Instantly, I knew I had blown the lid off our secret. Doing the beat-it-up dance to the fast-beat Southern soul song, I stared at my woman and cheesed. "Oops, baby, I'm sorry. I've been waiting to spill that sweet tea since the doctor confirmed it."

"Wow, y'all. Just wow. My little brother is ten weeks old." Rayne giggled as Lucas kissed her forehead while pulling her into his arms.

As our family congratulated us, I strolled toward my woman and secondborn child. The love smothering us and blanketing Lucas, my child, and my grandkids were everything. Everyone at the table was at peace, thanks to a phenomenal woman all confided in. Nyomi was the best thing to happen to everyone at the table. She was our glue, a rare gem I would always treasure and keep close to me.

"I love you, Nyomi," I confessed, rubbing the side of her face.

"I love you, Richardo." She lovingly breathed, gripping my neck and pulling me to her.

I thought I would place a peck on her lips. I was wrong; a loving, tear-forming sensational kiss was created once I wrote my name on her tongue, gripped her neck, and deepened the kiss. The eroticism of the peck made me eager to tell our family to fix a plate and go. I was hot and ready for her as the wind blew harshly, tickling my neck.

"Alright, Dad and Mom. My arm is hurting while we shield Zanning's eyes." Rayne giggled as I provocatively removed my tongue from my wife's starving mouth.

Remembering a bet, I decided to fall through to surely erase the sadness from the intense apology to Lucas. I gazed into her eyes and stood erect. Happily, I smiled. "You are going to stay pregnant because that mouth … verbally … that is … is everything. Oh, how I love you. Nyomi Richards."

"What the fuck you called me, nigga?" she nastily stated, glaring at me.

Everyone, minus my crew, gasped; those idiots laughed along with me. Hurriedly, I dragged two fingers down her face and laughed. "Nyomi Mets, an idiot felt you wouldn't cut up if I did that. So, baby, hold out your hand for your bet money."

With the most embarrassed facial expression, she quickly apologized to everyone before looking at Avery and extending her hand. All laughed heartily when he planted eight crisp one-hundred-dollar bills into her soft palm.

"I can't believe y'all are still this childish." Dad chuckled, shaking his head.

"It'll never change, Old Bones," Avery goofily voiced, causing us to chortle as we settled in our chairs.

"I love you. Thank you for taking the biggest risk to be in our lives, especially mine," I softly voiced as Momma tenderly rubbed the back of my woman's hand.

"I love you, and no thanks are needed," she cooed, eyes becoming glossy. "I pray for nothing but greatness and much happiness for and from you and Lucas."

"We will have it," I sincerely responded, never tearing my eyes from her.

"It's been a long time since I've seen this much love in our family," Donovan stated proudly. "Finally, the hellraisers can express the one emotion they could never do openly. I am proud of y'all's growth!"

"Can we get a toast to that?" Momma giggled, raising the glass filled with bubbly champagne.

"That's a must!" I happily replied, grabbing my glass as the others did so. Ashley, who was newly pregnant, breast-feeding Rayne, and my wife had apple juice in their glasses.

"Ugh! I wish I could have a little sippy sip," Ashley sassed, rolling her eyes.

"Well, if you hadn't decided to let Req knock you up after you had just given birth to Raquel, you would." Donovan chuckled, causing us to laugh. "So, you will be pregnant two more times. I suggest it's time to get used to apple juice, Ashley."

"Whew, I can't believe y'all in this peculiar situation like … how does it work? Don't y'all ever think about sucking up the other's cum when it's your day to be with her? Y'all are some true suck-mouth dudes," Rayne seriously voiced, causing me to howl in laughter as Momma clamped her grand-daughter's lips.

Rapidly shaking her head, Momma calmly voiced, "I'm going to get my damn toast out of the way because I, too, have questions about that … um … relationship. There's a lot of different breaths on those titties. It's seven days out of the week. It's four of them. How do you handle them on their birthdays? Are they lining up and just waiting for you to get done dating and loving on the other brother? How are you maintaining your PH balance? How do you not call or moan the wrong name? What do you do when they all want to lay up with you? I mean, how … how are you maintaining which cock to suc—"

A red face, laughing, Avery clamped Momma's lips while looking at us. He simmered while sincerely voicing, "First of all, Momma Donna, it's either a penis, dick, tool, pipe, assault rifle, grenade, pussy plugger, or shrimp. Never in your life say cock. Where was I? Oh, yeah. Respectfully speaking, love is a motherfucka. It got us at this table. Five people are in a unique situation because of love. My brother and goddaughter have two beautiful, begging-ass, always-hungry kids who always seem to be on molly. All because of love. I damned near killed my brother at his request because of my love for him. Ma and Pop have three children and a daughter-in-law because of love. Yeah, I didn't leave out, Maysha. I really think she's Rayne. Another topic for another day. Donovan and Cruella de Vil…"

I slumped on my wife as tears poured from my eyes as I had returned to laughing after the fool called that man's absent wife, Cruella de Vil. I was weak when Ashley clamped his mouth, looked at us, and sincerely said, "What Avery meant to say was, we are here because, without love, we wouldn't be anything. Just a shell of a person with no purpose. Life is durable and beautiful when surrounded by people you love and genuinely love you. I so happen to love amazing, silly, hardworking, caring, and loving quadruplets. I don't care who knows it. I don't care what people think or say behind my back. Let's face it, they won't speak their opinions because they know bullets will rain from all angles. Off the topic, I went. Anywho, we are sitting here because of love herself, Nyomi Mets. So, the toast needs to be given to her!"

As we hopped to our feet, we looked at my woman and eagerly yelled, "To love herself, Nyomi Mets!"

When my overjoyed woman stood, shoving her glass into the air, she beautifully choked up. "I'm honored to be thought of as love herself, but without y'all's open heart and arms, going through major movements, and eager to receive me, none of this would've been possible. I must send the toast right back at y'all by saying to love because y'all make it so easy to express the most powerful word in the world."

"To love!" we enthusiastically shouted as I tightly hugged my wife.

While our family hugged, I separated my wife and our secondborn from our family. Planting us on the farther side of the porch, I rested the tip of my forefinger under Nyomi's chin. Searching eyes that I proudly pried open when she slept too long, I lovingly whispered, "I'm so glad the toast didn't make it to me."

"Why?" she probed, eyes sparkling the more she smiled.

"Because it would've gone a little something like this. Love is a motherfucka when you are with the one who keeps your mind in the gutta. Love is the best thing that could've ever happened to me. Love is why I drove my day ones and me crazy each day, just to be with the one who makes my heart feel like it's about to bust a split. Love has me not wanting to sleep just to pull your drawls down with my teeth. Love, have my dick up in you as if it's a tampon. Love is why I'm looking forward to cracking your back when our family leaves and our son goes to sleep. Love is why I will smother you in fudge, whipped cream, ice cream, and sprinkles. Love is why you will be begging for God to make me catch a cramp while I'm slowly stroking the pussy from the back. Love is why I'll be sucking up my son's milk while I'm tootsie rolling in the coochie."

"All righty now. Time to eat because I'm ready for everyone to leave just so I can see you naked." She breathed erratically.

"Oh, how do I love you, Nyomi Mets. The love of my life," I announced, rubbing her stomach.

Observing my eyes, she cooed, "Oh, how do I love you, Richardo Mets. The love of my life. Us forever."

"Us forever," I quickly voiced before covering her mouth with mine.

. . .

THE END

Did you enjoy the read?
Let us know how much by leaving us a review on Amazon
and Goodreads.

Keep reading for a preview of…

Wet Dreams On Lockdown: The Male C.O

By Tamyra Griffin

CHAPTER 1

"Silence!" Officer Lewis barked. "This shit here ain't no sorority house. This is a prison! Single file line, inmates…and welcome home," he added with a smirk as he walked the line of ladies that had just arrived.

I stood there and shook my head as I watched this asshole act like he owned the prison – which was a daily routine. He wasn't the only asshole on staff though. Me, on the other hand, I lived by the motto – *do your eight and skate.* However, I didn't treat the inmates the way other COs did. Yeah, they were in prison for committing a crime, but it didn't make them any less human. I mean, I wasn't trying to be the cell block savior, but I did my job the way it was supposed to be done.

Today was Friday – which was dubbed New Arrival Day at Garden State Women's Correctional Facility. Most people looked forward to this because it ended the week, but for me, it was my least favorite day. Some of the women had never been to prison, so there were all kinds of tears, theatrics, passing out. You name it, it's happened. The existing inmates showed their asses as well. You would think some of them were niggas the way they acted as they sized up the "fresh meat' being brought in. On both ends of the spectrum, there was a lot of unnecessary drama and bullshit to close out the week. TGIF my ass.

After the new arrivals were processed in, searched, and given their gear, I stood at the entry of the tier with my counter, making sure everybody was accounted for. I only paid attention to 'em long enough to make sure my count was right at this point in the process. Although, you couldn't help but take notice of some of the women that came in. Of course, you could pick out the junkies right away. Then there were the privileged, scared white women that got caught up in some white-collar bullshit – and my least favorite, the repeat offend-ers. They were my least favorite – because they always felt the need to test your gangsta, and most times ended in the need to get physical.

This particular day, I happened to look up at one inmate when her feet didn't move, and I heard kissing noises. When I looked up at the stringy-haired white woman, she smiled, revealing a mouth full of brown-ish colored, rotten teeth.

"When I get all settled in, come find me. I'd love to taste your chocolate stick," she said flirtatiously before licking her lips with a white-coated tongue.

"Move your ass along before I write your ass up." I spat, offended at just the thought of my dick anywhere near her trash mouth. "I said **move**…inmate!"

"If you change your mind…I ain't going nowhere," she returned with a wink before taking her ass on her way.

Officer Lewis stood a few feet away from me, briefly laughing at the exchange before he went back to talking his shit to the women as they walked by. I continued my count until I heard him say, "Well damn, beautiful. Looks like you're in the wrong place. What's your name, sexy?" he flirted, eyeing the woman he was lusting over, who I couldn't see clearly.

"Inmate number 9237560," she replied with a bit of spunk before taking a step forward with the rest of the line.

"Aiight then. I'll give ya bougie ass a few days before you're begging to be in daddy's good graces," he spat. "Get ya ass on then."

When the woman finally came into view, I could see the reasoning behind his initial reaction. She was indeed beautiful. She wasn't quite plus size, but she was thicker than a Snicker in all the right places. Her long, naturally curly, red-ish colored hair was pulled up into a messy bun, and even under the poor prison lighting, her skin glowed. Sexy pouty lips, almond eyes, and a cute button nose were perfectly placed – making her one of the most beautiful women I'd ever seen. It also made me wonder what a woman like her was doing in a place like this – but you could never judge a book by its cover.

When she reached the front of the line, I couldn't help but look into her eyes. I could see more hurt than I saw fear, along with a hint of sadness. Those things alone made me want to know more about her, but that may never happen. After all, fraternizing with inmates was strictly forbidden – although other COs found ways around that.

I gave her a polite nod and she lowered her eyes before stepping through the door to line up behind the other ladies that were waiting to be shown to their new place of residence.

"Man! Did you see the bubble on the back of that bougie bitch?!" Lewis perked. "I bet that thang is beautiful bent over – all spread out for the spankin'," he added as he rubbed his hands together.

"I thought you had a girl?" I asked, annoyed with his ignorance.

"*Girls*, my nigga. These hoes are like Lay's potato chips. You can't have just one," he returned. "You get off your boy scout bullshit, you could have you a few biddies up in here; and it's the best kind of pussy to get. They test these hoes, so you know which ones are clean and which ones not. That right there is called *free fuckin'*."

"I think you do enough free fuckin' for the both of us." I returned with a smirk. That nigga got on my last damn nerve at times – mostly on Fridays.

"Shiiiiid. I can never get enough of free, disease-free pussy. You buggin', and making me question ya sexuality, my nigga."

"Don't worry about me. I'm good."

"Aiight. Well, if you change your mind…holla at ya boy."

Even away from the prison, I couldn't get my mind off of the mysterious beauty I locked eyes with. I couldn't concentrate on the game of *Madden* I was playing because I needed to know more about her. I logged into the Department of Corrections website to do a little research.

"Natifah Foxworth," escaped aloud from my mouth when her mugshot and information popped up on my screen.

Even in her mugshot, she was beautiful. Getting over the distraction of her looks, I looked down at the charges that had landed her at Garden State. Only one charge was listed, and it was a conspiracy charge. Wanting to know more information than the website offered, Google was my next stop. After punching in her name and county, a couple of news articles popped up on her. I sipped my ice cold Modelo as I began to read the first article on her after glancing briefly at the picture of her leaving the courthouse.

"Classic fuck boy scenario." I said aloud as I read the article.

From what I gathered after reading the first article, her man was a piece of shit drug dealer who left her in the dark about his bullshit. It also said that she was the owner of her own nail salon and beauty supply store, had been an honor student and homecoming queen, and graduated salutatorian. She was a bonified good girl. Towards the end of the article, it mentioned her man was sentenced to ten years, while she received sixteen months due to having no criminal background. Intrigued and wanting to know more about Ms. Foxworth, I surfed Google a little bit more. There were pictures of her at her salon's grand opening and Facebook photos of her at different events and charity functions. This woman seemed to be everything a man could ask for in his queen; but this queen was behind bars unfortunately, and off limits to me. Although that was the reality of the situation, I felt the need to get to know her better. For the first time in a long time, I was looking forward to Monday.

Monday was mess hall duty day for me, which I hated, but today it was welcomed. The tier Ms. Foxworth was housed in wasn't part of my detail, so it was my opportunity to get a glimpse of or even talk to her today. I low key looked around for her while keeping an eye on the other inmates. When she walked into the mess hall, I had to stop myself from staring. She'd survived the weekend and didn't appear to have a scratch on her from what I could see as I watched her walk over to the chow line. Once she got her tray, which she looked at and rolled her eyes, she walked past me with a book tucked under her arm towards an empty table. Even after washing with the cheap prison issued soap, she left a waft of jasmine and vanilla when she passed. After taking a seat, she almost caused my eyes to bulge from their sockets when she bowed her head to pray.

"Look at the princess over there," an inmate everyone called Big Meesh said.

Big Meesh was the resident bully, lesbian rapist, snitch, etc. If it was dirt to be done, Big Meesh had her hands in it. She got away with it due to an arrangement she had with certain staffers, so she acted as if she ran the joint.

"The Lord can't save you up in here, prom queen. Having the right friends can help you though." Big Meesh offered as she lustfully eyed her before licking her lips. "What's your name, pretty?" she asked when she got no reaction.

Ms. Foxworth nibbled cutely on a piece of bread, probably the only edible thing on the tray, and kept her nose in her book. I stood watch as Big Meesh got up front her seat, walked over, and stood behind her. Faster than I could blink, Big Meesh had grabbed a handful of Ms. Foxworth's beautiful hair and pulled her head back until she was almost looking at her. I was prepared to step in for the save, since Big Meesh had some size on her and would no doubt do her dirty; but as I took my first step towards them, Ms. Foxworth had already taken action. There was no fear in her eyes as she bent her arm and power thrusted her elbow in to Meesh's midsection, causing her to let go of her hair and double over in pain.

"Don't fuck with me and we won't have no problems." Ms. Foxworth said in a sweet voice, but her tone let you know she played no games.

"I'mma kill you, bitch!" Big Meesh roared before standing straight and rushing towards her.

Side-stepping Meesh's outstretched arms, Foxworth stuck out her foot, tripping Meesh and sending her to the floor. The commotion in the mess hall was so loud from the other inmates that you could hardly hear the alarm blaring, alerting other officers of the incident. Seeing Big Meesh getting up off the floor and some of her flunkies surrounding Foxworth, I rushed over just as a punch was thrown and connected with her face. Ms. Foxworth paused a moment to shake the lick off before coming back with an uppercut of her own that sent another flunkie to the floor.

"Damn!" I exclaimed at the Mortal Kombat style punch before I had to regroup and be professional. "That's enough, inmate! Break this shit up! Back up! Now!" I barked as Big Meesh, and her minions circled like sharks.

I grabbed Foxworth by the arm, placing myself between her and her attackers as I waved another officer for Meesh and her crew. When they arrived, I turned my attention back to Inmate Foxworth.

"Move, inmate!" I said sternly but couldn't bring myself to speak as harshly to her as I had the other inmates.

She didn't resist, but she had one request.

"Could you please make sure I get my book back?" she asked sweetly.

I waited until we were away from the commotion and ears of the other officers before I spoke.

"Are you okay?" I asked with concern in my voice.

"I'm fine. Thanks," was all she offered.

"You don't look like you belong in here, so I'm gonna give you a few words of advice. You see Big Meesh or any of her flunkies coming, you might wanna go the other way for a while. Either that or keep delivering those super punches." I said softly.

That got a cute little chuckle out of her before she glanced my way.

"Thanks for the heads up, officer."

"Jabril. Officer Pratt formally."

"Natifah Foxworth."

"Nice to meet you Foxworth."

"Where are you taking me?"

"To solitary – until the warden is ready to see you."

"Solitary? For defending myself?"

"It won't be for long after I make my report. I tell you what, if the process takes too long, I'll come by to check on you."

"You'd do that?"

"I got you."

It wasn't until the next day that I was sent to solitary to retrieve Inmate Foxworth, and I couldn't believe she was kept in there overnight. When I opened the door, she shielded her eyes from the bright hallway lights as she stood.

"Good morning," she said softly after clearing her throat. "It is morning, isn't it?"

"It is." I replied and stepped into the doorway. "Here, sip this before I put the cuffs on you. It's just spring water."

"Oh God, thank you," she said as she took the small flask I offered.

I didn't believe in all that electricity and sparks flowing through your body crap – until her fingers grazed mine. She had the softest skin I'd ever felt, and just that simple touch sent currents through me. I stole a glance at her as she finished the water, placed the cap back on the flask, and handed it to me.

"Thank you again," she said in that sweet voice. "Where to now?"

"To see the warden, then to your bunk. Your belongings are already there, and I put your book in there for you."

"Are all COs as nice as you?" she asked seriously.

"Not even – unless they want something from you. If you catch my meaning, and before you ask, that's not what this is. I'm one of the rare ones who doesn't feel like you should be treated like an animal since you're in a cage. Just keep your eyes and ears open, and your neck on swivel at all times. You never know which direction the bullshit is gonna come from."

"I appreciate you. Thanks again."

"Thank me by staying outta trouble and staying safe." I returned and offered a slight smile. "Let's move."

Touching the silky-smooth skin on her arm had the same effect on me that it had the day before. This woman had me ready to risk it all. I had to tell myself to pump my brakes –

getting this excited over an inmate. I wanted to know more about the mysterious Ms. Natifah Foxworth, but seeing the effect she already had on me, that may not be such a good idea. Especially if I want to stay employed.

Available Now On All Platforms

ALSO BY TN JONES

If My Walls Could Talk

Her Mattress Buddy

Santa Sauce: A Kinky Christmas Tale

I'm All Yours, Do Me Baby

Tasty Love, Acquainted & Possession

In the Arms of a Devil

In the Arms of a Devil 2

'Tis the Season: Smitten by an Assassin

'Tis the Season 2: Loving the Opp

'Tis The Season 3: Assassin vs Assassin

Thug Passion, Extraordinary Love

Entanglement: Gutta Love Lifestyle

His Little Pussycat

The Opp's Daughter

You Oughta Be with Me

Pressure: Loving a Real One

Tainted Love, Enticed by an Alabama Felon

Rehabilitating a Hustler's Shattered Heart

Dark Tunnel of Pleasure

13 Days of a Hot Girl Holiday

Rockin' around with Love for the Holidays

Deck His Halls

OTHER BOOKS BY

URBAN AINT DEAD

Tales 4rm Da Dale

The Hottest Summer Ever

Hittin' Licks For The Holidays: Atlanta

Wet Dreams On Lockdown: The Nurse

By **Elijah R. Freeman**

Despite The Odds

By **Juhnell Morgan**

Good Girl Gone Rogue

By **Manny Black**

Hittaz

Hittaz 2

Hittaz 3

Hittaz 4

Coldhearted

By **Lou Garden Price, Sr.**

Charge It To The Game

Charge It To The Game 2

A Summer To Remember With My Hitta

Snatched Up By A Hitta

Santa Sent Me A Real One For Christmas

Wet Dreams on Lockdown: The Unit Manager

By **Nai**

A Setup For Revenge

Wet Dreams On Lockdown: Librarian

By **Ashley Williams**

Ridin' For You

Trickin' on a Heaux for Christmas: A BBW Love Story

Homie Hoppin' For The Holidays

By **Telia Teanna**

The State's Witness

The State's Witness 2

The State's Witness 3

By **Kyiris Ashley**

Stuck In The Trenches

Stuck In The Trenches 2

By **Huff Tha Great**

The Swipe

By **Toōla**

Melted the Heart of a Menace

By P. Wise

Merry Trapmas: Ice & Frost

By **Mia Sky**

Thug Me The Right Way

By **DiamondATL & Nai**

Wet Dreams on Lockdown: The Male C.O

By **Tamyra Griffin**

Wet Dreams On Lockdown: The Counselor

By **Paris Iman**

Wet Dreams On Lockdown: The Warden

By **Shawnice**

Ridin For You, Too

Wet Dreams On Lockdown: The Female C.O

By **Telia Teanna**

A Setup For Revenge 2

By **Ashley Williams**

A Gangsta's Last Kiss

By **Mia Sky**

Pretti & The Beast

Wet Dreams On Lockdown: Lieutenant Grace

By **P. Wise**

BOOKS BY

URBAN AINT DEAD's C.E.O

<u>Elijah R. Freeman</u>

Triggadale

Triggadale 2

Triggadale 3

Tales 4rm Da Dale

The Hottest Summer Ever

Murda Was The Case

Murda Was The Case 2

Murda Was The Case 3

Hittin' Licks For The Holidays: Atlanta

Wet Dreams On Lockdown: The Nurse

STAY CONNECTED

Follow
Elijah R. Freeman
On Social Media
FB: Elijah R. Freeman
IG: @the_future_of_urban_fiction